These Pictures of Us

LIFE CHANGES. LOVE HURTS.

TOMMY COTTON

Tommy grew up in the countryside of eastern Victoria, Australia, where he learned to love nature, animals and creativity. He now resides in Melbourne City with his partner and a vocal calico feline.

Other books by Tommy
Just Went Out For Milk (a novel)
Wandering Through a Wondering Mind (quotes and poetry)

Contact Tommy:
www.facebook.com/TommyCottonAuthor
Instagram @tommycotton
Twitter @tommycotton
www.tommycotton.com

THESE PICTURES OF US

ISBN:
9780992592745 (Paperback)
9780992592752 (Ebook)

For Mary.
None of this would be possible without you.

Love never gets easier.

Chapter 1

(NOW)

I'm numb. I can't feel a thing.

It's not because I'm a quadriplegic. This isn't physical – it's inside me, my heart.

Each night I want to die in my sleep and then wake up in the morning with a new life, but I don't.

It hasn't always been this way, though.

There was a time when I couldn't imagine anything but sunshine. That was a long time before things got so cold I lost feeling. Before I was stuck in this chair, limited to movement from the neck up, and weak efforts from my left forearm and hand. Before That Sunday.

Now, there isn't much to do. Except remember, and regret.

The photographs I still have are faded now. Most are hidden away. A few cling to the bubbled paint on the walls of this shitty townhouse, a reminder of what once was. Sometimes when I see them I think I can recall the moment behind the image, or the man who took them. But I just can't feel them enough to know if they were real. If they were part of my life, or someone else's.

Chapter 2

(THEN)

My memories of my birth parents have only ever been vague.

The thing I remember most is the last time I saw them. They were leaning over and saying goodbye to me. I had on a backpack. There were children running past me toward a building.

"We'll be back to pick you up later," my mother had said.

Then there was the police station.

The officer turning off the news. A car crash.

"He doesn't need to see that."

I had one photo to remember them by. A shot taken just after I was born, cradled in my mother's arms, my father beaming at the camera. It was something I held onto, even hugged at night to get me to sleep. Something that reminded me that I was loved.

I always wondered why I didn't get a foster home. Why I ended up in the cold halls of St Madeline's.

Those early days in the orphanage were frightening. I didn't know anyone and didn't know how to. The nuns smiled, and tried to connect with me, but nothing worked. I was scared to talk to anyone, to get to know them. If there was never a conversation, there would never be a goodbye.

Inside my shell was my place to be.

That was until a stifling summer afternoon when I was about ten. One of the sisters came to me as I picked tomatoes.

In her hand was a dusty black object. "Cody, this is for you," Sister Margaret said. "We thought that maybe you'd like to try taking some photographs."

She showed me how to load the film, aim it, the button to press to take a photograph.

The framing of the shot, the click of the shutter, the picture coming from the slot and slowly forming in front of my eyes … with a simple picture of a tomato on a vine, an obsession was born.

Photographs were comfort. My parents lived in one. Photographs could make things stay. And so in photos there were no goodbyes. Nothing to be scared of.

I snapped everything. More tomatoes, nuns, the other children, grass, leaves, dirt, windows, the sky, ants, and the sunshine on the pavement.

The thing that I snapped most, though, was the people who walked by the orphanage – the life outside the fence. I'd aim my lens through the diamonds of the wire fence and capture them – sometimes just their feet. I'd wonder where they were going and who they were going to see.

This occupied me for years. The sisters would find me film in the basement and when that ran out, they'd stretch their budget to get me more. By the time I turned thirteen, my room was covered in photographs, and I was running out of things to capture.

But then one spring afternoon out in the courtyard, something new walked in front of my lens.

They were private-school girls. Blazers and skirts, high socks. A well-to-do looking adult leading them. It was the girl at the back who stole my attention.

She was tall and awkward – her uniform seemed to hang off her – and when she smiled shyly her braces showed. It was her eyes, though, that held me. The hazel seemed to shimmer different colors in the sunlight.

I aimed my lens and snapped.

"Hey!" Her friend was pointing at me. "Mom. That boy is taking photos of us."

Her mother glared, and then came toward me.

"Why are you photographing my daughter?" she asked.

I was hugging the camera to my body. "I … I wasn't …"

"Don't lie to me."

"I wasn't …"

"Well, then what were you talking photos of?"

My eyes caught the tall, gangly girl, her lips sealed to hide her braces. "Her."

The mother's eyes followed mine.

"Isobel? Why would you take photos of Isobel?"

I mouthed her name silently. "Because she's beautiful."

The mother scurried off, huffing. Funny thing, people. She took her daughter's hand and led them away.

Isobel held back, then came over to the fence. She bent down and pretended to pick up something from the ground.

"You were lying, weren't you? Just so Kate's mom wouldn't be mad at you."

My heart had started to beat fast. "Lying about what?"

"Photographing me."

"No. I wasn't." I held out the photograph of her that had now dried. "Do you really think what you said?"

I nodded.

"Nobody's said that for a long time."

"Then they're stupid."

She smiled, and then dropped her head and tried to hide her braces.

"I like that you took pictures of me."

"I like taking pictures of nice things."

The mother called to Isobel.

"I've gotta go," she said. As they walked away, Isobel turned to me, those hazel eyes meeting mine.

I knew nothing in that moment other than the fluttering in my stomach, and the urge I had to take more photographs of the tall, awkward private-school girl called Isobel.

She walked past the next day, and the next, and every weekday after that. And I took more photographs of her, day after day. My walls became a shrine.

Days turned to weeks, and weeks to months.

Soon we were meeting up several evenings each week at a seat by North Pond in Lincoln Park. My camera in one hand, her hand in the other. We'd roam everywhere through the park. All around North Pond, South Pond, the Zoo, North Avenue Beach, through every trail. I took so many pictures. Photos of Isobel, everywhere.

She was the only person I loved talking to, and the only one who I yearned to listen to. With each meeting, I learned more about her, and learned that there was always more I didn't know. She was light, optimistic and innocent on the surface. Beneath it all, though, there dwelled a darker girl. As time went by and her walls lowered, I saw more of the darkness in her. She could drift away from any moment, her mind somewhere else. The look in her eyes would be so cold, making me want to hold her and bring back the warmth usually there. She'd become quiet, hug herself, and close off. I wondered about what she thought, how something behind such beautiful eyes could be so sad. My own fears itched in the back of my mind in those moments. The wall I built between myself and other people … that wall torn down by Isobel … I wanted to put it back up, shut her out, scared of the goodbye that might come.

But I just couldn't – every time I saw those hazel eyes, every smile that made me love braces, was worth the worry and fear.

As thirteen-year-olds under September moonlight, we shared our first kiss. In that moment, it felt as though I had never lost anything, never had to say goodbye, never had to miss anything. It felt as though I had everything, and everything made sense.

Months passed and gradually we revealed the innermost parts of our young selves. I tried to remember my parents, how it felt to have a family, and told Isobel about my trouble trusting people and getting close to them. She listened, she cared, and eventually she opened up about the darkness inside her.

About a year and a half before, her mother had passed away. She didn't say how, but it haunted her.

"I dream about her so often." Her eyes seemed to be somewhere else when she stared into the stars. Somewhere her mother might be. "I wake up, forgetting that she's gone. It feels as though I lose her again when I wake up enough to remember what happened … that I'll never see her again."

I held her the way I wished someone had held me when I found out that my parents had died.

We became closer than ever after this, and I felt a level of affection I had never felt.

She understood what it was like to lose someone. We felt the coldness of loss together. With each other we were home, warm.

She reached a part of me that no one ever had. I trusted her.

And then one day Isobel stopped walking past the orphanage. She stopped meeting me at night, too. She became a ghost to the Chicago I knew. After a year of having someone, I felt alone again.

Three months later, with a wallet full of photos, I ran away from the orphanage.

Every night I searched the places where Isobel and I would hang out. To survive I'd sell photographs I took of the city. A good day meant Chucky Cheese; a bad day meant snatch and run from the markets, or an angry stomach.

I'd been on the street a year when a staunch, middle-aged man stopped to look at my Polaroids. Most kids who wind up sitting on a crate on the sidewalk grasping at scraps of change don't get much of a chance, or a turn of good luck. Most street kids don't get a Larry Foreman.

"Spectra, huh?" Larry said, gazing over a snap. "Look more like you stole these."

"Paper was lifted." I jingled the coins in my hat. "Pictures are all mine."

Larry laughed, that deep baritone chuckle I would come to know so well.

He took me in. Just like that I had a home and a family. I think for the most part I was the kid that Larry and Janine never got to have. They sure as hell treated me like it.

I got an education, and learned how to take photos properly. When I was good enough, I worked under Larry and traveled the fashion capitals of the world with him. I became a professional out of some part skill and a massive part of luck.

So it was because of Larry that years later, at twenty-two, I wound up in New York, photographing one of the biggest spring fashion shows of the season.

✺

Inside the tents in Central Park was a congregation of fitted suits, indoor sunglasses and painted-on dresses. Beauty and privilege. Celebrities and models.

Bright lights shone down on the runway. To the side of it, Larry and I waited with our Nikons cocked.

A brunette model strutted down the walk. Snap. Another came, this one blonde. Then a strawberry blonde. They were all beautiful. Women out of most people's league, including mine. One after another they came, music played, the MC chimed in every so often, and soon the show had moved on to its last set.

I started to daydream about the after party. Perhaps I'd gather the courage to talk to one of them. Maybe have enough champagne that those first words would just come naturally. Maybe there'd be nothing to worry about.

One-night stands and first dates had made up most of my experiences with women to this point. Only occasionally was I drawn to see someone again, and if I was, many times they weren't interested to see me. Any relationships that did happen had been punctuated by guardedness, worry and mistrust. I was a honeymoon dater, nothing lasting more than a few months, and over time it grew tiresome. Goodbyes were logical when it came to relationships. I always had it in mind that any connection would end.

I thought this as I considered how I might fail later on. Or if I succeeded, how empty that one-night stand would feel the next day.

Model after model. Snap after snap. No hellos. No goodbyes. Just work.

For as far as I'd come in life, from orphan to street kid to professional photographer with a loving home, I'd moved nowhere inside of myself.

Then I paused.

Larry nudged me in the side. "Kid, you're meant to be snapping."

Butterflies fluttered in my stomach, and all the way up to my throat. I gulped.

A new model had appeared on the runway. In among all the beautiful women who were far too good for anyone, she seemed far too good for them.

"Cody ya little shit, get on with it."

My finger became overactive. I snapped over and over again. It was as though there was a magnetic pull between my camera and her.

That sandy blonde hair. Wavy, in a way that it looked like it was made for hands to run through it. Eyes of hazel that seemed to change color in the light: sparkle of green, ice-cool blue, warm brown so comforting.

Then I stopped again, this time frozen.

It was those iridescent hazel eyes.

The models rotated through once more, but she didn't come back out. My mind was playing tricks on me. It couldn't have been her …

The last of the models disappeared backstage and the MC leaped onto the runway to bring the show to a close.

We packed up our equipment.

"You want to get a bite?" Larry asked.

I had taken my camera out again, and was flicking through the photos. It was hard to believe my eyes. "Take my stuff," I said, handing Larry the camera. "I've gotta go."

∽❦∼

Out the back, some models laughed and chatted to rich hangers-on, already wooing them, while others did interviews or sipped champagne. All the girls from the show were there. All except the wavy blonde with hazel eyes. Then through a gap in the tent I saw her, changed into street clothes and already a few hundred yards away. Her head was dropped, her bag slung over one shoulder.

I pushed through the crowd and out of the tent.

Through picnics and over paths, I ran. The sweetness of cherry blossoms flashed by as I descended the stairs. I weaved through people in the arcade, under the Minton Tile ceiling, and then burst out onto Bethesda Terrace.

"Isobel," I called as I gained on her near Bethesda Fountain.

She turned.

"Hi," she said, a quizzical expression on her face. "Do I know you?"

"It's been a long time."

The smile wouldn't leave my face.

And then her jaw dropped. "Oh my god, Cody?"

I nodded. "Looks like people ended up liking taking photos of you."

She beamed momentarily before dipping her eyes. Her teeth were white and straight, not a hint of braces. There was barely a hint of the awkward girl who was the first to take my attention.

"I guess I grew into my body."

That was an understatement. She was tall and slender, her skin golden. In fact, everything about her was golden, from her smile to those eyes. Looking into them, I remembered the enigma of a girl I fell for.

"Do you maybe want to go for a walk?"

Isobel hugged herself with one arm. "Sure. Do you know your way around town?"

"Not really."

"Well, maybe I can show *you* some places this time."

That spring afternoon was reminiscent of our times shared as two curious teenagers. We strolled around Central Park for hours, talking, laughing and catching up on everything that had happened.

Isobel modeled full time and in her spare time she drew and volunteered at Morgan Stanley Children's Hospital. She'd gone to college at NYU, and lived in an apartment on Fifth Avenue.

"I always wondered where you went," I said.

Isobel sighed. "Dad thought we needed a change … it was sudden."

I told her about my path, too, from running away to the streets, to a turn of luck named Larry. I told her about the travel, and she smiled, reflecting on her own experiences roaming the world.

As the sun began to fade, we stopped by the cherry blossoms near Delacorte Theater.

"You know I've never forgotten how you were the first person who made me feel like I was pretty," Isobel said. "You made me believe I was worth being photographed."

The sweet scent of the blossoms came to me for the second time that afternoon.

"You were the first person I ever felt comfortable talking to. I loved taking photos of you, but it was the time without the camera guarding me that I enjoyed the most."

We shared a smile, some silent moments.

"How long are you going to be in town?" Isobel asked.

Clouds passed, and a flicker of dying sunlight hit me. In the middle of Central Park, it felt as though there was not another soul around. "I think I might stick around for a while."

Chapter 3

(NOW)

I'm groggy. The meds.

I roll my head side to side and cough. It startles Isobel as she comes through the front door. Waking up, I tend to forget everything that's happened for a moment, as if it's five years ago. Isobel could be walking through the door of our New York apartment, or the one we had in North Central Chicago. When the blur of the magic eye clears, though, I remember it all.

"Sorry," she says and puts down her bags on the sofa. "I just had to get some things for dinner."

She's so plain and worn down. Cooks more than ever. Cleans. Cares for me. Works part time as a receptionist at a law firm. A shadow of the enigmatic supermodel who once graced the most lavish runways in the world. She's worlds away from the woman she was.

I'm barely a finger push of the photographer I used to be.

The pictures of us then and now are polarities. A rollercoaster of passion and feeling then. A flat plain of apathy now.

"Okay."

The rasp and strain in my voice is prominent.

Isobel was the one person who made it easy for me to talk and open up. Now talking to her is harder than talking to anyone else. So I don't say a hell of a lot. I don't care to, either. I can't care.

I don't hate Isobel, but I definitely don't love her anymore.

I don't know if she still feels anything close to love for me. Maybe she persists with this out of obligation, or guilt.

My chair whirs as I drive into the kitchen. I stop by the sink and reach pathetically with my T-rex left arm for a glass from the drying rack.

I'm weak – a child would destroy me in an arm wrestle.

The glass falls out of the rack, hits the bench and smashes. In the reflection of the window I see Isobel on the couch. She snaps her head up. Again, I've startled her.

She hurries from the couch, collects the dustpan from the hook and frantically sweeps up the glass. I consider saying sorry, but that's where the sentiment ends.

I'm a jerk. But I don't give a shit. It's hard to when your wife, or a man you're paying, has to wipe it from your ass.

Some glass landed on my lap. Isobel notices it, and after emptying the pan into the bin, leans over me and picks the shards piece by piece.

Her cleavage shows.

This used to get me hot, and hard. Now it's just meat to a wolf who's gone vegan.

Isobel looks up at me. "Are you okay?"

Her eyes are sorry, and tired, like wilted hydrangeas.

"I'm fine."

She stays there for a moment and a scent wafts into my nose. First, it's hers – Chanel No. 5 – then the Chanel is supplanted by a thicker, tangier scent.

A man's.

"You smell different." I cough, a dry wheeze, which grazes my throat.

Those wilted hydrangeas look away.

I know what's coming. Of all the parts of me that no longer work, my brain is not yet one of them.

Isobel takes the handkerchief that hangs out of my front shirt pocket like a spit-covered identity tag. I never used to wear shirts much, except when going to high-end parties, and they were part of a suit. The ones I wear now are the cheap kind. Plaid, checked, striped ones that come in packs of three. My fashion sense is that of a five-year-old boy whose mother dresses him to look neat.

She wipes the saliva from the sides of my mouth, and then replaces my slop towel.

The same scents waft one by one into my nose. Sweet Chanel. Tangy man.

"Cody ..."

"How long have you been seeing him?"

"We met about six months ago."

"That's a while."

"I only wanted to tell you once it really became something."

I cough and splutter.

Isobel wipes my mouth.

"What's his name?" I ask. "Where did you meet?"

Isobel clears her throat and looks around, unwilling to catch my eyes.

"His name is Jake." She glances at me. "We met at the grocery store."

How easy it is for them to revisit their special place.

"Which aisle?"

"Laundry."

Silence lingers between us. The electric hum of the kitchen light is audible. The buzz of the refrigerator.

This is what I've been telling her to do since it happened.

That Sunday.

Early on, when I was still angry – angry enough to still feel something for her, angry that I couldn't love her how I wanted to, that we couldn't have the life we wanted – this is what I told her to do.

"Don't stop living," I told her. *Leave me behind. Let me go. Move on.*

Now she's started to move on. Maybe she's fucked a few people since we stopped. Maybe lots. I don't know. She's been seeing this guy for six months, though. She started moving on a while ago.

I've paid no attention to anything.

I've never moved on. Just stopped moving.

Eventually Isobel speaks. "Do you care?"

My head is turned to the side. The direction in which I look is one of the few things I can control.

Over on the wall beside the refrigerator there is a photo. It's as if the buzzing of the refrigerator leads me to it.

It's tucked away, as if the person who placed it there doesn't want it to be prominent, but wants it visible enough for them to see when they choose. A cry for help written on a diary page. Look but don't look. Help me, but I can't ask you to. Horizontal scars on the inner forearm under a long-sleeve top.

I want to cry right now. No, I *want to* want to cry.

"No. We don't love each other. Why would I?"

She gulps, swallowing her tears. It does nothing to me. I'm emotionally impervious.

She's good at putting up a strong facade, even better than she used to be. I know she still hurts. Still has appointments. Still takes her meds. She hasn't discovered how to feel nothing yet.

She strokes the back of my left hand. A lonely tear splatters on my skin.

There used to be a poetic sadness and raw beauty in the black squiggle of her tears. I photographed it once. A single teardrop, just before it left her cheek. In black and white. It was the bleeding of everything that made her so completely beautiful. A captive spectrum of her. Nature. Depth. And plastic. Superficiality. Outward confidence disguising her lack of self-esteem. Just saline and Max Factor. I saw it all. Now, I see a photograph. Blurred for some reason.

"I'm making roast lamb for dinner." Isobel sniffs. "Potatoes and all."

She hasn't started it yet, but I can already smell the rosemary.

I'd feel excited and jump up and down if it was five years earlier.

But I can't jump.

I can't feel a thing.

Chapter 4

(NOW)

"Ducks are an underrated animal, I think," Joe says.

We're in Lincoln Park, at North Pond. Joe is in flip flops. I'm not much shorter than him, even in the chair. He's been my caregiver from the home ever since I left hospital.

The home's where I go when things get too much for Isobel. When she needs a break to keep caring for me …

She's got someone else to care about now.

Through the archway in the trees, the water spreads out in front of me. Waterlilies float atop, deep reeds sprout from beneath, thick forestry hugs the pond all around, and the gray city watches over it all.

A duck retreats when I turn my chair. "They seem pretty stupid to me."

"Maybe they are." Joe rolls a piece of bread into a ball. "Seem like they know how to hope, though. There's no way they're all going to get a feed from this bread, but that doesn't stop them trying."

"They have no idea. They just take a chance. They're stupid."

He rolls his hands over his bowling-ball stomach. "Taking a chance isn't a bad thing."

"Could get them killed." I steer at another duck that's wandered near my chair.

Joe shrugs, smiles at me and then tosses the bread ball to the grass.

The ducks scamper after it and tussle until one comes out winner.

Joe rolls another ball of bread and hands it to me. "I'd never have loved if I hadn't taken a chance."

There looks to be a million miles behind his wizened skin, worn like old boot leather. His eyes are big and brown, bright and round like buttons. Through them his story shows. A good part of his lifetime spent being something he wasn't.

After he was taken from his parents by the Australian government when he was four, he was raised in affluent suburbs to be a white kid, because he could pass for it. He says he has flashes of the homestead's tin roof as the car drove away. The man in a suit telling him things are going to be better. The confusion.

A human being. Stolen.

He was told that indigenous Australians were dirty; was raised to dislike them, only to find out when he was twenty that they were his people. By the time he found his blood family, his father had already passed on and his mother was very frail.

Once she had died too, he left the country. Roamed the world until he fell in love with an American woman, Rebecca. Here in Chicago, the strangest of places.

Feebly, I toss the ball of bread. "Ducks don't know what love is. Don't know what it is to get hurt."

Joe throws another ball into the water. It sends circles out like a perpetuating target. The ducks still haven't seen mine.

"Maybe ignorance is bliss." Joe tosses another ball into the water. "As long as you know north from south for winter time."

I stare at the one duck who is lingering on the outside of the group as the others scamper for each successive bread ball Joe throws to them. "Either way, they're insignificant. How does something so insignificant hope?"

The bread is finished. Joe dusts his hands off and wipes them on his khakis. "Everyone and everything's got hope, mate."

A bug is crawling over an arched blade of grass near my chair. If I could move my leg I would stomp on it. I used to love nature.

"You like animals, don't you?" I ask.

He nods. "Lived on a farm with my blood family for a while before I came here."

"Was it confusing?"

"Farming?"

"No. Being made to believe you're one thing, then finding out you're another."

"Well, after I found them it made much more sense why I didn't quite fit in with the white fellas growing up. The farming was probably harder."

"Do you know who you are now?"

Joe's gaze is off in the distance, well past the water. "I'm me, all I can ever be." He sighs and pinches his nose. "Miss it sometimes. The open land, paddocks by the roadside, blue mountains in the distance. Fresh air with the smell of eucalyptus. Kookaburras laughing just after dawn, willy wagtails singing in the moonlight … loved that I could see too many stars in the night sky to ever count them all."

The clouds above have darkened. I want to see the fields filled with hay, which Joe calls paddocks: the land he misses, a place Isobel and I never visited. "You miss home."

"I don't know where home is. There's the place I was born. The place I grew up. And the place I fell in love. Same place I buried my missus."

"You've never told me she was dead."

"You've never asked."

"How did it happen?"

He circles his thumbs over each other. "She got sick, mate. Motor neuron disease … death was inevitable. We got married right away. Brought it forward, because it was something she wanted to do before her time was up. She lasted our honeymoon and passed shortly after we got back."

"I'm sorry." I mightn't care, but no one deserves to see their soulmate die. "Life sucks."

He stares at me with those big brown buttons. "Depends how you look at things. Am I unlucky because I lost the love of my life, or am I lucky because I got to love her?"

I think of Isobel and me. Which are we?

"Only thing I regret was that I didn't help her see more of the world. Didn't take her to my homeland. Got complacent here."

There's something stuck in my throat.

Isobel and I saw the world. We're not dead, but we are further apart than Joe and Rebecca. Something starts to eat at me inside. My spine, deep down. My lungs. Weakness, tightness.

Joe's looking at me with concern. The pain meds are in the bathroom cabinet.

"Come on, mate. Let's get you home."

That stain of a house.

This conversation, the thoughts, even the pain, it's all just echoes as Joe wheels me toward the van. Just for a moment, I wasn't the person I've become. For an instant, I remember being something else.

He steers me onto the lift and into the back like a horse into its float.
Echoes, fading.
Home.
Echoes, barely audible.
Joe fixes me in place.
Echoes, moving from a sound to a memory.
Joe buckles his seat belt, starts the engine and begins to drive.
More pain. Just physical.
Joe drives through the streets. Toward that shitty little townhouse, long and thin. A skeleton.

My street appears. The hallways and rooms are in my mind. So are those of New York. Our north-side apartment in Chicago. Those images. Stills of my life then, and my life now. Polarized Polaroids.

Joe parks the car.
Echoes, gone.

Joe and Isobel talk on the front step while I wait inside. They murmur the words they don't want me to hear. I'm a kid again. Adults talking about me. People who know better for me.

They'll leave eventually.
Everybody does.
"Sorry about that."
Isobel is standing in front of me.

I'm drooling. Isobel sits in the armchair beside me. She wipes my mouth. Her fingernails are coated in red shellac. Fresh, like tomatoes on the vine …

I've only ever loved one woman.
It's a past tense.
She was the only one, though. Together we grew, came out of our shells, became ourselves more than ever. Only to lose ourselves in a whole different way.

"Your nails. They're fresh."
Isobel brings them up in front of her, and spreads her fingers. "I got them done while you were out. You like?"
"They remind me of blood."
She scrunches her face, though I didn't mean it as an insult.
"What's the occasion?"

Isobel entwines her fingers and hides them away between her knees. She fixes her eyes on the wall ahead. "Jake's coming for dinner. I would've told you earlier but it was really last minute. I hope that's okay."

Something just got bent inside my head.

She's finally doing what I want her to …

Leave me behind. Let me go. Move on.

… but this sits in a weird way.

"Okay," I say.

Isobel rubs her palm over the back of my left hand. It's soft. I used to think her touch was magical – that if I died, it could bring me back to life.

"I'm going to put dinner on now."

She stands and is about to walk to the kitchen when she stops. She looks at me for a moment. Through the window, white sunlight shines off her skin. In that light, she almost looks like the woman she was. I almost see her here.

For a moment, it seems as though she's about to say what she always used to. *I don't want to move on, Cody. I'm where I need to be with you.*

I ready myself to respond the way I always have. *You have no choice. Happiness isn't with me. I don't love you anymore.*

She doesn't say anything, though. Just stares through me.

Then she shakes herself off and heads into the kitchen.

I watch her scooting back and forth and organizing the baking trays.

I smell paprika.

I used to hate paprika.

Sitting in the living room, in my spot beside sofa, I think back to the first time she cooked me dinner, a week after we reunited. She was still living with Kate. She didn't know I hated paprika and so she sprinkled it everywhere. I sat in the living room and made small talk with Kate while I watched Isobel dash about the kitchen. I had no idea what Kate was talking about – Isobel had my attention. She captivated me.

I wonder if Jake will sit here and make small talk with Isobel's housemate as I did. I wonder if he'll gulp down the food and pretend to like it just to make her feel better about her lousy cooking. Just because he knows how beautiful she is, and how fragile she is, too.

I wonder if he'll see what I used to see.

The woman behind those tired eyes.

I wonder if he'll find something I lost.

❧

The doorbell wakes me.

A blurred Isobel strides past me, a hint of that catwalk strut in her gait. It's been an age since I've seen her hips talk like that.

When my vision clears, I can see her properly. She looks good – better than I've seen her for a long time. The red dress is glued to her body and her figure shows. With most of her time spent in baggy tees and unflattering jeans I thought it had gone.

She opens the door. The corner of her lip rises, her smile profiled to me. Just a teaser. Like a trailer for a great movie. It's the hint of something extraordinary to come. A story.

No, it's not.

Remember where you are, Cody. Remember? Everything.

It used to be that.

You used to be in front of that smile, not to its side.

She has on heels. They match the dress. I don't remember her buying the dress, but the heels she's had since a runway show in Amsterdam back in 08. They were brilliant that night, when they were all she had on.

The indentation in the side of her leg shows, running from her dainty, pin-like ankles up toward her knee, as even in heels she has to push a little higher to meet the man I still can't see.

Jake.

The house falls silent for a moment. Then the sound of a kiss.

I feel it.

But I don't love her. I can't love her. I don't even hate her anymore. The feeling … the pain medication … it's that. Messing with me.

A tall, good-looking man enters the house. Dark blonde hair parted to the side. Smooth, tanned skin. A white-toothed smile, crystal blue eyes. He looks like a model. The type of guy I always thought Isobel would have been with. The handsome guy she deserved.

Standing in front of me, they look perfect together.

Something doesn't fit, though.

"Cody," Isobel says, "this is Jake."

Even if I wasn't so aloof, I couldn't shake the hand of the guy who'll be fucking my wife soon.

"Hey Cody." He smiles. "It's nice to meet you."

What do I say to him? Have fun …? Pretend to like her cooking …? She likes …

"You too," is all that comes.

We stay here awkwardly for a moment. Isobel seems unsure of what to do. We're saved by the oven timer.

"Dinner's ready." Isobel grazes her hand over the back of my left and then takes Jake's for an instant. "Why don't you two wait in here while I serve it."

Jake sits in the armchair opposite me.

This would be torture to someone who cared.

His eyes struggle to leave Isobel.

"Isobel tells me you're a great photographer."

"Was."

"I'm a lawyer. Arts law. Have done some copyright cases for some photographers. Quite interesting." Every word from his mouth makes me want to hate him more. It makes me want to disappear even more.

"It's ready," Isobel calls.

Jake stands and steps aside, ushering me. "After you, buddy."

In the kitchen Isobel has made space for me on the side of the table. Jake is on the opposite side. Isobel sits on the end, between us.

I try to glare across at Jake. That want to dislike him is nudging me. I should dislike him, shouldn't I?

"It's roast lamb," Isobel says, glancing to both of us.

Who was the dinner intended for?

"I made the potatoes how you like them."

It was made for Jake.

They share a moment. A brief one, an exchange between their eyes. Speech that only they can hear. They look as if they are alone right now.

Then Isobel breaks from it and remembers I'm here. She begins to cut up my meat and vegetables. "I didn't use the herbs on your potatoes, Cody."

I'm still staring at Jake. He can't decide where to look, his eyes wandering around the kitchen. He knows I'm staring, but seems unwilling to enter a contest with me.

"Ready?" she says and lifts a fork toward my mouth.

This is our ritual for dinner. She'll switch between me and her, though she always feeds me first. I once had a massive appetite. For food. For sex. For Isobel. For life. Now on my plate, the serving size resembles a Third-World meal.

Usually I feel handicapped. Now I feel like a stupid child with an airplane flying toward my mouth.

Jake has finished observing the architraves and skirting and is now watching Isobel feed me.

Isobel puts down the fork. "Did Jake tell you that he's a copyright lawyer? Has worked with lots of artists and some photographers you might know."

"Is that meant to impress me?"

"Was just trying to make conversation." Isobel shakes her head. "Geesh Cody."

It's not often that I piss her off. This dinner seems to mean something to her.

"It's fair enough, Bel," Jake says. "With everything you accomplished, Cody, I'm sure you're not easily won over."

Bel? He calls her Bel? She used to hate that. Always said that she wasn't a Disney Princess.

And win me over? Who the hell is he dating? Beguiling son of a bitch.

"Isobel has to wipe my ass." The words just fly out my mouth without a thought. "My accomplishments aren't what they used to be."

"Cody," Isobel scolds. "What is wrong with you?"

What's not?

I'm diffident and insolent rolled into one obtrusive package on four wheels.

"Nothing," I say. "I've just never been that fond of lawyers."

Isobel's forehead is crinkled. "I'm aware of that. Does that mean you need to be a dick about it?"

"Maybe I should leave for a little bit," Jake says. "Let you both talk."

As he pushes his chair back, Isobel grabs his hand. "No, don't. Cody's being a jerk. If he has a problem, he can leave."

Her eyes pierce me. Isobel was never one to put up with effrontery from anyone. She'd use a few words to put someone in their place, or she'd go find another place where assholes weren't. Either way, she didn't tolerate it. That girl's been incognito for a while.

Yet here we are.

Awkward silence fills the room for some time.

We resume. The airplane comes. Open, chew, gulp and repeat. Isobel and Jake talk. I'm no longer here.

I become thirsty. I don't ask for water, though.

My eyes waver between Jake and Isobel. Their words are polite and careful. Their body language speaks loudly. Then on the wall behind Jake I notice the photograph that doesn't want to be seen.

My left hand twitches as I try to steer out of the room as fast as I can.

"Cody?" he asks.

"Cody?" she asks.

I push the bedroom door closed with my chair.

The room is dark and cold. My breathing is heavy, fogged in the moonlight.

The clock on the wall ticks. Thoughts tick over in my mind.

There was a time when our hearts pulled us together … now, with no working limbs I've managed to push her away.

Everything I ever feared I've chosen.

Chapter 5

(THEN)

I did stick around New York for a while.

That while became permanent about a year later when, in the spring of 2006, we moved in together. We'd been almost inseparable since that afternoon in Central Park. She was my person. The one who got me, and I was hers.

Our apartment was a third-floor loft on the corner of Fashion Ave and West 59th. It was lavish, filled with ornate furniture and artwork – photos upon photos. It was the coolest place within spitting distance of Trump Rink.

"Are you almost ready?" I called from the living room.

The party had started an hour ago.

No reply came. I went to the bedroom.

Isobel was sitting on the bed in a little black dress that hugged her figure as if painted on. In between her breasts hung the necklace I had bought her to celebrate moving in together. In it there were two pictures of us.

The silver of the necklace shone off the bedroom light.

"What's up, baby?" I asked, sitting beside her.

"Dunno," she mumbled. "Just don't feel like going out."

"I don't get it. Fifteen minutes ago you were excited and running around the house."

She stayed silent.

This was how she was. A yoyo.

"Come on, hon. We'll have fun."

Still, silence.

"Isobel, seriously. You can't do this. It's New Year's Eve."

When she got like this it scared me. She'd close off, become someone else. It would feel as though we weren't those two people falling in love more with each day. There was distance. Coldness. Apathy. Not us.

I wrapped my arms around her and kissed her. It changed nothing. It killed me to feel that I could do nothing for the woman I loved.

I sat there blankly for a time, then noticed my digital camera on the dresser.

I got up and turned it on.

"Isobel," I said, "look at me."

She peered up through her lashes. I snapped her once and then again.

"Why are you taking photos?" she asked.

"Because I like taking photos of you."

Minutes went by like this. Eventually Isobel relaxed her arms from shielding herself, and leaned back, smiling up at me.

There was the girl I knew, all darkness in those hazel eyes gone.

Isobel stood and came over to me. She held my head in her hands and kissed me. "You always know how to make me feel better."

Though I smiled at the idea, truth was I didn't.

The first time it happened I had no idea what to do. After eighteen months, I still didn't. Sometimes the camera would work. Sometimes a cuddle might. Other times, nice words or jokes or just being silly. And sometimes, nothing worked.

Right now, though, I was just glad that something had.

On our way out of the apartment, I opened up the gallery on my camera and clicked through those images of her on the bed. Dark and hidden. Vulnerable and exposed. I felt as though I knew her better than anyone, yet still she remained a mystery to me in many ways. But in that mystery, that darkness, that vulnerability, she was still beautiful. I loved every part of her, even the ones that scared me, the ones that frustrated me, and the ones I didn't understand.

"I can tell you that you're beautiful, Isobel – you might even see it in a mirror." The lift rattled toward Ground. "I just wish there was a mirror you could see your heart and soul in. Maybe then you'd see just how amazing you are."

The snap of a New York December night hit my face.

Isobel took my hand, warmth and comfort in her touch. "You are my mirror, Cody."

The party was at Kate's, Isobel's best friend. The apartment was jam-packed with slick suits and tight dresses, trendy overcoats and leather shoes. Privilege that's only ever a birthright. The type of people who used to sneer at me when I was a kid on the streets with just an old blue Nike hat. If you drove a car that cost less than six figures, or wore anything with a price tag with less than three zeroes on the end, you were poor. In every hand was a champagne glass, each bubble a mortgage repayment for most of America.

This was our self-indulgent, over-privileged scene.

As a teenager on the street, any meal was sufficient. Now, I could have any meal I wanted. It never felt right, though. Mac and Cheese was just something I could never give up. Where I'd come from was ingrained in me, despite how well I played the part. Isobel had always found comfort in material wealth, but she didn't fit either. She didn't obsess about what she had, or what she could get. Experiences were what fulfilled and interested us, what we craved.

We were misfits who managed to fit. Revelers in one moment, detesters in another, and hypocrites in all.

It pulled us in, though – the scene, the rush of it all.

Larry had told me about it. He'd done the same thing – this was New York, after all, the scene had existed as long as the city itself.

"Simon is handling the Swanston account now," Kate said of her new fling. "I have no doubt that partner is on the horizon."

Her prize was on display for the rest of the circle to see.

"Oh, that's wonderful," replied Tania, a raven-haired underwear model. She toted her own new toy on her arm. "Marcus owns a boutique – he's a designer. It's down on 11th Avenue. You can't miss it. And you're opening up another two this fall, right?"

Someone was always doing something, or going somewhere higher than where they were. The driven are always driving, never checking out the scenery. I could read most of their minds. They were like mine before I reunited with Isobel. Before I fell in love. They only thought about which contacts they would make, who would help them make another million or climb another rung. They only thought about the physical – money, clothes, cars, the body of the person they'd be screwing that night.

Isobel and I drifted away from the group as the show and tell continued.

"Are you as bored as me?" I asked, closing Kate's bedroom door.

Isobel locked it. "Those conversations drive me insane."

Her dress unzipped so slowly that I heard each groove of the zip click. The black Chanel fabric fell from her body. What lay beneath was a masterpiece to me. The indentations and silk-like skin of her body. She stood there in sheer black Journelle lingerie and six-inch stilettos.

I took out my camera.

"Bring your eyes up," I instructed her. "But keep your head down."

She did, similar to what she'd done earlier, but now it was confident, sexy. Not just for how it looked, but for what was behind those eyes. That was the real turn on.

The camera was like a security blanket for Isobel. The moment it came out, she was confident, secure, and knew how to put on a show for the lens. I snapped her – click, click, click – as she altered her position in every minute, tempting way.

"Bend forward." Her breasts accentuated, and then she held them, circling slowly. "Now turn around and bend over."

My instructions were decisive. The camera was confidence for me, too.

But when she turned her face back to me, elbows almost on the floor, butt in the air, and bit her lip, with a look that would've made a monk break his vows, I completely forgot about my camera.

In seconds, I was behind Isobel.

Suctioned to her body, my hands corseting her waist.

She stood straight, fronted me, and wrapped her fingers around my throat, kissing me with control, pushing me to take it back from her. I threw her on the bed and pinned her hands, my lips burying into her neck.

Where passion took over, we forgot everything we thought we weren't.

Isobel moaned lightly. "Fuck me until we're no longer two different people."

The door handle jiggled, and then a knock came. Both Isobel and I groaned.

I rolled off her, my clothes untucked, her hair frazzled – that perennial beauty of sex hair that men love and women blush about. We fixed up in seconds then I answered the door.

"Was wondering where you two went." Kate smirked. "We're going to bump if you'd like to join?"

"Sure," Isobel replied.

She took my hand and we followed Kate down the hallway.

In the bathroom, Tania was already waiting. On the sink four lines of blow were readied. "Cocktail. Half blow, half molly."

The girls bumped first. Each line vacuumed through the same hundred-dollar bill. Each one of them rising as though they were about to take off.

My turn, and I did the same.

A sniff, and then came the drip at the back of my throat.

Then fervent energy and pace. Time on fast forward.

"Where are the guys?" I asked.

Tania shrugged. "Talking stock or some shit."

"I don't get it how they always just carry on – money and bullshit." Kate clenched her jaw between sentences. "Damn it, I forgot the magnesium; they just talk about stock, about profile; fucking men, it's all they care about."

"Where's the fun, hey? Where's the good times?" Tania added.

Isobel sat on the edge of the spa, quiet. Eyes up at the ceiling. Body open.

Kate sniffed and then wiped her nose. "How the hell are we meant to be young forever if we start being boring when we don't have to be?"

"They don't get it." Tania threw her arms up. "Where's the fun?"

Isobel climbed into the empty spa.

Her legs stretched out.

Kate and Tania stopped jabbering.

Isobel ran her hands over her own neck and through her hair, up and down her thigh.

"You're so damn beautiful, honey, so sexy." Kate climbed into the spa.

Isobel sipped her wine and leaned back. Kate crawled on top of her and took the glass. She kissed Isobel's lips, her neck and her breasts and then moved lower, hitching up Isobel's dress.

Kate's tongue melted into Isobel's skin.

Euphoria.

My cock hardened, throbbing against my zipper.

Ruby-red lips working up Isobel's thigh. Panties to the side. Kate's tongue, massaging Isobel's clit.

My fly unzipped.

Tania was on her knees. Her lips wrapped around the head of my dick. I became harder and harder until I couldn't take it. Frantic kissing, bodies driven by heat, mind floating higher. Tania turned around. My lips found every part of her skin. She bent over and pulled up her skirt – no underwear.

Soft and already wet, she writhed with first contact. Slowly, entering, making her feel my girth. Every movement deeper, her moans growing louder. She clawed and clenched at the vanity, tendons showing. I twisted her free arm behind her back. Lust, alcohol, stimulants: driving me on, higher, harder, faster. She tightened around me. Pulsing, clenching, coming; moaning.

Tania sighed, and collapsed on the bathroom floor. She picked herself up. With a glass of red in her hand she watched.

Into the spa.

Isobel and Kate tangled, sixty-nine. A race to make the other come first.

Isobel's waist in my hands, gripping like a belt. Leaning in to tease her ass with my tongue. Her whimpers and moans, growls of sexual tension. Her, reaching back and pulling me in. How tight she always was. We were unguarded, uninhibited, free …

While music played, and the rest of the party swooned around, swapping braggadocio, I had an orgy with two beautiful models and the woman I loved. They gripped my skin the way Tania had the sink. Their shellac-coated nails cut my flesh, leaving me with scarred reminders of this night.

Every position.

Everyone connected at once.

Spectating.

Swapping partners.

Everyone the center of attention.

Snorting until the bags were dry …

Once it was over, we sprawled out on the cool tiles.

So much pleasure. So much sensation.

This was my life. Confused and guarded in some hours. Passionate and free in others.

I pinched my leg to see if this was real. The feeling was dull from the drugs and alcohol. Someone else feeling something – someone else's leg. My knee bent and then flexed in the air and then rested back on the cool tiles. I looked around the expansive bathroom.

Three beautiful women draping one another with their naked bodies.

Life was so good.

Chapter 6

(NOW)

I'm being lowered out the back of the van. It's customized for me. *Pimp My Ride* for the handicapped. The lift hits the ground with a jolt. The horse is out of the float. That's not right – if I was a horse, I would've been put down.

Isobel rounds the side of the van and unlocks my chair.

The front of the home, much like the back, is populated by evergreen gardens. Free natural surrounds. Inside is a place for people who can't be free anymore.

This is where I come when Isobel needs a break.

"Are you sure you're okay with everything?" Isobel asks, kneeling down in front of me. "It's only for a few days. I'll be back to pick you up on Monday."

This is my first day of kindergarten all over again.

Isobel kind of looks like my mother for a moment, with the glow of sunshine off her cheek – my birth mother. It's one of those rusted old photos with color bleeding in spots the way rainbows form in oil. I see it in my mind. That one photo I had of my parents. It's locked away in a cupboard in the townhouse. I haven't looked at it for years. Isobel might not even resemble her, my memory sullied.

There's still that memory, though. A vehicle. A woman I once loved asking me if I'm okay. Telling me she'll be back. Sunshine and sandy blonde hair.

Trust, belief.

She'll be back.

But will I see that van on the six o'clock news at the police station? Is this the last time I'll see those eyes beyond a photograph? The contorted wreckage of that van, smashed glass, smoke, wrapped around a street light.

She's not coming back. I'm never going home.

"Cody?" Isobel's hand is on my left.

My mind is flickering between two moments. Her touch is in both. I don't want it to be the last.

Wake up!

"Yeah … I'll be fine."

Joe bursts out of the front entrance as we approach. "Perfect timing, you two troublemakers."

We were troublemakers once. We were wild little shits. Wayfarers. We're not anymore. We're sensible. Routine.

Isobel thanks him as he takes my bags from her. He turns back through the door, calling that he'll be out in a moment just in case I need him.

"I'll see you in a few days." She leans over and kisses my forehead. "Have a good time."

"Okay."

Her hand touches my left before she leaves. It's habitual. I don't think she realizes that she still does it. Old habits.

She climbs into the van. The big old horse float swallows her.

My mind doesn't flicker again – I'm here.

That old rusted photo is probably lost, or ruined so much the people in it can't be made out anymore.

My mother's gone.

The van tires crunch over gravel.

That van might come back. It might not. I don't know what I want it to do.

Either way, Isobel's gone, too.

❧

The afternoon outside the window is fading, the night sky appearing. A cosmic graveyard of yesterdays. Many of the stars I can see aren't even there anymore. Impressions of what was. Memories.

The moon is just visible. On it are footprints that will still be there long after we're gone. Remnants of something magical that might never be seen again.

Thinking about the enormity of the universe always gave me hope. I was so insignificant to the world, but so large in the worlds of those I loved.

People were my hope.

The universe is nothing but space to me now.

Stuck inside myself.

Stuck inside this home.

I'm so insignificant. The only way I'm large in other people's lives is the burden I bring to them. My farts will have more impact on the world than anything else I do.

Bony fingers rest on my shoulder. "What're you doing there, Cody?"

It's Sophie. An old lady who moved into the home about a year ago.

"Just thinking." I rotate to her, and the cosmos disappears.

Her smile is bright but everything around it has been worn by time. Her face is like a flower at spring's end, a colorful bud for a smile, encased by wilted petals.

"Some men spend a lifetime doing that."

I grunt. What else do I have to do with the rest of mine?

"What were you thinking about, dear?"

"Nothing."

"Well, you weren't really thinking then, were you?"

"You know 'nothing' usually just means that someone doesn't want to tell you something."

"Why didn't you say that? I'm old, don't have time for pussyfooting."

"I'll keep that in mind."

The sky outside the window is now dark.

"Was that your wife who dropped you off?"

The question makes me want to squirm. I can't squirm. My neck stretches side to side. "Yes, that was Isobel."

"She's beautiful, dear."

This makes me want to disappear.

"When's dinner?" I ask.

"Oh, I think it's here now," she says, glancing over her shoulder. "Shall we fight for the least stale bread roll?"

She has a sense of humor. I think she'd have been something in days of black and white. There are whispers that flow along the home's grapevine. Gossip never stops, even when people are getting ready to die. I've heard things. How she was in her day: legs kicked up high, dresses like Marilyn's, driving all the boys crazy.

I start to steer my chair toward the dining room. Crackled laughter whirs past my ear. "Oh, Cody, even with a head start, you can't beat me." Her voice trails off as she disappears into the dining room. "I'm still the fastest girl in the town."

⌘

My bread roll looks stale enough that it could be classed as a blunt weapon.

Viktor slides his plate alongside mine and sits beside me at the big communal dining table. He's been here longer than anyone, even the staff.

We always sit down one end, the guys' end, where Viktor heads the table and exchanges looks with Sophie, who congregates with the girls at the far end. It's juvenile. Everyone knows they have the hots for each other. Sophie says she doesn't like pussyfooting, but she and Viktor can't manage to just get it on.

I'm hungry. Joe's gone home, and Caren's not working. They're the only two who pay any attention. For the rest of them, we're a drag, or entertainment.

"Why no eat?" asks Viktor, sawing at his thin slice of meat as if it's still alive. "You no hungry?"

"Waiting for someone."

He scoffs his mouthful and makes a noise from the back of his throat. "They no good. I do for you."

Before I can object, he is cramming meat and vegetable into my mouth. This plane is a kamikaze.

"You know, back in Russia, we eat a lot of meat. Good for energy."

I'm trying to chew through the food stuffed into my mouth without choking.

"It was good time. Happy for me."

He starts to collect more food for another attack on my mouth. The knife and fork in his hand look like part of a child's playset. "I'm fine, thanks Vik."

"That why you so small, little Cody."

I roll my eyes.

He returns to his meal, his knife and fork squeaking on the plate.

"Do you miss Russia?" I ask.

His eyes become dreamy. "I miss the air. The freedom. Russia? No, just the air."

"I think everyone here misses their freedom, buddy."

He continues hacking at his meat for a moment longer, and then stops.

When he brings his brick head up to look at me he has gone completely. His bottom lip drops and his eyes vacate. Gravity brings down his expression, and then confusion overwhelms him. The hunched-over Viktor becomes a tower when he stands. He looks around, his eyes darting about, full of fear. His breathing deepens and he begins to wheeze.

"Where?! Why I am here?"

He surveys the room in paranoia and then throws his food tray into the air. "I not belong!" he roars as he starts away from the table.

Sophie calls out, "Viktor, please."

He stops and turns, his eyes catching hers.

"Come on, honey. Sit down. Sit with me."

If anyone can placate him, it's Sophie …

Dementia supersedes starry eyes – he breaks into a lumber, straight toward the illuminated green sign above the door, the fire exit.

The nurses are prepared. The caregivers get out of the way. Needles come out and so does Philomena, the head of this show. That's what it is, a goddamn show.

It takes three of them to pin him. Two to sedate him. No words are used to try to mollify Viktor, just drugs. Poor Viktor. He's like a scared animal being captured. He really is like an animal. He's been captive here as long as I've been coming. Signed away by his family to die here. Too demented for the outside world he misses so much. Too much for them to care for.

My dinner has decorated a good part of the table, carrot and peas splayed out like Lego pieces. Viktor moans as he drifts away into a sedated pile of flesh.

I reverse and steer out, passing the nurse who was meant to feed me. It was better to be fed by Viktor, even with the kamikaze plane.

Philomena glares at me as I pass. "What did you do to Viktor?"

"Nothing."

She comes around and stands in front of me, her cheeks as red as her hair. "You're back for one evening and you're causing trouble, upsetting Viktor. He only gets like this when you talk to him."

"Maybe if you let him out of here every so often then he wouldn't lose his mind and need to escape."

"Your wife has dropped you off because she needs a break. Have you thought about that?"

I feel the need to stretch my neck when she says wife. Why does everyone have to say wife? Why can't they just say Isobel?

"Well, have you, Cody?"

I consider saying something smart-ass, but don't. When you can't move ninety-five per cent of your body, you pick your battles. "Yeah, I know that."

"What does that tell you?"

I can only shrug my forehead.

"It tells you that sometimes you can be trouble."

"How much trouble can I make when I can't move?"

Philomena raises her eyebrows. "Plenty."

"Is there anything else?"

"Just try not to upset Viktor while you're here."

I steer off to the window.

This whole place needs to be upset. Everything does.

✢

The room becomes visible as I wake fully with a short, sharp gasp.

A large weight plonks beside me, depressing the lax floorboards beneath the lounge carpet, and causing my chair to rise as if on the other end of a seesaw.

"Why I have to stay here, Cody?" Viktor's head is drooped, as though he's trying to use his knees as earmuffs. "There is big world out there. More story."

Dust has built up in my throat – I cough. "I don't know, Vik."

"Why you stay here?"

"To give my wife a break."

I surprise myself. I never call her that anymore. Hearing it must have been infectious.

"You married?"

"Yes, Vik. You've met her before."

A few eye squints and he extracts a memory. "Oh, yes. Tall blonde woman. Very pretty."

I grunt. Why are people so observant of Isobel today?

"You think Sophie is pretty too, though, don't you?"

Now he grunts.

"Don't lie to me, Vik. I've seen the way you two look at each other. You've got a crush on her."

"You cheeky, little Cody. My father would have clipped your ear for remarks."

I wonder about my father, and what he would have done in response to my remarks. Not my birth father – I mean Larry. He'd probably just have laughed, or come back with something even smarter … I try to think of him and Janine as little as I can. Guilt is an insidious thing.

Viktor leans back on his chair, an assured look on his face. "You know, Cody, I get out of here one day."

"And you'll take Sophie with you, right?"

He shakes a fist. "You watch it now."

It's meant to be threatening, but I know Viktor. He's a teddy bear.

I feel sorry for him. It's difficult not to pity this old, naïve fool. There's no getting out of here for him, or for anyone else. Once you're a resident, the bed you sleep on at night will be your deathbed.

"One day I make plan," he continues. "And then no one can stop me."

I want to see him get out of here, and drive away into a blood-orange sunset with Sophie. See the fight he'll put up to break free. Do his best Chief Bromden impersonation. Stick it to Philomena and the nurses.

I really hope he proves me wrong.

I want to be wrong about everything.

Chapter 7

(NOW)

The shelves are stacked high, as though I'm moving along city streets lined with skyscrapers. No, I'm a kid, again and again. I'm going to get a toy. Home will be forgotten along with this toy … one of my handful of memories before that day that Mom dropped me off at kindergarten.

Now here I am, a thirty-two-year-old boy, being taken to get another toy. I won't play with this toy, either.

Joe told me that Isobel had shown him some of my albums. He's decided it's time I "got back into it". He says he knows a way it can work. That he's got a friend who can fit this or that. He doesn't understand, though; it's not my inability to move that's stopped me photographing.

Passing camera after camera, fancy playthings for stupid tourists that used to be instruments to me. My tools. My weapons. My art. Every passion of life captured in this passion of my art.

And I see them now, plastic and batteries. Acid.

"I won't use it," I say as we hurtle on toward the new digitals. "I don't care what you get."

We stop at a case. "Maybe you won't, fella, but maybe you will."

He really doesn't understand. I haven't snapped anything since a bump called Holi. Colors, everything. Celebration. And then a fucked-up moment in time …

"I think this Canon looks good." Joe's pointing to a camera in the middle shelf.

"It's a piece of shit." I'm not lying. The lenses have never been good.

"I guess they're all pretty crappy, right mate?"

I don't respond. The Nikon beside it is much better. Just as useless to me, though.

A store clerk who looks like he's just discovered the wonders of internet porn comes to Joe's aid. He asks in his breaking voice if we need any help.

"Cody here used to be a bloody great photographer," Joe starts. "And he's looking to get back into it."

The clerk looks at me with bewilderment. "Okay …"

"So, what's best?"

The boy rubs the back of his neck. He's got no goddam clue. "This one is pretty hot right now. It's got all the specs you want." He points to the Canon.

"What do you think, Codes?" Joe is grinning.

"I could take better pictures with a pinhole camera."

Joe claps his hands together. "Excellent. We'll take it."

The clerk opens the cabinet, takes out the camera and then leads Joe away.

He's left the cabinet open. A memory flash, away I go … there's laughter on the wind, some energy somewhere else …

Slink through the aisles. Keep your eyes on the target.

My legs went from a solid to liquid as fear rose within me. Young, homeless, desperate, but in love with life. A rambunctious little shit. A camera cabinet not locked properly. There in it, the sleek-looking Polaroid. So much in the world, on the streets and parks in which I lived, so much to capture and hold onto. Snap a moment in the infinite timeline of the universe. Keep it safe and beautiful. Hell, even sell one or two.

Those watery legs found strength, became solid. That boy snuck closer, slid his hand in and retrieved the Spectra.

The call of the store clerk, the pounding feet of security. The dash as I ran. Those watery legs turning to tidal waves. Out into the stream of a Chicago afternoon.

A teaspoon of courage changed my entire life.

Larry.

Isobel.

And right back to a cabinet ajar. The better camera sitting there. I could snatch it …

Those watery legs … it's the Dead Sea.

I'm back, the sound of store music, overly bright floodlights.

Joe is nowhere to be seen.

The aisles are narrow. It'll be hard to make it around the corner.

I push the joystick and begin to roll, but I'm stopped.

"Woah!"

A can drops, and clinks when it hits the floor. A black pool forms. A teenage boy is standing in front of me, his arms raised and spread like he's covered in something poisonous, Coke all over his shitty jersey. Who wears a Wilkins in Chicago?

"Relax, it looks better now."

Another smart-ass remark – I surprise myself.

"Fuck you, retard," the boy snarls.

Two boys join him. "What's up Craig?"

"This spastic ran into me and made me spill my Coke."

I reverse and then try to steer around him, but he steps in front of me. Damn these skinny aisles.

His lips twist into a nasty smirk. His friends step to his side, the same delinquent grins on their faces.

"Look at this fucking retard. Going somewhere buddy?"

They laugh. Hyenas sound better than these chirpy kids. My hand shakes as I reach for the horn. It'll do nothing, but in the most ridiculous moments I have some sense of humor.

The boy wipes his jeans and then spreads it across my face. "You put something on me, so now I'm gonna put something on you."

His friends cackle and step back. The boy unzips his pants and flops out his dick.

I go to reach for my joystick, but one of them grabs my hand.

The boy breathes in, and his friends encourage him, "Think waterfalls, Craig."

"That thing's pathetic, does it even have the range to get me?"

Why I'm goading them, I can't fathom. Yet I'm about to pissed on by a boy half my age, and I'm laughing.

"You think this is funny?"

I'm shaking with laughter, incredulous of my own behavior. "If I didn't have a catheter and a leg bag to drain my piss, I think I'd actually piss myself."

He stops trying, his face scrunched in anger and shock. "Fuck you retard!"

His pin-dick has retracted back inside his pants like a scared tortoise hatchling. With the same hand that was just aiming his cock, he slaps me. "Bitches get slapped like that."

It stings. The pain is riveting. Though when the next comes, it jolts my head and I feel that spot in my upper spine. Shock through my body. My breathing shallows. The boys are jabbing me, slapping me, prodding and laughing. My breathing …

"Oi!"

Joe is hurtling toward the boys. They laugh. For a man who could impersonate a hobbit, he appears ferocious.

"What, you want some too little man?" one of the teens goads.

One. Two. Two kicks, and two boys are on the ground clutching their thighs. "Come on tough guy." Joe is bouncing up and down. "I'm just getting warmed up."

The boy looks seasick. He fumbles for words as his friends try to stand. They laugh like hyenas when they scavenge, and now they retreat like hyenas when a lion arrives.

"Bloody cowards," Joe says, as the boys disappear through the aisles. "You right mate?"

I'm wheezing. "Yeah."

"Can't let little bastards like them push ya round."

"What the hell am I meant to do?"

"I dunno. Was justifying my violent outbreak. You could do something, though. Maybe ram them with your chair."

"I tried – they stopped me."

"Then beep your horn."

"Tried that too."

"Then spit like a llama."

I roll my eyes. "And what's that meant to do?"

"Dunno. Just confuse them, maybe delay them until I get there." Joe places the camera on my lap and steers me out of the store. "Maybe we'll get Dave to fix a battering ram on this thing. Then it'd do some damage."

"Wouldn't have happened if you hadn't taken off, you know."

"Wouldn't have happened if you'd kept up."

The water runs through my hair, tingling my scalp. I try to follow each drop. Onto my head, down my cheek like a tear, then hurtling down my neck, and then it's lost. Every single drop, lost at the same point.

Showering is worse than toileting. It was difficult to get my head around both at first – having someone do them for me. Emptying my piss bag, supervising me as I crapped through a hole in my commode chair – at least I didn't need a bag for that – wiping my butt. Washing my dick, my butt, bathing me like an oversized infant in an oversized baby's chair. It was all hell to begin with. Losing care has made them both better. But the showering still gets me.

The shower was where something magical once happened. Passion. Sheets of water caressing our naked skin. Now it's perfunctory and mechanical. Hoisted by pulleys into a special commode chair so someone I once loved can bathe me because I can't. It looks more like a torture chamber than a shower.

Isobel always wears a swimsuit. Not a sexy one, an old one-piece. She wears gloves too, like they told her to, as if I'm something toxic. She needs them to get into the cracks of my lifeless body where other life forms have probably taken up residence. I'm like a rock at the beach that's covered in mollusks.

"It's nice Joe got a camera for you." Isobel holds up my arm and runs the loofah up and down, getting into my armpit.

"I paid for it. He just stole my card so he could get it."

"Still, nice of him to think of you."

I don't reply.

"He said the way it's attached you can move it in all angles with your hand."

It's attached right beside where my phone sits. A phone that no one texts or calls next to a camera that won't take any photos.

"He thinks you'll start photographing again. Reckons it'll be like riding a bike …" She says it so nonchalantly, then realizes. "Sorry."

"It'll be exactly like riding a bike for me."

The conversation ends there.

Water running through my hair.

I start to detach as Isobel moves to the back, the way she always does when she is cleaning my ass through the hole in the chair. I close my eyes, leaving this shower for another one that's happening five years ago.

Warm water running between bodies. Hair slicked. Droplets dotting the most beautiful face I'd ever seen.

"Cody."

My name – and I'm right here in the shower of now. My name – it must be serious. I swear I didn't leave the toilet seat up.

"Can we talk?"

"What about?"

She's in front of me again. I hate that stupid red swimsuit. It's like looking at a washed-up *Baywatch* girl trying on her old costume. "About Jake."

That jerk is the last thing I can be bothered with.

No answer from me is good enough for Isobel when she wants to talk.

I remember another woman who once inhabited her body being so concise – away from the public, anyway – and careful with words. She'd speak so little but say so much. Now she speaks so much and says very little.

"Things are getting more serious with us."

"You've only been seeing him six months."

The water seems louder.

"I know, but things are moving quickly. We're older, you know."

"Just tell me what you have to tell me."

Isobel places the sponge on the rack, and then sighs, rubbing her hands nervously. "I want to make sure you're okay with it beforehand."

It's as if I'm her kid, not her husband.

"It doesn't bother me." My voice has become crackly. Fatigue. "I've told you a million times to move on. Now you're doing that. Good for you."

It sounds like a waterfall in here.

Water runs over my lips but my throat is bone-dry.

The steam is making it harder to breathe.

"Okay … I was going to ask you, but since you don't care, I'll just let you know. He's going to move in."

I had to break down walls to meet the real Isobel, all of her. It was my greatest achievement.

He's moving into our house after what, six months? Does age really precipitate knowing someone that well? Does *he* know her that well already?

Isobel turns off the shower. The waterfalls become silent. "I didn't want to say anything to you before I was sure he was going to be part of our life. I'm still going to care for you, Cody."

Jake. Isobel. Our life?

"Whatever. I don't …"

"Yeah, I know, Cody." There's fire in her eyes again. "You don't care. Maybe I'm finding it hard to give a shit, too."

She's been tired for so long, drained by me.

Now he's here, charismatic and benevolent. Energizing her again.

And I'm pissing her off.

She's here more than I've realized, the ardent Isobel who I once knew.

The man who once knew her …

We're out of the shower now, Isobel dressed in her robe. She opens the bathroom cabinet and takes out the bottles. Two pills from this one and one from that one. With one gulp and no water she swallows them. Sometimes I think to ask how that side of her is. Mostly, I try to believe those three pills with no water each night work.

Breathing deeply, I start to sink into my abyss of apathy as she dries me. But I can't – thoughts are pinging off the inside of my skull. Jake. His body engrossing hers. The body that I would massage moisturizer into, that would feel supple with the scent of cucumber as she shed her robe to lie against me … It doesn't matter now, though. I can't do anything for her anymore. She's still alive. She can find pleasure.

When did I let this happen?

No, I can't think like that. Concentrate and tune into the white noise of the bathroom fan. Let it distract me. Blur everything else.

Something's interrupting this too, though, something irritating like an itch that can't be reached. Isobel's drying me too roughly, maybe? I can't quite catch it.

Try again. Get into your abyss, as she gets you into your pajamas.

The bathroom fan shuts off. The white noise is taken with it. Now there's no noise, nothing. Just here, rolling down the hallway. The cold wooden floorboards creaking under the weight of my obtrusive carriage.

I'm in my abyss now.

Echoes come and go … that fan starts up again! No white noise, just the fan. No nothingness here. No comfort. Everything's mixed up and not how it should be.

That fan is loud for a moment, not just an echo. And then something takes my attention. The whirs of the fan recede back to echoes. There's something else, now loud, taking over. Blaring in vision to my mind's eye.

In the distance, a shadow of a man.

My eyelids have anchors attached as we approach my room.

My room.

The room just for me. My special room. My special bed. My hoists – my hired limbs.

Me, a corpse in an abyss.

Trying to ignore the echo of that fan, ringing in its ear. That shadow in the distance.

A corpse being transferred into his bed, being tucked in with cold hands. Pillows being fluffed so he can lie at the right angle.

He – a man?

The man of the shadow? It's hard to tell if he's there. But there's definitely a shadow, there in the distance. The shadow, the fan, I can't get them out of here.

The fan, still spinning to create that echo.

Something, creating that shadow.

Chapter 8

(THEN)

There was nothing other than the beautiful woman I loved occupying me, shining brighter than the city lights.

There was no insecurity in us. I felt no fear for her. There was just light. The city lights and the sparkle of her eyes. The darkness in her thoughts was somewhere else. Any worry I'd found since falling in love was eclipsed by her smile.

The happy version of us on a warm Parisian night.

Hand in hand, we navigated the streets until we reached Boulevard De Clichy. Passing tour guides with groups at their heel, suavely dressed men and elegantly clad women, we neared the red windmill on the rooftop of the Moulin Rouge. It made no sense to me, but it was cool, eclectic, and so I snapped it like a tourist on the way in.

The interior made me think that perhaps this was what Vegas wished it looked like. It was on fire. It was everything good about anything classic. It was passion and sophistication in drapes and fashioned wood. The main room was a forest of glowing bulbs.

The show was something else. The costumes, the legs, the garters, the frills. We sipped champagne, the price of which should've made me feel guilty. We cheered, and whistled, and struggled to keep our hands off each other. Lust and passion seeped from our pores – we just didn't care who else was around. The smell of pheromones was strong when I ran my lips over the skin on Isobel's neck. No smell ever beat that, not even freshly mown grass in summer time.

The cancan didn't leave my mind the entire night. In the bar afterward, an impression of those long legs kicking up in front of me, almost close enough to touch, was playing over in my mind as I noticed Isobel lock eyes with a woman across the room.

She pushed back the stool and joined the woman at a booth. Their lips moved, soft pink, so sweet and alluring. Things went in slow motion watching them.

I sipped my martini, and relaxed as much as I could with my imagination now taking hold.

It was a game of wait and see. I just had to stick it out.

Finally, Isobel said something that made the two of them turn to me. The curl of the woman's brow as she spoke from her eyes told me all I needed to know.

They stood, the woman lending Isobel a graceful hand, and passed me on their way to the door. Their butts moved side to side, ever so slightly. The woman nodded to a man by the bar. Isobel turned and winked at me. I followed them out into the night, as did he …

It was still night when I woke.

Icy moonlight beamed in through the high lattice windows. I lay on a mattress on unpolished wooden floorboards. An almost-empty bag of molly was beside my head. "Fuck," I thought …

There were arms draped over my chest. One from each side.

I was stuck in the awkward time between being high and not yet coming down. New consciousness and a fading buzz, which still made time surreal.

Nestled up on my left shoulder, Isobel breathed quietly. Prone, to my right, was the woman from the bar. Only as I surveyed her naked body in the moonlight, from head to toe, and back over those legs did I realize who she was. That cancan really did stick with me the entire night. Those legs. Up in my face. Over my torso. Around my head.

Over Isobel's waist was another hand. I slid from under the girls. The man behind Isobel grunted and turned the other way, snatching as much blanket as he could.

I tickled Isobel's feet and she sat up with squashed, overtired eyes.

She raised a hand to say what the hell.

I flicked my head toward the door. She looked around the room and then out the lattice windows, and then back to me, and nodded.

We dressed messily, collected our stuff and crept out of the apartment, navigating a dungeon-like hallway system.

The curvature of the walls. Was I in the Catacombs?

I opened the heavy oak door for Isobel and we burst into the night.

The fresh air flowed through my nostrils and the night flowed back through my mind.

The girls together. Toys and a show. Higher and higher. With Isobel, and then swapping … how hot it had been to be with someone in front of Isobel, while I watched her be with someone else. Uninhibited sexuality. Explosive lust.

Isobel laughed as we ran down the street in bare feet, our shoes in hand. "We are awesome."

Through the quiet hum of night, a disgruntled call came from a man on the opposite side of the road.

Isobel called back in French. This caused him to yell and point, turning that beautiful French tongue into something poisonous. He waved his arms and waddled off down a cobblestone alleyway.

"Pfft." Isobel waved hers. She didn't give a shit right then. She was irresistible.

"What did he say?"

"Reckons we're dirtying up Paris. I told him his wife's doing that right now."

"You're such a smart ass."

"Some guys think just because they have a dick, they have to be one. I don't care for it."

At the foot of the stairs of Rue Foyatier I grasped her hand and pulled her in, then lifted her up onto the metal handrail.

I lunged for a kiss.

No lips.

I opened my eyes.

Isobel was off and running up the stairs.

"We've got fire on our feet, Cody," she called. "And we're running around this crazy world with passion and blazing a trail that someone'll read about one day."

This was the upside of her yo-yoing.

I told myself that I just had to appreciate these times when I had them.

Let the passion run free when it's felt.

At the summit of Montmartre, I caught up to her. The Sacré-Cœur Basilica stood to one side and to the other the overgrown village of Paris spread out to the end of the earth. In the distance the Eiffel Tower rose out of bubbles and boxes, faint in the light of the stars.

We were alone, at the highest point of the most elegant city in the world.

So high, and less and less because of MDMA.

I pulled her in by the waist and then slid my hands up to cradle her head gently.

Isobel giggled. "I'm a fruit loop."

"No, we're fruit loops," I said.

"We're fruit loops."

"Like the cereal, right?"

"Yeah!" Her eyes flared. "We're *Froot Loops*. Let's never become oatmeal."

I fell in love with her more.

Our lips connected.

The world could've crumbled around us and we wouldn't have noticed. It did. Everything disappeared, and I was alone with Isobel looking over the universe. Holding hands, connected beyond physicality, and with the knowledge of a secret that no one else knew. That no one before us had known and that no one after us could ever know. If there could even be an after.

Forever.

This moment seemed forever.

Looking in on everyone stuck in their ruts, stuck in their nine-to-fives, stuck with their regrets and their cowardice to go after what they wanted, what they went to bed at night and dreamed of. We weren't sleeping. We weren't stuck in dreams of yearning for something else.

We were up, living it.

And that's how we'd always be.

Together.

Chapter 9

(THEN)

"Ain't it somethin', kid?" Larry was gazing up to the towering points of the Milan cathedral in front of us. "Like stalagmites."

We were standing on a small footbridge looking over the square.

Earlier, we'd photographed a runway show, in which Isobel was one of the lead models, the first time Larry and I had worked together in a long while.

Milan was something all right. A city made to be photographed.

A small cluster of fluffy white clouds, which looked like poodles' tails, had gathered in the sky behind the cathedral. I lifted my camera and took a snap. A tall woman with skin fashioned from olives strode by, as if she was on the longest of runways. Most women in Milan walked like this.

"Only thing more beautiful than the architecture here is the women," Larry continued. "Was kind of glad you weren't a girl when I found you. You'd have been more of a worry than you are."

"Why the hell are you worrying about me? I'm doing well. Come on."

"I hear things, kid, and I know the scene, remember? I've been down that way of experimentation and all that."

"My feet are anchored. I'm just enjoying life, that's all."

Larry held his eyes on me for a moment longer and then nodded. He lifted his camera and snapped the cathedral, and then admired the photo on screen. "And how's the most important part of your life?"

Isobel was out shopping with Janine in the Quadrilatero d'Oro. "She's great. We're great, but …"

"But what, kid?"

A myriad of scenes ran through my mind: those peaks we climbed, and then the lows.

"She scares me, Dad. Scares the living shit out of me."

"Why's that?"

We relaxed our cameras and leaned on the railing.

I exhaled a long breath. "To be honest, there's a lot of things that scare me about Isobel, but it all comes back to the same thing. I'm scared of losing her."

"You two seem pretty peachy to me, kid."

"It's not that – I know Isobel is far too good for me – it's more …" This was difficult. I'd never talked to anyone about Isobel's problems. "She's a yoyo. And sometimes I get scared that she'll make a rash decision. Just leave. Disappear like she did when she was young. Or …"

Larry was taken aback. "No, no way. She wouldn't."

Isobel walked through my mind. First like she did past the fence of the orphanage, then on a runway, and then, like she did when she approached me while I sat handcuffed to the bedpost. I surveyed the town square, where thousands of tourists scurried.

"I don't think so," I said, gulping as insecurities flooded my thoughts. "But I don't know. These things just come into my head. I figure I'll lose her some way in the end."

Larry gripped my shoulder. "You lose people in life, but while you've got them you've gotta make the most of your time with them. You might lose her, but that might be when you're old and gray and more senile than me."

"You've always known what to say."

"That's why I'm your dad."

This filled me with a feeling of warmth and belonging. If I'd never known otherwise, never lost, I'd have thought he had always been my dad.

We cased our cameras and started from the square.

Larry stopped by the open window of a café, ordering two coffees in Italian. "Have you ever talked to anyone else about this?"

"No."

"You thought about it?"

"I've never had a clue what to do. This is all new to me. I spent my childhood years with next to nothing, but I've always tried to be positive.

She spent hers with anything she wanted, but she's always had this darkness about her."

"Don't think it's that simple, kid. What most people want isn't something that can be bought or sold. It's something they've got to find in themselves and in their life. It doesn't matter how you grew up, either. Mental illness can affect anyone."

Larry passed me my coffee. I sipped it, mulling over those words. Mental illness. "What do you think I should do?"

"You love this girl?"

"I do."

"You see a future with her?"

"I don't see a future without her."

"Then you need to do the right things by her, and that means supporting her through everything. Helping her to be the best she can. If you're concerned I think you need to get her to talk to someone."

Isobel came to the forefront of my mind – she never fell far back into my thoughts. Her heart. Her enigmatic mind. That confusing head of hers. Her wild side. Her dark side. I loved every single part of her – even the ones I didn't really understand.

"There's a guy in New York I know," Larry said, taking out his phone. "I'll give you his number. I suggest getting in touch with him."

I punched Gary Wildemere's number into my phone.

"And for now?"

"Just enjoy Milan, kid. It's a damn good city."

⁂

Milan was a great city. But the best thing about it was someone.

"Eyes closed until I say." Isobel untied the blindfold. "Okay, open."

I'd never seen legs look so long.

She had on fishnet stockings, six-inch stilettos, a garter belt, and lace bra with matching panties. All black, except for her silver necklace and cherry red lips.

I went to move my arm, but I was tied fast to the chair.

"I see shopping went well."

A stiletto shot up and stomped on the chair in front of my bulging briefs. "Shut up. You don't talk unless I tell you."

Nerves and excitement shot me through. I shut my mouth.

She turned away from me and, with her legs straight, bent down and held her ankles. I felt my cock pulsate and break free from my underwear. My teeth grinded, fists clenched. I needed to feel her. Her waist verging inward from either side like an upturned chalice. The small indentation of her labia showing through the silk. Her butt, round and perky, always drawing in me like magnets to the iron in my blood. And her eyes, when she glanced back at me. Those eyes, the window into the realest part of her.

"Seriously, Isobel, I need to fuck you."

Slowly, the way a wave builds, she rose and stood tall. In her hands she held a strip of cloth. "I told you to shut up."

She gagged me, then dropped to her knees, hands resting on my thighs. I began to hurt as she massaged up my leg, and stopped short of touching my erection. Over and over again, she continued to tease me to the point of insanity. She smiled from her eyes, her moist lips held still.

I groaned and tried to break free.

She slapped me.

Once more she tickled the inside of my thigh, but this time she continued higher. I nearly lost it on her first touch.

She sucked slowly, and every slight movement or hum from her throat sent a buzz reverberating through my body. She took me to the edge. Right when I was about to come. And she stopped.

Isobel stood, kissed my lips, the cloth still in between them, and then lay on the bed with her legs apart. She made me watch as she pleasured herself, massaging her clit, slipping inside just a little, biting her lip as she moaned. With each breath in, the light shone on her stomach, highlighting her smooth, flawless skin, the thin, shadowed lines pointing from her abdomen to the top of her panties.

Then her stomach tightened, contracting as she climaxed.

A heavy sigh exited her lungs as she sat up. She crossed her legs seductively and made me hate Sharon Stone.

From the bedside table she took a bottle of wine. She filled a glass, and then swirled the wine as she surveyed me.

She stayed there for a while, sipping wine and staring at me with the minutest elevation in the corner of her lip. My hard-on ached.

Eventually, she stood, crossing her feet over as she approached me, that alluring strut that distracted me every time I photographed her.

She towered over me. The stain of her red lipstick on glass. The lace of her lingerie, creeping up onto her breasts. The line of her panties ... *just another inch lower, please.*

Her fingers tickled my chin. She opened my mouth, removed the cloth, and trickled wine onto my tongue. I gulped it down, and then drank some more, then tasted something sweeter and more intoxicating than the tipple. Isobel's lips easing onto mine. Long deep kisses.

Then she gripped my back, her nails etching into my skin like a cat's claws, and climbed on top of me.

Nothing came close to the warmth that came when we connected like this.

In the same way she had worked me with her mouth, she grinded on me slowly. With each moan, she clawed harder and made me bleed. Settling after she came, she paused and kissed me, running her hands through my hair. Then she sat up and started grinding again, pushing herself to another climax, and edging me to the point of erupting. But she stopped again, and left me alone, sitting on the bed with the bottle, scanning me for every little flicker of pleasure and frustration.

This happened three more times before she allowed me to come. My orgasm was more intense than ever before, more explosive and relieving.

In bed, I held her as though I'd die if I let go. Nothing was said as we fell asleep on silk sheets, skin glued with sweat.

⁂

A cold gust woke me. My hands searched for Isobel, but found only the coolness of the sheets. Moonlight shone in, pale on the polished floor. The window was open, the white voile curtains moving with the breeze to look like a wedding dress. The sound of quiet weeping carried in.

I rose from bed and wrapped myself in a robe. The door to the balcony was ajar.

Outside, balled up on a bergère, Isobel had her chin resting on her kneecaps, wearing my gray hoodie as a dress.

The door creaked as I pushed it open. Isobel's eyes didn't move from the cityscape of Milan.

I pulled the other chair up to where she sat and took her hand.

"Babe?"

She sniffled, but didn't answer. Her mascara had turned to ink, black rivers running down her face.

I tried again. "Isobel, talk to me."

It took minutes of silence for her to say anything. When she did, her eyes turned to me. Those beautiful hazel eyes, bloodshot and drained.

"I don't want to be here."

"What do you mean? In Milan …?"

Her face disappeared into her knees.

"Isobel."

I pulled at her arms, trying to get her out to look at me.

"Isobel look at me."

Nothing.

I wrapped her up, hoping my warmth would bring her out. Help her remember.

Minutes passed, what felt like a long time.

Nothing.

I got up and found my camera.

"Isobel, please look at me." She wouldn't. I snapped once, then twice, waiting for her to look up at me with a nervous smile. Then over and over again. Dozens of photos of Isobel, all the same. Balled up on that chair. Dark night sky. The coldest image I'd ever photographed.

My arms were useless.

My camera was useless.

I was useless.

I was becoming distressed. "What the hell do you want me to do? You won't talk to me, look at me, or say a fucking word. How am I meant to help you when you're like this?"

Finally, she brought her head up. Her eyes were bleary and now lit with frustration.

"Just leave me the fuck alone, Cody."

"I'm not leaving you when you're like this."

"You're making it worse," she said through gritted teeth.

My stomach felt as though someone had taken the wind out of me. Stunned. Jaw dropped. Unable to speak.

Isobel returned her head to her knees.

I'd never felt so far away from her.

I listened to the voices in my head, the doubts and fears, when they told me what to do, and I listened to Isobel. I walked away from the woman I loved when she needed me.

I sat on the side of the bed and buried my head into my hands.

The coldness of the silk was depressing.

That position on the bed. That feeling. I sank into it so deep that I thought
that was what my life would be like. As though I'd never be anywhere else,
or feel anything else again. As though we would actually stay that far apart
forever.

Chapter 10

(THEN)

It was as though nothing had happened.

The next morning, we awoke together, Isobel's arm draped over me. Memories of the night before were there, but the sun was out and the day was new. Isobel was smiling at me, happiness in her eyes. We kissed. I got lost in her touch.

I fell into those moments and left behind the fear and distance of the night before.

For the rest of the time in Italy there was no sign of the dark Isobel, and three weeks later in the Swiss Alps for our last shoot of the tour, that night in Milan was as good as forgotten.

Outside were clear blue skies, sun shining a gentle yellow on the lush green grass and reflecting off the snow-capped mountain tops.

Isobel shouldn't have been able to look so gorgeous in leggings, big furry boots and a faux-fur jacket. She did, though. When her eyes caught me and she smiled, there was nothing that could ever be more beautiful. She was her.

The walk from our cabin on the lake to Giessbach Falls was short, and Isobel made it quicker by taking me on a musical journey, backed by her iPod. She could play piano and sing, but she found it more fun to be an ass.

First off, she ran rings around me to the tune of "I Want to Break Free", miming Freddy Mercury's mop microphone.

"I love how you entertain me instead of helping me carry my gear."

"You're the photographer."

That was it, and then back to the performance.

Prince's "Raspberry Beret", for which Isobel frolicked and pouted her lips off, singing in falsetto and then the deepest baritone she could. Her hood was the beret, and when the chorus arrived she bumped me, using her pubic bone as a nudge bar.

Then there was "Rhiannon".

And "Tiny Dancer" – a myriad of pirouettes and arabesques.

We followed the rocky trail at the foot of the mountain until we reached the bottom of the waterfall, where Larry and the rest of the crew were waiting. The sound of the crashing water drowned out the iPod, but not Isobel.

They laughed when they spotted us.

Isobel dumped her stuff with me and bounced over to Larry, greeting him with a big hug and kiss. She went straight to makeup and kept singing while they worked on her, though now in the presence of others she was singing much more sweetly than before.

"She's a ball of energy today, hey," Larry said.

"Yeah. Knows how to put on a show when she wants."

"How's she been?"

I looked at Isobel, her eyes closed, quietly singing "Ironic". "She's good."

"You still got those concerns you told me about?"

Thoughts of Milan came into my mind. I'd pushed them back since it happened. The abyss between us that felt insurmountable. "Yeah."

"Did you get in touch with Gary?"

I started setting up my gear. "Not yet."

"Well do it. You need to take care of her, kid."

I continued setting up, letting Larry's simple words sink in.

My eyes made their way to Isobel again. She'd finished in makeup and was getting into position.

I focused my camera on her. She stood there up against the rock, middle finger raised. This was customary for most shoots with me.

"You're a class act, Isobel."

Larry chuckled. "Shoots would be boring without her, ya know."

"Life would be too."

She blew me a kiss and then got on with the shoot.

She was everything to me. Such a big part that I didn't know what I'd be without her.

Life would not be boring without Isobel – it would be nothing.

Isobel did her thing, the professional she was, and we finished within an hour.

We thanked the crew and helped them pack up.

"You two coming to the bar?" Larry asked, starting along the trail.

I glanced over my shoulder to Isobel, who was leaning up against a rock. "I think we'll stay up here for a little bit. Nice day, might make the most of it."

Larry and the crew disappeared.

"Should we start the real shoot?" I asked, uncasing my camera again.

Isobel nodded, a cheeky smirk on her face.

The fun began.

Camera set to auto-capture.

Clothes shed piece by piece, photo by photo.

Entangled, we became hot and immersed in passion.

Then for some reason, in the quiet of nature, with just the waterfall crashing behind us, I stopped.

"Isobel."

Her eyes opened. They were magic to me.

"What's up?"

"I think we need to talk about something."

She relaxed, lowering her hands from my face. "What?"

"Milan. The times before, too."

Her eyes narrowed. "Why now? Why now in the middle of making out? Why can't you just go with it, Cody. Be happy."

"That's what I want for you."

"I am happy."

"Maybe … but we need to talk about what happened that night in Milan. I've let it go too long, to the point where it made me feel so far away from you. I don't want to feel that again. I don't want either of us feeling the way we did that night."

"It's just how I get sometimes." She ran her hands over my face. "Can we just leave it?"

Usually, any request of hers was irresistible, especially when she asked so gently. I had to stay firm, though. "No, I want to talk about this."

Isobel withdrew and stepped away from me. She paced, scuffing her feet on the rock.

"I'm not leaving this, Isobel. You don't have to talk to me now, but I want you to talk to someone."

"I don't need to talk to anyone!"

I tried to touch her but she backed away. "Isobel. Please."

"We have this amazing life. We adventure. I let you fuck other women. Why when we're in the middle of a beautiful moment do you have to ruin it?"

"I'm not trying to ruin anything. I'm trying to communicate something that needs to be addressed, whether you acknowledge it or not."

"Acknowledge what? That sometimes I get down? That sometimes I'm erratic? That's human, Cody. Big deal."

"It's more than that and you know it."

"Just leave it."

I stopped her pacing, and held her arms. "Why don't you ever talk about your mother?"

She sank down onto the rock and began to cry.

Part of me wanted to sit beside her and wrap her up in my arms, tell her it was okay. Leave it. The other part of me was tired of being scared. Tired of living with the fear of losing her. So I just stood and watched her as she sat there in her underwear, shaking with tears.

Her face was florid, and her eyes bleary when she finally brought her head from her hands.

"Don't talk about my mother ..." she seemed to choke the words out of her throat.

"Why not? Why have you never told me anything about her, huh? Why do you keep half of your life a secret and ..."

"Shut up!" She stood and swung her arms at me. "Shut up!"

Her hands hit my chest, my shoulders, my face, but they were weak, and became weaker as the shaking sobs took her strength. I gently took hold of her arms and pulled her in close. She tried to resist for a second longer, and then relinquished and buried her head into my chest.

I felt like a jerk for making her feel this way, for bringing up her mother. But it wasn't about the moment, it was about the future and the moments ahead. That there'd always be moments to have.

"I'm sorry, I didn't want to upset you like this. I'm just scared. You scare me. If you ever decide not to be here, there'll be no you. No us. I'll have nothing. I can't lose you."

Isobel continued to cry. I held her, ambivalent about myself, trying to stay strong in my conviction that this was the best thing despite her tears.

"*I'm* sorry. I don't want to scare you. I hate that I do. I hate that I have so much but sometimes I feel like I don't have anything. I hate that sometimes I don't want to be here, and that I say it to you. I shouldn't do that to you."

"It's okay, honey." I kissed her forehead.

It wasn't okay, though. It hurt me like hell to think that she could feel that way. That our love wasn't enough for her.

I tried to swallow that pain, gulp it down like bourbon.

Larry was right. I didn't understand.

"I'm scared, too, you know?" she said after a time. "I'm scared that I'll be my mother one day."

"Why do you say that?"

Isobel slipped carefully from my embrace and sat on the rock. I sat beside her and wrapped my arm around her.

She rubbed her hands nervously up and down her legs. "I'm scared that what's wrong with me was the same thing that was wrong with her. That it got passed down to me."

"What was wrong with her, baby?"

"She used to write me letters all the time, some of them I didn't read until after she was gone. She'd go away for days at a time. Leave the city and go out into the countryside. She'd sit under this tree in a place that no one else knew about. I could read the fear in her words. I could hear how dark she got sometimes … just like me … I'm scared I'll end up doing what she did."

She stopped rubbing her hands and looked up at me.

"She hung herself."

Suddenly everything made sense.

"I'm so sorry. I didn't know …" I held her with desperation, my face buried in her hair, tears pressing at my eyes, wishing that I could squeeze the pain from her.

"We all just become our parents, don't we?" Isobel gave a bittersweet laugh. "Newer versions of them, but we just make the same mistakes."

I brought her face up so our eyes connected. "You don't have to be your mother. You're not. You're you, Isobel, and you can beat what you have to beat. Larry knows a guy that can help you. I'm going to call him and when we're back home you're going to go talk to him. Agreed?"

She nodded and then wiped her eyes, sniffling. "I'm a mess, a snotty mess."

"And you're still beautiful. You always are, baby." I kissed her swollen eyes, wiping away residual tears with my thumb.

When her lips found mine, there seemed to be another level of connection. I had never felt closer to Isobel.

Stripped away of all the bullshit we thought made us happy: the drugs, the alcohol, the excess, the women and sex, there was just us. The rawest, realest versions of ourselves together in a valley of snow-capped mountains. More honest and bound. Each laid bare for the other to love completely, with absolute truth.

Isobel picked up her coat and reached into the pocket. She brought out the iPod, smiling cheekily at me.

Bowie's "Young Americans" came on.

I kissed her like her lips were oxygen.

We fell into each other, and drowned out the sound of everything.

The world meant nothing.

"Never forget the passion," Isobel whispered to me as we made love. "Never forget us."

Chapter 11

(NOW)

The living room is a city of boxes, stacked high and low, streets through the middle.

The weekend's come. Jake is here.

Life was a weekend once upon a time.

Even after I got like this, weekends still encompassed something peaceful at least. Maybe Lincoln Park with Joe, or whatever part of greater Illinois Isobel thought would help me see something except emptiness.

Trees I couldn't climb.

Picnic rugs I couldn't sit on.

Trails I couldn't walk.

Still it was something. At the time, I tried to drown out how much Isobel cared and how much effort she put in to make me happy.

Now, between the box skyscrapers, I see her flash past.

Then comes Jake.

They pass me by.

I think back to her kneeling on the picnic rug to feed me strawberries, helping me sip wine through a straw. Steering me along a trail when I was too tired to move. Staying with me at the bottom of a tree and trying to help me remember when we climbed the highest heights. She tried, she really did. And I didn't care.

Now I have to not care. There's no other way.

As Isobel passes by again, Jake catches her in his arms. "I'm so glad I found you, Bel."

Isobel rises on her tiptoes and gives him a peck on the lips. Something just pecked at me. They pause for a moment and then go ahead with a longer kiss.

I tell myself I don't care.

I can't look away, though.

Isobel takes his melon head in her hands. "Come on, babe, more boxes to go."

Bel.

Babe.

They've got names already.

She never used to like being called Bel. Said she wasn't a princess. Maybe I just never made her feel like one. Maybe he does.

Babe.

That's not me anymore.

Reaching for a box, Isobel catches sight of me. The third armchair. For a second it's as though we're talking silently again, through our eyes.

Isobel drops hers.

Reality pervades her tiny, manufactured place of happiness. She's trying, still. Just not for me. Trying for herself. For some small part of what life was meant to be about.

"Sorry – everything's a bit frantic today." She gulps down something the size of a golf ball. Her eyes are polished. She releases a defeated breath for me, and then inhales a new burst of air, I guess for Jake. "Do you need anything?"

"I'm fine." My voice is weak.

Isobel resumes unpacking boxes. Jake goes into the garage. Isobel and I are alone.

Time alone was one of the most sacred, exciting things we had. Then after That Sunday, we weren't together for a while. Then we were surrounded by help. Then we got to be alone again. That alone was loneliness for us, together. Discomfort. That beautiful alone time, it sits with nostalgia in my mind.

"I'm sorry if this is too quick." Isobel has stopped again. "I'm just trying to do what you …" she stops and internalizes that thought. "I'm doing what I need to do. I still want what's best for both of us."

I reverse, but I'm stopped by the wall. There's not a place far back enough to go. "Neither of us know what that is."

"I have to try, Cody. This is what you wanted."

"Just do what you need to do to be happy."

She comes over to me. "I want you to be happy too."

Our eyes lock. They want to talk again. Hers might want to tell me something. I think she can read mine, too, I'm just not sure how legible my writing is.

"For me to be …"

"That's everything in." Jake comes to her side, his arm coiling around her waist. "Let's have a quick break."

"Okay, great." Isobel feigns a smile. Once a model, now she could be an actress.

Jake notices me. "Sorry, Cody. You've been so quiet I thought you were out."

"Yeah, I went for a walk."

He looks to Isobel awkwardly. "Sorry, I didn't mean to …"

"It's okay." Isobel squeezes his hand, and looks to me. "Maybe we'd all like a glass of wine?"

"I'll get the bottle." Jake goes into the kitchen.

"You want to join us, Cody?" asks Isobel.

"I'll pass."

She stays there for a moment. The way she is framed is made for a photograph. This is the picture I'd take of this experience. Those iridescent hazel eyes, caught up in calamity and the clutter of cardboard. Relics of glory in a suburban empire.

"Okay," is all she says, and then turns away.

Just one word, so terse like a girl I once knew. The way she walks is youthful, full of energy, her feet moving faster as she approaches him. She's excited to be around him. He makes her feel young.

They embrace, kissing slowly. Lips dancing.

Look through the boxes, I tell myself.

Stop watching them.

Why do I have to look?

Why does a legality scream at me? *She's your wife!*

Pride. It has to be pride. It's disturbing – I can't survive on pride. And why pride, when I have nothing to be proud of? Everything I had was taken …

Given away.

Pushed away.

Isobel's head is pressed into his shoulder. Her hazel eyes are staring at me. Through me. Past me – into yesterday. She's looking at me like I've so often looked at her. The Isobel of that time sometimes resurfaces when I look at her like this. Is she seeing the Cody of then, too?

I'm not him.

I'm old. I feel it.

She deserves to feel happy. Feel young like he makes her feel.

⁂

"How are you adjusting, fella?"

Here we are at North Pond. Joe's not going to let up until I take a photo. May as well have my funeral here.

"I only have to see you twice a week," I reply. "Can't ask for much more."

"I've missed you too, mate. But the new fella – talk to me."

The ducks have congregated near an old man two benches over. Old people are duck magnets. They must have wallets filled with loose change, pension cards and bread.

The ducks scamper after each bit he throws, and each time a different duck gets a piece. All of them except the little one at the back. He has no hope.

"If he makes Isobel happy then good."

"I don't get it." Joe leans one hand on his thigh and stares out into the white abyss of a standard Chicago sky. "I see the odd photo, hear the odd story, get the odd impression of something bloody brilliant with you and Isobel. Why is it that your pawning off your responsibility to help make her happy?"

"It's not my responsibility."

"Not completely, but you've got a part in it."

The old man leaves and the ducks finally notice our pile of bread. They waddle over and fight for their share. Again, the little one misses out.

"I can't make Isobel happy anymore."

"Why not?"

"Look at me. Listen to me. There's about as much feeling in my heart as there is in my left shin."

He rolls a bread ball between his fingertips. "If you say so."

"Give me some more bread," I demand.

Joe ignores me, and throws another ball to the ducks.

"Seriously, I want some bread to throw. At least give me that."

"It's not me that needs to give you anything, fella. It's you that's gotta stop taking it from yourself. Whole time I've known you, you've tried to play the corpse and ignore what's still here … and now you've lost her. I think about my girl. I've never got the chance to see her again. And you? You've just pissed that chance away by feeling sorry for yourself. If you truly loved her, there's nothing that could have come in your way."

A small sizzle inside me builds, and then I burst. "You have no fucking clue. No goddam idea how we got to this point, so just shut up and leave it."

Joe's smiling … smiling?!

I'm apoplectic, beyond any anger I remember.

"You know, that's the first time I've seen any sort of genuine emotion from you. Might be anger. Better than nothing, though."

It feels as if I've raised up out of my chair, and now I'm dropping back into it.

The distant traffic, the fluttering of feathers as the ducks squabble over the bread.

This isn't meant to happen.

Detach.

I gulp. There's something in my throat, my jaw, my temples. The nerves behind my eyes. The bags under them.

"What would you do if one day you found yourself loathing what you saw in the mirror? What if you tried to put the images of others in place of you?"

"What specifically are you talking about?"

I hear him, but I'm not talking to him.

I see other faces.

"What if a mansion of happiness had been demolished, and left behind rubble – everything shitty? Would you still try to live there?"

Joe tosses another ball. "I'd probably get out of there."

"Yeah, exactly." Maybe he gets my goddam point. Maybe he can keep his mouth shut about what he has no idea about. "There's no other way."

"But then, maybe I'd get to work starting to rebuild that mansion from that rubble. Mightn't ever look the same but it would still be somewhere to live."

"And what about the man who can't move to build anything?"

"We're not talking about an actual mansion, fella, we're talking about love, so it's got nothing to do with your arms and legs, but everything to do with your heart."

Joe rolls the last of the bread into a ball, and then offers it to me.

I open my palm. "I told you …"

He goes to drop it in and then reconsiders, tossing it into the water instead.

"Yeah, I know. You might say there isn't any feeling left in yours, but the fact of the matter is that whether you know it or not, your heart is still beating. As long as you're alive, you've always got hope."

None of the ducks notice the bread ball in the water.

None except the little duck.

The door closes behind Joe.

The house is awfully quiet. No chatter, just the sound of the oven humming.

Jake calls from the kitchen, "Isobel's out. Gone to get potatoes for dinner."

I ignore him and park in my space.

I'd have asked Joe to stay if I'd known Isobel was out.

"Do you think we can talk, Cody?" Jake's standing in the archway, munching on one of his shitty protein balls.

I don't answer, so he comes and sits on the couch.

"I know this must be hard for you …"

I turn my head away, staring blankly at the front door. "What?"

"The fact that I'm here. It's easy to see that it makes you uncomfortable."

"I couldn't care less."

My left hand is tired. All I muster is a twitch from my index finger. I'm stuck here with him.

"Be honest, Cody. It's just us here. I know you don't like this situation. Or me."

I roll my head over the back of the head rest to fix on him. "I told you, I don't care."

"I'm not here to change anything between you two." This almost makes me laugh. "I just care about Isobel, that's all, and we've grown close."

"How long have you known her? Eight months?"

He shrugs. "Yeah, about that."

"And you think you know her?"

"I feel like I do."

"You don't know shit."

I close my eyes and wish for the front door to open. Better still, to be away from here.

"I know it would kill me, if it were the other way around. If I was in your position. I'm not your enemy, though, Cody. We can all get along."

Now my eyes flare open. "Yeah?"

"I think so. I don't want things to move too quickly for you, or Isobel. It's a lot to cope with."

He thinks he knows a lot. What the hell does he know? He hasn't journeyed with Isobel. He didn't grow up missing her. He didn't grow through the best years of his life with her. He doesn't know her like I did. He didn't lose what I lost.

"And what do I have to cope with?"

"Well … seeing another man with your wife. Not being able to do things for her … you know? I don't know the feeling, but I imagine it must be hard for you."

The room is blurry.

That picture on the wall, the one that doesn't want to be seen … I want to look at it. See it. Feel it. This gel-covered lens can't focus, though.

My jaw is clenched. "I don't care …"

"Maybe you don't. I do care, though, Cody. Isobel deserves the best."

"She does …" I choke the words out. "She does …"

For a moment that picture comes into focus, a presage from another time.

He's right. She deserves what I couldn't give her.

My eyes stay on the picture. "What makes you think you can give that to her?"

"I don't know …" He pauses.

The room falls silent.

Jake stands, towering over me. "Maybe I can't. Maybe she's one of those women who no man will ever be good enough for. I guess at least I'm trying."

It's Isobel's voice that wakes me. Her sounds. I'm parked in my bedroom, still in my chair from the night before. Isobel was too preoccupied to get me into bed. The kitchen light is the only one on in the house. Its yellowy-white beams bleed through to my room. I push the joystick and follow the noise, parking in the lounge room.

When I see where it is coming from, I rouse completely.

I'm awake. For a moment. More awake than I've been in a long time.

It's like an old analog television that just can't quite get the tuning right on a station. A picture jolts between one thing and another.

What is in front of me.

What is in my mind, behind me.

Their door is ajar. Those are Isobel's legs, kicked high into the air. The sides of her body, the indentations of her waist. Her soft, golden skin. I see just a little of her face. Her eyes closing with each sensation. And his ass, ramming into her as if it is a battering ram trying to smash down a door. His strong arms. Ripped back. Her hands clawing into that back.

Sleep, let me sleep. I don't like being this awake.

It was in a Parisian apartment with high lattice windows when I first saw Isobel have sex with another guy, while I screwed someone in front of her. We did it more after that night. After Isobel told me we have fire on our feet, running around this messed-up world so fast.

My feet can't feel the fire on them. They can't run on the spot, let alone around the world.

The scenes continue to play beside one another. Inebriated, passionate swinging. A beautiful French night. And now. A dingily lit Chicago bedroom. Half-dead, half-alive. Cuckolded by a man who seems better than I ever was. Hearing my wife make the sounds with another man that she used to make with me.

Sleep.

I need to go to sleep.

I can't move, though. My eyes are fixed.

Somewhere else?

Apathy is hanging on by its blunt claws.

The abyss is still somewhere I can go. But it's not the same. It's invaded. Corrupted.

That bathroom fan, the shadow of something … now the shades of light, those legs in the air. Different pictures coalescing into one.

Isobel moans, reaching climax.

I can't stand this anymore – I need to move! Back into my room …

The joystick is so close. My hand has weakened, though. Tired from clenching.

It can't move.

I'm stuck here, a eunuch. Listening, watching, the foul taste on my tongue growing.

Chapter 12

(THEN)

We returned to a party.

First was our welcome-home party, hosted by Kate, Tania and the rest of Isobel's friends. Then there was someone's birthday, then someone's engagement, then just house parties and clubs every other day.

Intoxication. Higher than the man on the moon.

After everything that happened in Europe, it was as though we hadn't skipped a beat. After I'd gotten to know Isobel to a deeper level than before, I let it all slip because things felt great.

It continued for months. We stayed high for so long on that return home I would've felt confident walking a tightrope. In fact, that's what we were doing.

It was a Monday afternoon when I walked into our bedroom.

"Isobel?!"

A pile of sleeping pills on the floor. Her necklace splayed beside them.

I rushed over, sliding on the carpet, and grabbed hold of her shoulders. She wouldn't look at me, or say a word.

"What've you done Isobel?!"

I gently shook her. "Baby, please." I was panicking now, ready to call 911. "You need to tell me if you've taken any."

I kept asking, shaking her lightly.

Eventually she shook her head.

"Do you swear to me?"

She nodded, rubbing her arms while she hugged herself. "I'm sorry."

I counted the pills and checked the blister pack. She hadn't taken any.

"We're going to see someone," I said, pulling her to stand. "We've put it off long enough."

Isobel blinked, her eyes vacant. "I'm fine."

"No, you're not!"

Fear, frustration, anger. They went off inside me like fireworks.

I marched to the bedside table and took a bag of molly out of the drawer. "And this shit – we're done with it. Kate, Tania and whoever else, if they want to be our friends, they can learn to love us sober.

"Get your coat."

Isobel stayed standing in the bedroom, hugging her elbow to her body, sobbing.

I grabbed her coat and held it out. "Put it on, we're going now."

She stayed stationary.

I put the coat over her shoulders, and she clutched it like a blanket.

"Now take my hand, or I'm carrying you."

She reached out and took my hand. Hers was cold and clammy.

On the way out the door I called Gary, something I should have done a long time before.

The whole way there I couldn't let go of her hand. The warmth of our connection wasn't there. Just cold hands hanging on.

I hung on tight, as though she'd fall off of the earth if I let go.

"Now you need to tell me if you were serious about taking those pills?"

Gary's voice was warm and soothing.

Isobel was seated on a shrink's lounge.

She shrugged.

She'd gone so far into her shell I didn't even recognize her eyes. Those usually resplendent hazels were dark. Daylight shone in through an opening in the curtains. In the pale afternoon light Isobel looked like someone else.

"Please, honey," I said. "Gary is here to help."

We stayed at that impasse for some time. The grandfather clock's tick filled the room.

"Cody." Gary turned to me. "Perhaps it would be better if I spoke to Isobel alone."

I kissed Isobel on the forehead before I left.

I don't remember my birth parents' funeral, or how it felt to walk away from their coffin, but for some reason I thought of it at this moment.

Isobel wasn't dead, but the loneliness was overwhelming.

The loneliness felt familiar.

And I was frightened, like I remembered being frightened as a child. She's not coming back, I thought. The woman I love is lost. She's not coming back.

Chapter 13

(THEN)

Therapy became a regular thing, and after six months it felt as though we had a handle on things. Isobel opened up to me more. The lows became less frequent and less severe. We changed the way we lived.

Isobel meditated.

We did yoga.

She drank water.

Occasionally a wine.

We exercised – Central Park became a sober morning walk, rather than an inebriated night stagger.

The crazy sex continued and got a little crazier. But more than anything, it got deeper – the pure lust and physicality of our sex, the connection and coalescing of our souls when we made love.

We did so much, but there were some things we didn't do. The parties became an occasional pastime, the drugs and alcohol non-existent to us. Our friends learned to live with it, while they continued their diet of canapés and blow.

There was more oxygen in the air living this way.

My heart only beat heavily when Isobel made it do so. When her eyes captured me and her heart took hold of mine. When she stood at the door with a whip in her hand. When she ran her red fingernails down my chest. When she smiled and the world seemed to make sense, and life seemed as if it couldn't get any better.

We had run around the world, blazing our path with fire on our feet. Now we blazed our path in a new direction, our fire stoked by different highs.

She wasn't lost to me.

I'd found her more than ever.

We'd found each other more than ever.

I'd planned it all well, I thought. Stay with my parents in Chicago for a week, and then make an impromptu trip out to the country because, well, nature was nice.

We'd been driving for an hour out of Chicago city. My heart rate was like I'd been running for an hour. I couldn't calm it.

"Where are we going?" Isobel asked, rolling her fingers through her hair, a cheeky smirk on her face. "You seem a bit murdery: doors locked, shifty eyes and not much coming out of that mouth of yours."

The steering wheel was moist.

"Habit." My voice crackled. "City life."

Along field-lined highways, we drove into the free air of the countryside. Grass deserts met the horizon to either side, alternating with archways of trees. The Illinois countryside seemed like it knew the secrets of centuries before, when concrete cities didn't consume the earth.

We passed the sign for Ostenvale and I took the second left. The road became windy. We passed the broken-down tractor, then up ahead I spotted the abnormally large oak. I turned right down the dirt road, riddled with bumps and potholes that made the car jump and its suspension groan. The forestry grew denser, and soon we were canopied by luscious green, with the twinkle of yellow sunlight breaking through gaps in nature's roofing.

Isobel gazed out the window. "It's so peaceful out here."

"I've always been a city kid," I said. "I've always loved city life. When you come out here, though, I guess you really get it."

At the mound of rocks, I made a left. The track was only big enough for one car. At the arch created by two trees I pulled over and cut the engine. "We're here."

I got out of the car and went to the trunk.

Isobel got out and looked around. "Where exactly is here?"

"You'll see soon."

In one hand I carried the picnic basket and with the other led Isobel. Hummingbirds and sparrows sang as we followed the makeshift path. Sunlight showed the way ahead. From the dense woodland we emerged into an opening that had been hidden by the forest at its front. Endless waves of green grass ebbed and flowed in the summer breeze.

The only shade outside the forest was a lonely oak tree about thirty feet away.

Isobel was peering around curiously, like a detective at a crime scene. Then she spotted the oak. "Cody, where are we?"

"I think you know, honey."

I led her to the shade of the tree.

"This is the tree where your mother used to write letters to you. You said you'd like to find it one day. Well, I found it."

I wedged the basket between two protruding roots.

"But how – how did you find it?"

"It was hard. When you gave me those letters to read, I pored through them to find clues. A town forgotten by time, a relic of simpler times when food was grown locally, an oak fit for dinosaurs, an archway created by angels, with light from heaven, an arena of green, hidden from the world. It took me a long time, and a lot of wrong guesses. But I'm quite sure this is it."

For a moment, she hid her eyes from me, but then returned to me with a smile of wonder. She came to me and kissed me. If nothing else happened that day, the effort was worth it for that kiss.

"Baby, I seriously don't know what to say," Isobel said as we broke, her palms still warming my cheeks.

"You don't need to say anything. Just relax, eat, and drink a lot."

Isobel laughed. "Maybe a glass or two."

We settled on the picnic rug. Isobel looked around at the tree, the fields. "You have no idea what this means to me."

"You have no idea what you mean to me, Isobel. I could try to tell you and show you forever, but I still wouldn't get it right."

She leaned in and gave me a peck on the lips. "You're the best, Cody. You make me happy."

I brought her in once more, this time for a long kiss.

We ate fruit, crackers smothered in cranberry sauce and camembert, and chocolate – lots of chocolate. We drank wine and talked about anything and everything.

There were photos, too. Of her, of us.

Full of food and wine, I leaned back against the oak with my arms wrapped around Isobel.

The wind swooshed the waves of green.

"She would've sat here just like this." Isobel's voice was peaceful, as if she'd just realized something that settled everything inside her. "Her life still had so much light in it. At least in the early letters, the ones she wrote here."

"I never knew her, but I know she loved you. It's impossible for anyone who knows you to not."

"And what about my father?"

The afternoon I had spent with him recently in New York came to mind. Where I'd asked him what I had to.

"He's a broken man, babe. He lost his wife, the woman he'd been in love with for years. And, yeah, he stuffed up by not being the father he should have been for you. At the end of the day, though, he still loves you, and he wants you to be happy."

"How do you know?"

"Because he told me. He just doesn't think that he can help make you happy."

There was no point telling her that in his mind a big part of why they grew apart was that Isobel reminded him of her mother. She scared him, too. He couldn't bear it, he said. I saw it mostly as his own weakness, and his inability to understand that he still had someone to love, that let them drift apart.

"I don't really care to be honest ..." Isobel brought my left hand up to her lips and kissed the back of it. "Because I have all the love I need from a man in you, Cody."

I gripped her hand tightly to let her know it was true. What our hearts could see in one another was as a real as anything our eyes could see.

"I'm not much of a writer," I said. "Pictures have always been my thing. But I'd love to write you a letter one day. Tell you all the things I think about you. What my mind can say but sometimes my mouth can't."

"I'd like that."

At this moment, I'd arrived at the point of the whole trip. "I need to stretch my legs, babe."

I stood and helped Isobel up. I might have stumbled, or walked around in circles as I collected myself, I'm not sure.

Isobel was stretching high when I decided I couldn't wait any longer.

Next thing I knew I was kneeling, and the moment Isobel's eyes caught mine looking up at her, I blurted out everything I might have written in a letter.

"Isobel Claire Green ..."

"Cody, what the hell?"

"Just shut up and listen, I'm nervous enough as it is …

"Isobel, I've loved you since before I knew what love was. You were the highlight of my childhood. And then you came back into my life when I didn't think I needed anything else. I thought I was complete, but then you showed me what this truly means. You're unpredictable. You're insane. You are perfect for me, and I treasure everything about you. I want to ride this rollercoaster with you.

"I will love you more with every beat of my heart, and the only time I'll stop is when it does … Will you marry me?"

Isobel dropped to her knees and threw herself onto me. Our lips found each other's and the day became scorching hot. Steam rose from our bodies in the shade of the oak.

We made love, and then lay on the grass to cool off.

"I guess I'll take that as a yes," I said.

Isobel snickered and nodded her head.

Once more we kissed. I couldn't get enough of her. Upon releasing, I fell into her eyes like I always did. Lost in her.

Under that oak, I felt so alive.

"Never forget the passion, Isobel."

She ran her fingers through my hair. "I never will, Cody. Never."

I vowed to myself that I'd never make the same mistakes as her father. That I'd never forget how to love this once-in-a-lifetime woman.

Chapter 14

(NOW)

The days have melted into one. It's hard to tell how many times I've been reminded of my mentally induced castration. Isobel's moans run through my mind, one continuous symphony of yesterday's glory, remixed as today's incompetency.

The morning birds are singing their melodic song.

Another night spent in my chair. Isobel was too busy having fun with Jake again … At least I'm up early for once.

Everything is still in the house. A deep-blue dawn waves at me through the window; in the distance it's a beautiful morning, somewhere.

Light pattering, and Isobel sneaks out of the bedroom. At the sight of me in the chair at the kitchen table she jumps and gasps, and her hands shoot to her mouth.

"God, you scared me."

"I'm preparing for Halloween."

Isobel giggles. I've surprised her. Since I've been the reticent one, a response like this has been rare. It even surprises me. My wit hasn't completely deserted me.

"Well, you're early. First for everything."

Tardiness was always inevitable for me. I wouldn't have just been late to my own funeral – I probably wouldn't have shown up.

Jake's snores come from the bedroom.

Isobel and I are alone.

"Big night?"

"Just a few drinks." Isobel clutches her elbow to her body, and then swiftly sits at a kitchen chair.

The morning birds take over. Is this the part where I tell her that I'm glad she's finally moving on? That I'm happy that she's happy? Or do I tell her I don't care?

"Are things okay with you?" she asks.

I shrug with my brow. "Fine, I guess."

She doesn't need to know what it feels like … she doesn't need to know I hear them fuck. That I see them kiss. That I understand the way they look at each other.

She's happy right now – and that's something.

"Honey!" It comes from the bedroom. Jake has awoken. "Come back to bed."

Isobel's fingertips graze over the back of my left hand.

It's a new day. I can feel her, just a little. She touches the camera. "You'll have to use this sometime. I can still pose, you know."

With that she walks back to the bedroom, to Jake.

The bed springs squeak and groan. Isobel squeals and moans. Jake heaves. The sound of skin smacking skin. Him smacking her butt. Bodies clapping against one another.

It goes on and on.

On the table I notice Jake's car keys.

Does it matter at all that he drives a Bentley?

Autopilot takes over me. Temporary insanity. I'm steering to the side of the table. Getting my chair close enough to reach the keys. Taking the keys. Driving to my customized trashcan.

My wheel moves over the sensor and the chute slides out. I put the keys in it and reverse off the sensor.

I park back where I was.

For some stupid reason, it's just a little more bearable hearing them now that his keys are in the trashcan. *God, I'm petty*, I think for an instant. Then I smirk to myself. A shallow victory is a victory nonetheless.

"I swear I left them on the table."

Jake is running around the house. Lifting sofa cushions, looking in the fridge, hitting pockets on any bit of clothing strewn around the place.

Isobel is searching too.

I'm parked in my spot beside the sofa, just watching them. I wonder if they'll think to look in the trashcan. Probably not. Who'd leave their keys in the trash anyway? Especially for a Bentley. Expensive cars, those. Probably expensive keys too.

"Where did you last have them?" Isobel asks, kneeling near me and peering under the sofa.

Jake throws his arms up. "If I knew that then I wouldn't be looking for them, would I?"

I laugh. Three months into this thing, and the honeymoon is over.

Isobel throws me a scolding glance.

"I swear I left them on the kitchen table." Jake is getting flustered. "I've gotta meet the guys for golf. I don't want to miss tee-off."

Isobel stands and goes to him in the kitchen. "Relax. I'll drop you off if you need."

He golfs. A dark blonde lawyer who drives a Bentley and golfs. That's whose taken my place. It dawns on me – breaking me from the entertainment I was getting from this – he's the guy who Isobel probably would have been with this whole time if I'd never been in her life. If I'd never known her when she was younger and more lost. What is she now? Is she any more whole and confident, or is he just being the same opportunist that I was, capturing a woman who just doesn't know that she's too good for anyone? Maybe he is good enough for her.

My eyes catch them, a couple in the middle of a useless, meaningless squabble about the most generic of things. Lost keys.

"They're in the trashcan."

They turn to me.

"Pardon?" Jake looks confused.

Isobel goes to the trashcan, opens up the lid and fishes out the keys, brushing off an old tissue that had stuck to them.

"Really, Cody?" she says, raising an eyebrow to me.

"What the hell?" Jake darts his eyes between me and Isobel. "Is that meant to be some sort of joke?"

The humor I'd found in the joke has deserted me. I'm somewhere wandering mentally through a stream of thoughts. Here, there, now, then. High, down. Mountain peaks. Valleys. And that abyss I found.

"Guess it depends on who's telling it," I say, my eyes dropping to the floor. "It's all a joke, isn't it?"

The kitchen faucet turns on. Isobel is washing Jake's keys off. He has his back to me. The air in between us is thick. They're a long way away. They're done with me.

I think to say sorry to Jake as he passes on his way out.

Nothing comes.

Isobel follows.

I think to say sorry to her.

Nothing comes.

They stand at the door and kiss goodbye. He is happy – he's going golfing, how great. She's happy too. He's going golfing.

The door closes and Isobel's smile drops.

He's gone golfing.

It's just me and her. She doesn't seem so happy now.

The house becomes a library.

Isobel goes back into their bedroom.

Their bedroom. It's not even just Isobel's anymore.

Time passes and I wonder what I'm doing. What I just did. Why?

Through a crack in the door I can see into the bedroom. There's the bed, part of the bedside table, the mess of clothes on the floor. Isobel's knickers hanging from the bedpost. Bright pink lace.

And Isobel.

She takes over the space. Her track-suit pants drop and the profile of her naked butt shows. The curve is still there, though it hangs lower than it used to. I can see the start of the line that veers toward her pussy. Not where it goes, though, and so some wonder comes. As she reaches high into the wardrobe, her lower half is q, the top a p. It's been so long since I've seen her naked.

There's only so long a woman's beauty can be suppressed before it finds a way to prosper.

Why am I thinking like this?

In the time I drop my eyes to the carpet, gather myself and look back up, she has dressed and is standing in front of me in yoga pants, Nikes and a hooded sweatshirt.

"We've gotta get groceries," she says, prompting me to follow her. "Can get you a Halloween costume if you like."

"It's okay. I'm already in costume," I say as I follow her to the door. Two jokes in one morning – they've put something in my meds.

"They'll make a comedian out of you yet, Cody."

Outside, the sun is spreading its beams like arms, inviting people into its warmth.

Isobel passes the van and heads down the driveway.

I follow. "Aren't we driving?"

"It's a nice day," she says, "thought we'd walk."

"*We'd* walk?"

"It's a figure of speech, Cody. Get over it."

I feel the sunshine warming my cheeks, and can't help but notice … I'm smiling.

We continue in silence for some time. Comfortable silence.

"I'm sorry for hiding Jake's keys."

"Hiding? You threw them out."

"Yeah, I suppose."

"I know this is hard for you, but you are going to have to try to at least be civil to him. You wanted this, remember? I wasn't the one who pushed …"

"Okay, okay! I get it. I don't need to be reminded of it. It is what's best."

"Are you sure about that?"

My chair rides a pothole, jolting me. "Yeah. I can't offer you anything anymore."

Isobel winds up and punts a soda can as if it's a football. "Maybe not … but I don't need to be told that anymore, either."

"What do you think is best?" I ask.

"Cody, I have no fucking clue. I'm just playing the cards I was dealt."

That ends that conversation.

"It was kind of funny." Isobel smiles as we near the front of the store. "I can't believe you actually put his keys in the trash."

"Bentleys were never my thing."

Her smile widens a little more.

My stare gets caught between the leaves of the trees that line the parking lot. I'm somewhere, trying to find the sky that comes through. The clear blue hope, I'm floating toward it.

I can still make her smile.

Isobel's message tone sounds. She swipes the screen and then snickers to herself.

"What's funny?" I ask.

She shoves the phone in her pocket. "Nothing. Just Jake sending me memes."

The branches are jagged and sharp. The sky is no longer in focus.

I have to leave it there at the door. Things have changed. This isn't the same grocery shopping. I've come with Isobel many times since it happened, but I've never thought about the groceries.

Now, I'm wondering if Reese's Peanut Butter Cups are in the same spot. I used to love those things. Ate them by the bagful. Isobel used to monitor how many I had, said they'd send me to an early grave. I lost the taste for them after it happened. She kept getting them for me for a while – she'd wave them in front of me like a bone to a dog. I always just thought of that saying about sleeping dogs.

Now I'm kind of hoping she leads me down that aisle.

We navigate the fresh-food section first. Isobel bags a cos lettuce.

"What do you think of Jake?" She comes straight out with it. No warm up, nothing.

"He's fine." It's programmed into me to respond like this. "Why do you ask?"

"Coz." That response is programmed into Isobel. It was her reason for anything she didn't want to answer.

The lettuce hits the bottom of the shopping cart and a leaf breaks off. "Cos is a lettuce, not a reason."

Isobel looks at me the way a teacher looks at a terrible student when they finally get the arithmetic on the board.

"Haven't heard that one for a while."

I nod my head to the cart. "Haven't bought cos for a while."

We carry on. Isobel adds to the basket. Fruit, vegetables, crackers, meat, cheese … The yellow and orange packet comes to mind … "You know what I haven't had in a while, either?"

"What?"

"Reese's Cups."

Isobel's eyes remain straight ahead, but from my chair I can see her face turn to reflect a fond memory. "Those things," she says. "They'll send you …"

"Yeah, I know. Blah. I'm three feet closer to six foot under anyway. Let me enjoy my final few feet."

"Don't talk like that, Cody."

We continue, but we pass the confectionery aisle, where I see a flash of yellow and orange. "Well are we going to get some?"

Her head dips. "We can't. Jake is allergic to peanuts."

⚬⌖⚬

Isobel and I are in the living room together when Jake comes through the door.

The episode of *Game of Thrones* comes to an end. The fourth we've watched this afternoon. This is the third time she's tried to make me watch it. This is the first time I've tried to get into it.

It's addictive. I get it now.

I want to watch more.

Isobel presses stop and then turns off the TV.

He's here now. Our time is over.

"How was golf?" she asks, standing to kiss him.

"Was good," Jake replies, and then glares at me over her shoulder. "Almost missed the tee-off, but just made it."

I can't be bothered with this shit right now. They continue to chat, arms wrapped around one another. I go to steer past them. They don't realize they're blocking the path. This stupid, skinny townhouse. Really, it's Jake blocking the path. Tall, strong, too big for in here.

I beep.

This shocks them.

"Do you mind?"

They murmur sorry and shuffle out of the way.

I go into my room. Park beside my bed. Beside the metal frame. The hoist. The commode chair in the corner.

They're out in the lounge room, still holding one another.

The bathroom fan is spinning. Who forgot to turn it off?

Spinning. Louder and louder.

It feels like a black hole in here. Everything being sucked in. No light.

They're out there.

I'm in here.

There's an urge inside me to steer back out there, and interrupt their mushy moment. Shoo away the love birds. Steer right at them. Beep, and beep and beep and beep. Ram them if I have to!

My hand is tired. My heart is too. I stay here.

Stuck.

Their voices become more audible as the fan disappears.

"I love you, Isobel."

A pause.

"I love you too."

Chapter 15

(NOW)

It happened, again. Right after Viktor proclaimed he was going to escape and then made a lumbering attempt to abscond. Something touched my left hand, and then it started.

Robert, my doctor, is leaning forward on his elbows looking over notes. He seems quite bleak. Perhaps he's going to deliver the bad news that I'm not going to walk again, again.

Some hours ago I was convulsing in my chair, pain splintering deep into my muscles, the air as thin as on top of a mountain.

I asked Joe not to call Isobel. She's going away – they're going away. It could be good to interrupt them – interrupt him, stop his little getaway happening. But it's not fair to Isobel. She deserves a weekend away. She deserves some sunshine, some respite from the gray skies of this city. Or maybe I'm just scared her phone will ring out.

Maybe I need to stop that. I can't be scared. I have to let go. Accept them.

The first time an attack happened I was terrified. Each subsequent attack got easier and I learnt how to switch to acceptance mode. While I'm gasping for oxygen, unable to call for help, I let myself reflect in a blur, wrapping up everything my life has been to that point. I prepare to leave this world.

Each time was easier, except for this last one. Acceptance mode never came.

"Today was lucky in some ways, Cody." Robert never tries to be funny, but he humors me sometimes. "We ran our usual scans and tests. Had the attack not happened, we might not have found the blood clots."

"Are they the cause?"

"No, the clots are unrelated to the attacks, but they are a serious concern in their own right. They have formed due to the inactivity of your limbs."

He pauses, looks down and around, as if he's looking for the best way to say what he is about to say.

"Your blood seems to have a tendency for clotting. They have formed rapidly since our last scans, which showed nothing unusual. And," he pauses again, "certain treatments are not suitable for you, given the state of your body."

As Robert keeps talking, I see the letters and words forming and falling from his lips …

Treatment.

Plan.

Hopefully.

If not?

Worst case scenario …

Hopefully not …

We shouldn't think about that right now …

He holds the door open for me and I drive out.

Joe takes an envelope from Robert, salutes him, and then walks alongside me. "So, no more high jump or ball sports, mate?"

"He said it'd be best if I got a new caregiver. Your shitty jokes sent me over the edge."

Joe laughs as we exit through the sliding doors. "In all seriousness, though, what's the deal?"

"Blood clots. There are a couple of scripts in the envelope, and I need new stockings. He's going to talk to you as well at some point." I look at him, looking worried for me. "It should be fine with medication. Don't worry, you don't have to find a new job yet."

"Bloody hell, mate. Don't want to think about that. Who'd make me laugh if something were to happen to you?"

"I'm sure you'd find some other cripple to make fun of."

The lift lowers and I steer onto it. Joe fixes me in place and raises me into the van.

He climbs in the front and catches my eye in the rear-view mirror. "You want to talk about it?"

I shake my head.

Joe nods – he gets me, despite his crappy jokes – and turns the radio up. He mutters to himself about the Top Forties and advertising, but then settles on a station, turning the volume up again to Gordon Lightfoot's "If You Could Read My Mind".

I feel my head shake as tears start to flow. The music is loud enough so that he won't hear me cry.

The world flashes by outside the window. I can barely see the photographs of yesterday, but what I do see is unsettling feelings that I've pushed down for so long. It was always easier this way. Suppress all of it. Be nothing. But now, the hurt pours from my eyes, and I feel the slicing of razor blades in my throat, choking me.

There's nothing they can do.

I gasp for air, and even it tastes sour.

Viktor looks like a vegetable.

Sophie has been knocked out by whatever cocktail of drugs she takes. A few residents cluster around the television, laughing husky laughs at a rerun of *Mork and Mindy*.

Joe has gone home.

With the sun barely set, I can't sleep like many of the other residents, despite the near overdose of pain killers. The meds make me feel numb.

I'm a thirty-two-year-old man surrounded by his grandparents' generation. Wilting alongside a bunch of flowers that bloomed for much longer.

I'm in here for respite. For Isobel … for Jake.

He'll be home from work now, getting ready for their weekend away. He's in my home. Who'd have thought I'd call that townhouse home? He's taken my place. A place I didn't think I wanted.

He's near my photos, my memories. Gorging them with every movement he makes in that house. Sullying them every time he touches Isobel. Every time he fills a void that I made in her life.

That I made.

I checked out of the hotel, I wasn't asked to leave.

I walked out of the front gates – rolled out – looked around and decided instead of moving forward or looking up at whatever sky was above that I should keep my short sight fixed on the gray concrete below my piss slippers.

I'm a goddamn moron. A self-imposed emotional eunuch.

My phone starts vibrating on the tray and startles me.

I drive over to the window, well away from anyone. It's a number I don't know. It's been a long while since I've received a call from anyone other than Joe, Isobel or someone at the home.

I slide to answer and then put it onto loudspeaker.

"Hello?"

"Hey Cody," Jake says.

I can barely feel where I sit but I feel uncomfortable hearing him. "Why are you calling me?"

"We're about to leave, and Isobel's been worrying a bit about you. This'll be the first time away since, you know, her and I have been together. She was wondering how you are."

"Well why didn't she call me?"

"She didn't ask me to, I just thought I'd check in so I could put her mind at ease."

"I'm fine."

"She still cares about you, pal."

In the reflection of the window I notice my face has scrunched.

"I'm not your pal."

He sighs. "Yeah, I'm starting to realize that."

There's movement on his end. The creaking of a door opening. The clap of it shutting. Breeze.

"I know you don't like me," he says quietly. "It's fair enough. I don't blame you. You've gotta realize, though, that I'm not going anywhere."

"Why'd you really call me, Jake?"

"I told you, to put Isobel's mind at ease."

"If she'd been that worried, she would have called me. I know her."

The breeze blows loudly through the speaker.

"You used to know her, Cody."

"What's that supposed to mean?"

He takes another moment, the breeze coming again.

"Nothing. I just want you to get your head around the fact that I'm seeing Isobel now. You need to accept that. That thing the other day with my keys was not cool. I don't want things to be like that, Cody. I want us to get along, not be enemies."

"How do you see that working out, Jake?"

"I don't know. But it has to. One way or the other. For you, anyway."

"Are you threatening me?"

He laughs. "No, of course I'm not. I'm just saying that if things don't work with the three of us being around each other, I won't be the one leaving."

"You're a dick, Jake."

"I'm starting to think the same thing about you, Cody."

"You're a pain in the ass."

"You can't feel your ass, pal. But you're definitely a pain in mine … Even when you're not around you're doing something to disturb my time with Isobel. Every hour her phone goes off with some reminder of something to do with you. You know how annoying that is?"

"I really couldn't give a shit about what annoys you."

"Yeah, probably not. But don't you care about what bothers Isobel? You think she wants to spend the rest of her life running around after you, doing everything for you? Don't you think she deserves to do what she wants and what makes her happy?"

For a moment, I was about to reiterate that he's a dick, but then it hit me like face-planting on the sidewalk. He's right.

"And you think that you're what she wants?" My voice is drained. Defeated.

"That's her choice, Cody."

My phone beeps when he hangs up.

In the reflection of the window I catch sight of Viktor.

Anything to distract me from Jake. From Isobel. From them and me.

Viktor's old and withered. He was young once, though. I hear the stories. Now he's dying in a home, and he wants to get out of here. Break free and feel the open air. He's staring at death and he's got a crush on someone. In his wonder years, he couldn't have pictured things turning out like this, could he?

Five years ago, I could never have imagined things would turn out like this for me, either.

But here we are.

I'm in the middle of a Talking Heads song.

Five years … do I have five years?

Wonder … can I still find it in the ones I do?

I unlock my phone and text Isobel.

Chapter 16

(NOW)

We're navigating the Maxwell Street Market.

I have some hours to kill. Isobel and Jake won't be back until later. Joe's packed my stuff and we've left the home. Not before Viktor tried to break out once more. He and Sophie had been talking, laughing, maybe reminiscing about when they were young and life was an adventure. And then with the opening of a door, he was gone from his mind. Lunging, fighting to be out of there.

I felt sorry for him. Even I can leave.

"Feels good to stretch the legs, ay Codes?"

I shake my head. "You're unbelievable."

"Better believe it."

"I'm getting tired of your cracks."

"I can have them change your primary caregiver anytime."

"I didn't say anything about changing caregivers."

Joe stops at a candy stall and points out what he wants.

"I haven't been home for a long, long time, Codes," he says as we continue through the makeshift aisles. "Miss a lot of things: Vegemite, the sound of cockatoos, the smell of a storm coming, the feel of soft dirt under my feet. But there's one thing that's kept me here." He reaches into the bag and pulls out a Reese's Peanut Butter Cup, unwrapping it and throwing it whole into his mouth.

"Guess we've finally found something we have in common."

"Open wide, fella." I obey, and Joe stuffs one into my mouth. "We've got lots in common."

Between chomps of sticky, salty, sweet peanut butter and chocolate, I reply, "Yeah, how so?"

"Well, at one point in our lives we were both prone to wander."

"Yeah, I suppose."

We veer away from the stalls toward a café, where Joe makes room for me to park and then settles on a chair.

A waitress takes our orders: a cappuccino for Joe and a long black for me. Wait.

I just ordered coffee.

Coffee was something I always loved. More than a drink, it was an experience. The aroma, the conversations, the feeling of warmth and coziness that would come from coffee catch-ups.

I haven't ordered coffee out since I've been in my chair.

I tried to drink it once at home, using a straw like I have to for everything else, but it just turned the whole experience into a Milli Vanilli song.

Joe reaches for a straw in his pocket.

"No," I say. "Maybe we could just do it half normally."

He nods, and tucks the straw back in its place.

"And it's not just the travel, mate," he continues. "It's the discovery of the journey. It's about not being stuck, willing to try new things, step outside your comfort zone and find yourself. Can you tell me you didn't find yourself, and Isobel, more when you traveled together?"

My mind runs through a loop. From Chicago to New York, to Europe, South America, India and back to Chicago. "We did."

"That's right. And me? I traveled so far that I met Rebecca. Found myself more than ever, too. So we're plenty alike, my friend."

"You're stuck in Chicago. You work at a nursing home."

This could be the first time I've made Joe think. His head drops. "Yeah, and I no longer have Rebecca."

His usual disposition of optimism has vacated. He's looking down the street and out to the city traffic that passes by like a hail of bullets back and forth in a never-ending gun fight.

"I don't have Isobel, either," I say. "Maybe you're right, maybe we do have a lot in common."

Our coffees arrive.

Joe scoots his chair over and helps me.

The first sip of the aromatic, thick, black coffee is bitter. A bitterness I've missed. Some spills over my lip and burns my chin. It's a wonderful feeling.

I've avoided coming close to the fire in fear of being burnt for too long.

Joe wipes my chin, and then relaxes and sips his own.

"I guess the only difference is that you lost Rebecca to death. She died loving you, and you probably still love her. I think because of that you'll always have her. I chose to push Isobel away. She's still here and loving someone else."

"You're right, fella, in both ways. Rebecca is with me, always. But I am doing everything that I wanted to be free from."

I stare at the whispers of fog in my coffee. "So am I."

"And the fact that Isobel is still here, at least means there's a chance for you."

I feel a strange ambivalence about coming home. I'd be lying if I said I wasn't looking forward to seeing Isobel. Missing her was something I didn't think I could do anymore. Even just to hear her voice would be a joy. At the same time, though, as I drive up the ramp I'm dreading the sight of Jake. Filling the space on the sofa where I used to sit. Warming the body that I used to keep warm.

The house is silent when we enter. Joe sits on the couch and takes out his phone.

"Isobel will be back soon." Jake appears from the bedroom. "Gone to get groceries."

"Great," Joe responds. "Was just about to text her."

Jake smiles. "Thanks for bringing him home, Joe, and for taking care of him."

"Not a problem, fella."

Joe's phone starts ringing. He answers it, says yep three times and then hangs up. "I've gotta head off. Bloody Viktor has done a runner and they need all hands on deck to find him."

For a moment I feel like being an annoying little kid and asking if I can come too. I don't.

The door closes with the smack of a bullwhip.

The whir of my chair's motor sounds like a Harley Davidson.

Jake's leaning on the frame of the archway into the kitchen, a protein ball in hand. He isn't smiling at me and trying to be friendly like he usually would …

Just when I thought I'd never have a new experience in my life again, here I am having my first adult staring contest. He's writing words on my forehead while I'm trying to read those written on his.

If uncomfortable and awkward could be defined by a scene, one photograph, this would be it.

He gulps down the protein ball, his eyes unmoved. I stretch my neck side to side. I don't want to be here – no, I don't want him here. I can't leave now. We're locked in the most uninspiring lock of horns.

Finally, it's Jake who speaks. "Thanks for texting Isobel the other day. Right after I called you."

"My pleasure." I reply with equal sarcasm.

He shakes his head. "Almost screwed up our weekend away. Thanks for that."

"No problem."

He's getting irritated. "You're really bothered by this, aren't you?"

"Something Isobel and I prided ourselves on was honesty. I knew she didn't know you were calling me. Maybe it's just habit that I tell her everything."

Silence. Each tick of the clock on the mantel sounds like a golfer teeing off.

"I've really tried to be considerate, to be nice to you," he makes a click-clack noise with his tongue, staring at the wall behind me, "but maybe I should just drop it and treat you how you're treating me."

He goes into the bedroom and returns with a box.

My heart is flirting with cardiac arrest. I know the box.

"Some beautiful albums in here," Jake says. He takes one from the box and flicks through the pages. "Some famous faces."

"Put them back. You've got no right to touch them."

"Kind of like you had no right to touch my car keys? Throw them away?"

I want to smack the shit out of him, pummel his stupid, pretty-boy head. Cut that fucking smile off his face. I picture a truck ploughing through the house and splatting him in front of me.

All that happens is my left hand shakes tremulously into a fist.

"That'd only be fair, wouldn't it? If I threw away something of yours like you did mine?"

"What the hell are you playing at?" I say through clenched teeth. "What do you want?"

Jake comes over to me, puts the album on my lap and leans in to me. "I want you to accept that I am with Isobel now. I don't want you interrupting our time together. I don't want you to burden her. I want you to make her life easy. She's not yours anymore. She's with me now. My girlfriend."

Nothing comes from me as I simmer, simmer and then boil.

RED.

It's all I can see.

I push my joystick forward and smash him with my chair.

He flies back, and smacks into the wall.

I line him up and drive at full speed toward him.

He jumps aside and I hit the wall.

"Cody, what the hell?!"

Wheezing.

I reverse and try again.

I fail.

Jake laughs. "Come on, stop it. You could have hurt me the first time. Now this is silly."

I try again.

Smash. The couch this time.

Jake's dodging me like a monkey climbing over the furniture and running around the kitchen table.

Laughing.

He's fucking laughing at me!

Wheezing. Panting. Shaking.

Jake runs into the bathroom. I go to trap him when he returns, but he leaps to my side.

"Shit," he says, disappearing behind me. "I didn't want to have to do this."

A hand whips around in front of my face.

He pinches my nose.

The pills flop onto my tongue. I try to bite him as he covers my mouth. Again, I fail. I gulp instinctively and swallow the sedatives.

"Isobel said you can have fits sometimes." He is breathing heavily, holding my shoulder. "I didn't realize that they were like this."

"They're not ..." My voice grows weary. "You just pissed me off ..."

"I'll know for next time to be ready with them."

"I'll hit you hard enough that you won't get up next time."

"Cody, you'll be the one moving out if this is how it's going to be."

"Fuck you, Jake."

The chemicals reach my brain. The room fades.

Chapter 17

(THEN)

We were married in Chicago Botanic Garden. The day was overcast, but nothing could stop the love flowing. In those moments, we were impervious to anything bad that had ever happened, to us or to the world. There was just happiness spilling out in celebration.

A wedding photo would come to live inside the locket on Isobel's necklace.

For our honeymoon we backpacked through South America. From exploring the temples of Machu Picchu, gazing upon the Milky Way over Lake Titicaca and photographing the River of Five Colors to driving the world's most dangerous road in Bolivia and snorkeling the Galapagos Islands, we ticked off everything on our bucket lists, and then found more things to add and tick off.

Seven months later we returned Stateside, tanned, feeling free, and more in love than ever. Five SD cards full of photos. A lifetime of memories.

On the way back to Chicago we visited Janine and Larry at their holiday house in San Diego. It was a place that was close to my heart. So many holidays had been spent there, and it was somewhere that my parents were their most relaxed, where their bond was most visible.

"I'm sure you've got a million stories to tell." Janine was bubbling in her seat on the sofa. "But don't let us pester you. Relax, you've just got in."

Larry leaned forward. "No way I'm letting you get away. I want to hear, kid."

"Oh, Larry, let them be." Janine slapped his wrist playfully. "Besides, you should be outside fixing the handrail."

I laughed. "That still not done?"

"Eternally, Cody," Janine said, shaking her head. "He'll never get around to it."

"Bah!" Larry waved his arm. "That can wait. I wanna spend time with my son and daughter-in-law. I want to hear about their adventures."

"We've had the most amazing time," I replied, and glanced to Isobel. "I think we have to share some."

"Don't let him get out of it, Cody."

Janine was smirking. It was always a joke, kind of, the handrail on the back steps. It had been rotten since they bought the house, but never got repaired. Every time they came here to relax, anyone who was around bugged Larry about fixing it.

"We'll let him off this time," Isobel said. "But one of you is doing it." She pointed a finger at both of us.

The four of us laughed.

We ate, sipped our drinks and relaxed in the airy setting of the family holiday house, telling stories, reminiscing and talking about what the future might hold for all of us.

"We're so proud of you two," Larry said. "Makes me so happy to see my kid all grown up and settling down in the right way."

Isobel and I nestled into one another.

"Look at you two," Janine said. "You just fit."

Later that day as the sun set in pinks and oranges over the water, Isobel and I strolled along the shore, hand in hand.

The ocean air was fresh, clean, just a little bit salty. Seagulls squawked in the distance. We were the only ones on the beach, this part of San Diego being quiet and removed from the hustle and bustle. There was something so incomparably serene about this.

Not a thing in the world clouded my thoughts. No fear, no longing, no abandonment, no noise other than the washing of the tide. The coolness of the sand between my toes was refreshing, massaging my skin as I walked. The hand in mine.

The woman by my side.

The love of my life.

My wife.

Isobel.

Nothing could ever be more than her. She was everything.

There was more for us, though. A more I'd started thinking about on our seven-month honeymoon.

It was just an otherwise innocent moment while we were snorkeling in the Galapagos Islands, just one look from behind my mask over to Isobel with her flippers on, mask covering her face. She was pointing at a turtle on the sea floor, yelling under water for me to look. In that one moment when she turned her eyes to me to see if I was looking, it was though a thousand convoluted thoughts all of a sudden aligned and formed into one clear, succinct idea. A desire. Something I was as sure of as my will to be with her for the rest of my life.

"I really enjoy coming here," I said, swinging our arms as we walked. "Seeing my parents here. So many good memories."

"The perfect way to end our honeymoon." Isobel bounced up and pecked me on the cheek. "With the perfect partner."

"I've always wondered about them."

"What have you wondered, babe?"

"I thought about it more as I grew up with them – did they ever lament that they couldn't have a child of their own? I mean, I'm their son, but actually conceiving a child. I wonder if they wish they'd done that."

Isobel shrugged. "It's hard to tell. They seem pretty happy. Maybe they've always just appreciated that they could have a family beyond just the two of them, even if it came about in the strangest of circumstances."

"I wonder, too, if they were yearning for a child when Larry found me. Was it by chance, or had they missed the boat and I was their best chance?"

"Does it matter?"

I thought for a moment, watching the tide roll in. "No, it doesn't. It just matters what actually came to be."

"And that was that they got to have a family."

The sound of the ocean took over for a while. My mind was clear. The thoughts aligned as easily as they had under water in the Galapagos Islands. The intent. The yearning. The desire to do it.

"I want to have a family with you, Isobel."

She stopped and gazed at me searchingly. "Do you mean that?"

"I want it so much, baby."

Her hand released from mine and she started to rub the back of her neck. Her eyes fell to the sand. "That means a lot, you know."

I took her hand back. "I feel like it's the next place for our love to take us. Creating a life, a person, together. Combining us to create something new. To love, cherish and help grow up."

She brought her head up. "I want that too," she said before her eyes disappeared again, her face masked with blonde locks. "It just scares me, though."

"It scares me, too." I looked to the horizon, down to the sand, and then back up to Isobel. "I barely know how to be an adult."

"I'm scared that I won't know how to be a mother ..." Insecurity was leaking from her pores. Her body closing up, fidgeting. Distant. "I've been better for so long, but what if things change?" The look she threw me could have broken any heart.

"What ... what do you mean, hon?"

"It's never left the back of my mind ... what if I just end up being like my mother? Doing to my child what she did to me?"

I took her head in my hands. "You're not your mother, Isobel."

Steely seconds passed locked in each other's eyes. From her mind I was trying to extract every concern and negative thought about herself. It seemed as though she was trying to inspect mine, too. See how I felt about it ...

Fear had erupted like a volcano inside me.

Had my worry just been dormant the whole time, too?

"Does what I said make you feel differently?" Isobel asked.

"Isobel, nothing could change that. I want this with you and I know you'll be an amazing mother. I know that because I know you. You are your own person. We both have no idea what it takes but we can do this together, babe. I know it."

Talking. Talking. Those words. I said them, trying to believe them as much as I could. And I did. But it wasn't without an uneasy feeling. The fear was always difficult to let go of completely. Time had helped. Now, though, it was reignited in some ways.

"Then I want to do it, too, Cody." Isobel looked like a part of her had found new life. There was a spark in her eyes. Desire. "Together, we can do anything."

Inside my mind, I pushed past the fear and remembered how far we'd come. Isobel had become a braver, more complete woman now.

How beautiful she looked with this new hope in her eyes.

How beautiful she was in every way. Her strength, what she achieved within herself.

I suddenly felt flattered, excited and nervous as I realized that someone this extraordinary wanted to start a family with me.

Isobel wanted what I did. We didn't need to be on the exact same page, but we were writing the most amazing love story. Together.

<h1 style="text-align:center">Chapter 18</h1>

(NOW)

It's been almost three weeks since Jake shoved sedatives down my throat. Since he threatened to toss away an album of beautiful memories.

Happy families.

I'm doing my best to restrain my urges to sabotage him. I believe him when he says I'll be the one gone if things don't work out with the three of us. I'm a third wheel on four wheels. An overgrown mistake of a baby with a bad attitude.

The irritation, though, gnaws inside my skull. When I take the new meds that have been added to my already burgeoning cocktail, I'm reminded of my fragile health. I can't leave it.

But the home? I can't be there, either. And even if I really wanted Isobel back, I'm not getting her. So what's the point? Maybe I should just get along with him. Be happy for them.

It sounds logical. Seems right.

Just doesn't feel it.

Jake's at work now.

Isobel's been cleaning all morning. Now she's in the shower.

Too much time for me to think.

The water stops. The bathroom fan continues spinning while she dries and dresses. She's taking her time – she must be getting ready for something. Jake, I suppose.

She must want to surprise him by looking nice. It's a wonderful thing. Caring about someone so much you'll try to be the best you can in every way, just to make them happy. She must love him enough to want to impress him. It was something I always appreciated, given that she was too good for me, or anyone, without makeup or fancy clothes, let alone done up. I always thought it unforgivable to let a day go by without telling her how beautiful she truly was to me.

"So, what do you think?" Isobel is standing in the bedroom doorway. She's dressed in a long, figure-hugging dress, her dainty calves peeking out at the bottom. She looks magical in a way. Like an old candle that has just rediscovered its flame.

"You look really nice," I say.

A gulp besets my throat, all the way down to my stomach, as I realize that this is all for another man.

Isobel looks pleased. I'm glad my opinion still means something. She slips back into the bedroom and then comes out with a long black coat on, and heels … goddamn heels.

"I'm glad I got you ready earlier," she says as she leans over and fixes my shirt. "Otherwise we'd be late. Remember when it was always me making us late? Couldn't decide on this stupid dress or that blouse."

This brings warmth inside me. "It was usually something very worthwhile that made us late, though."

"We were too horny for our own good …" Isobel's face is not far from mine. Close enough for me to gaze deep into her eyes and see the real her for a moment. She is happy right now, in a dangerous way. It's come about through memory.

This is the most we've said about our former sex life since we stopped fooling around. Even then, we didn't really talk about things. It was never the same in this chair. Sex was just a dick in a pussy, and that was just bland compared to how we once connected.

"Anyway," she stands, and shakes off whatever she found in being eye to eye with me, "we better get going."

"What are you talking about?"

"I'm ready, and I presume you are, too. Actually …" She flashes in and out of the bathroom and then sprays cologne on my neck, my wrists and down my shirt. "Now you're ready."

"Wait, Isobel. What's going on."

"Is that important?"

"Well, I presumed you got dressed up for Jake. Where are we going?"

"I'm dressed up for myself. And we're going to a fashion show … He's at work and I thought it was more your thing."

I'm stuck with words on my tongue, jaw slightly ajar, from the time she steers me out of the house, down the ramp, into the van and the whole way there. But I don't say them. It's too scary to think how they'll be received. They're there, though.

❧

This isn't the kind of show Isobel once owned with her strut and a figure that made other women green with envy. It's nice, though. We're in the mall. Isobel's on a folding chair and I'm parked by her side in what is a half-full audience.

The lighting is no help to the atmosphere – those harsh mall lights that reveal too much about an average person's skin – and the openness, shoppers scurrying all around, gives the show little coziness.

Still, it's something.

The MC, a man in a suit, some sort of pre-fitted get-up, leaps onto the stage and takes the microphone from its stand.

"Ladies and gentlemen," he says.

"I think he stole his suit from a manikin, and then had it dress him." Isobel hasn't said a thing about fashion for years. "Some men just aren't made for them."

"Some men aren't made for plaid shirts, either," I reply, peering down to mine.

She looks offended. "I thought they looked good on you. I thought you liked them."

"I've got the chair, the occasionally off expression and the rest of it. I'd love to at least not dress like I'm handicapped."

"Excuse me?!" Now Isobel is incredulous. "I dress you well."

I raise my eyebrows.

Isobel huffs, and pushes her purse into her lap, her forearms gripped in frustration. I've got to her. Something she used to do to me, but something I seldom did to her. She found it fun, now I kind of get what she enjoyed about it.

I find myself snickering. As I watch Isobel trying to remain focused on the man in a suit like off-kilter curtains, this snicker builds to the point where I'm wheezing with laughter.

"Stop it," she says, and slaps my left hand. "You'll disrupt him."

"What's the worst that would happen – he notices the only guy in the vicinity who's dressed like more of a douche than him?"

I'm just hilarious today.

Isobel remains staunch, though only for a moment. A tiny smirk creeps to the corner of her lips. I've got her again. "You know what? Screw you, Cody. I'm going to leave you with him after the show and you two can exchange dress tips."

I beam at her. "There you are."

"There you are." She nods her head at me. "You jerk."

"It feels good. Remember how you always used to get me? Rile me up, and poke me until I cracked into your stream of humor?"

"It was always pretty easy with you. Such a sucker."

"A jerk and a sucker. Double threat."

The MC finishes and makes way for the first model. She's okay. A not-quite-young woman who doesn't quite walk in the way to draw attention to how her legs move. The next comes out after her, and she's okay too. And then the next, and the next, and they cycle through. They're all okay. The outfits are okay too. Nothing special.

I'm paralleling this with the shows I used to watch and photograph. The ones Isobel headlined. She made the rest of the models in those shows look as average as this brigade when she turned it on.

"Are you going to take a photo?" Isobel asks.

I follow her eyes to the camera fixed on the front of my chair, which I've made considerable efforts to ignore.

The thought comes to do it – *just turn it on and push the button* – but is usurped immediately by another. "Doesn't feel right."

"It might be good for you, you know?"

"I used to photograph such amazing things. Nature that most people will never see, women that most people will never walk by … and you."

This catches Isobel's attention. She turns to me, a sparkle in her eyes. "What do you mean?"

"I can't photograph these women when I got to photograph you."

This makes Isobel blush. "Shoosh, Cody. What are you talking about?"

"Any other woman would just be disappointing to photograph. That's all I'm saying. I don't need to feel disappointed right now."

Shyly, she rolls her thumbs over one another. "I'm glad I never disappointed you in that way."

"You never disappointed me in any way."

She flashes a smile and then drops her head.

A moment passes silently. There are words forming in my mind. Are there in hers?

Keeping her eyes on the dime-a-dozen models walking by, Isobel says, "I was alright, wasn't I?"

Sentiments become words in my mind.

Do I say them? What have I got to lose?

I don't, though, so they stay there, a soft melodic ode to my wife, playing like a scratched record, over and over again, with just an ounce of regret for my own reticence.

You were more than alright, Isobel. You were amazing ...
You still are.

⚘

The whole way home there is a pleasant calm in the van. We don't say much, but this silence isn't awkward, it's an impression of a silence we could share long ago. It's comfortable and warm, like sitting and reading separate books on the same sofa in a cozy house in wintertime.

My thoughts are clear. Nothing is clouding my mind, I'm just enjoying the flash-by scenery, feeling still, being here.

Isobel parks in the driveway, lowers me out of the van and we head inside.

Inside is where the stillness ends.

Jake is on the sofa. "Hey," he says and stands to greet Isobel. "Where have you been?"

"Just went out for a while," Isobel replies.

"What did you get up to?"

"Why the twenty questions?" Isobel's hands have fixed on her hips. The tone in her voice reminds me of a quiet, strong and crazy woman I knew. Standing tall.

"Sorry. Didn't mean to pester, just excited to see you."

"It's all good. We went out to watch a fashion show."

"Ah okay." His head dips momentarily. "That would have been nice. That was kind of your thing."

"I haven't completely lost my fashion sense." Isobel smirks at me. "Though some would disagree."

It's impossible to not beam back at her.

Jake looks lost. "You two really had a fun afternoon, didn't you?"

Isobel's hand finds his cheek, comforting him. His hand finds hers. My smile fades.

"As much as Cody has to accept that we're together now," Isobel says, "you have to accept that we are still friends."

"Okay. Just feels a bit funny … seeing you have so much fun with your ex-husband."

"I know this is a weird situation." Isobel switches her eyes between the two of us. "But you two have to accept the situation. I want you Jake …"

Those words punch me in face.

"But I also want you here, Cody."

Though my eyes are trying to burn dry, I raise my head. "I still want to be here."

Isobel's hand soothes over my left. Tears of pain wanted to come a moment ago, now tears of relief want to flow. Neither come, though. I hold them in with every bit of energy I have.

"Anyway, enough of this. I'm going to start dinner." Isobel touches my hand again and gives Jake a peck on the lips, then walks into the kitchen, leaving him and me alone.

We stay there for a moment.

"She's not my ex," I say. "She's still my wife."

I steer into my place beside the sofa. If we're making moves, right now I feel as though I've got him trapped.

He doesn't reply.

He responds to my move, though.

He walks into the kitchen. He wraps his arms around Isobel from behind, as she stands at the kitchen sink, and kisses her neck.

"I care for you so much, Bel. Sorry for being funny then. Maybe you're just so amazing that I get jealous if someone else gets to spend time with you when I can't."

He tickles her neck with his nose.

She giggles.

I feel sick.

"I'm greedy, Bel. I want to spend time with you all the time. I love you so much."

Several moments pass with the quiet murmur of the television the most audible thing in the room.

Then Isobel turns and wraps her arms around his neck. "I love you, too."

That sickness in my stomach rises up through my throat and wants to pour from my eyes.

It's harder to stop.

Stop it!

They hold each other, Isobel's face to mine, her eyes closed.

They open.

Those resplendent hazel eyes.

They grip mine. My pathetic brown eyes, which feel like a sink that's rapidly filling. Growing closer to overflowing.

She blinks. Her eyes shine. Not just in color. Like they're polished.

Isobel releases from Jake and kisses his forehead. She leaves for the backyard.

Fresh air, a great idea.

I drive out of my spot and begin toward the kitchen. But then Jake flashes past. He reaches into the pantry, collects a protein ball, and joins Isobel in the backyard. He wraps his arm around her shoulder.

He stands side by side with her.

Something I can't do.

Gazing out the window at them, I take myself back to this afternoon. How it felt to laugh with Isobel again. To remember something. To have those thoughts. To have those feelings.

When we sat side by side.

Chapter 19

(NOW)

"Did you ever ride one of them?"

We're at the kangaroo enclosure in Lincoln Park Zoo.

"If I had a buck for every time a yank has asked me that … Of course I did, mate. It's what all Aussies do."

"Really?"

He's smirking. "You're not getting any sharper in your old age, Codes."

"You're not getting any wittier, either."

"Put it this way," Joe leans on the railing, "if you tried to ride one, even you'd lose feeling in your face."

"That's low, even for you."

"Roos don't take crap. They fight. That's why they are so loved back in Oz."

The kangaroos are just lying around, chewing tree roots and scratching their heads. The joey in the mother's pouch is kind of cute, though. Jack I heard his name is.

It'd be a wonderful feeling to be that protected when you're a child.

"They seem pretty boring. Can we move on now?"

"Give me a minute."

"Come on. You've had your time getting reacquainted with the most boring animal on earth. Even sloths are better than these lazy bastards."

"Hey fella. Watch your tongue. These animals are beautiful, noble and strong. If you want some entertainment from them, steer your carriage into the enclosure and run over the tail of the big guy in the corner."

"I get it, kangaroos are the Rambos of the animal kingdom, but I want to see something else."

"Kangaroos mean a lot to my people. Having some time to remember and reflect. It used to be hard to get you to talk. These days I can't shut you up. Don't know which I like more: you internalizing everything or the jerk that's taken over."

"I'll shut up and let you meditate to these shitty animals, but just be clear that you are the biggest jerk in this scenario."

"In terms of mass, you're definitely a bigger jerk."

I roll my eyes.

The joey pokes its head out again, and then awkwardly climbs out of the pouch. It stumbles and resets, trying to hop around with little success. Learning to move is not bum-shuffle, crawl and walk, for them it's stumble, stuff-up, fall and get back up until … it's bouncing, little unbalanced hops.

Tiny hops compared to the big kangaroo that's just gotten up. It approaches a medium sized one that's standing by a tree.

"Oh, this could be interesting," Joe says. "I'm not sure I like the way Old Red is moving."

A tour guide is talking to a group of tourists just beside us. "And you can see they are sometimes quite social animals," he says with a chime.

Joe laughs, "He doesn't have a bloody clue."

The kangaroos meet, and it's on. They throw paws at each other, grapple and lean on their tails and with both legs kick each other in the stomach.

Oohs and ahs come from the group, and the guide tries his best to explain what is happening and that sometimes they get into "disagreements".

"What did I tell you? They fight."

"They've just gotten a lot more interesting."

Finally, they finish. Contrary to what I thought would happen, it's the little guy standing tall as the big kangaroo retreats.

We start toward the tigers. They've always been my favorite animal.

Strangely, though, I'm thinking about the kangaroos as the roar of a hungry Bengal sounds.

Kangaroos: calm, settled, boring, then resistance, pride, heart.

"I kind of see why you like them," I say as I park.

Joe leans a hand on my shoulder. "You liked that fight, didn't you?"

"I did."

"You know something else about them – they find it very hard to move backwards. They're built to move forward. Move on."

A zookeeper appears and tosses a huge piece of meat to the tiger. It leaps on it and begins to tear shreds from it, which is met with raucous applause from the crowd. It's beautiful, and depressing, a glimpse of what might occur in the wild, contained in a show for human entertainment. She's safe, but she's in a cage; she has attention, but mostly from humans.

"Let's go," I say.

"Thought these were your favorites … Where you wanna go now?"

"I don't know. Just somewhere else."

"Monkeys? Lions?"

"No, I mean, let's leave the zoo."

On our way out we pass the souvenir store. Joe tells me to wait and ducks in. Moments later he waddles out with a black cap, and slaps it on my head so that it's sitting loosely.

"Take it off."

Joe laughs but doesn't take it off.

"I look like a complete retard."

"You can't see yourself. Besides, if you don't like it, fella, do something about it."

I shake my head as much as I can, side to side, and try to flick the hat off. My neck is tired and sore when it eventually falls onto my lap.

Sewn onto the front of the black hat is a brown animal that looks as if it's in motion. Bouncing high, and forward. What I thought was boring because it was still, was simply lying dormant until it needed to fight.

Often, when I could still feel the sand between my toes, I would come down to the curling arm of North Avenue Beach. I'd let myself be pleasantly fooled that I was looking out to the ocean and an endless horizon rather than just Lake Michigan. Although I knew it wasn't so, dreaming wasn't such a bad thing.

I'm parked in the sand, my chair loaded onto the platform dolly that lives in the back of the van. With its balloon tires the dolly makes beach trips possible, as well as making my carriage even more obtrusive. Joe is barefoot next to me with a handful of seashells, sliding them over each other like coins. Behind me is the green guard of Lincoln Park, which divides the light-yellow sand and the gray city.

"You ever wonder where you really are, Joe?"

A deep sigh exits his lungs. "It is something I ponder. Where are you, mate?"

"I feel like I'm stuck between today and tomorrow."

A bevy of women in bikinis pass us and join the crew crowded around the beach volleyball nets. Joe's eyes follow them. "Metaphors are pretty but a waste of words sometimes, Codes."

Conversations on the breeze fill the gaps in ours. The sun is blazing onto the left side of my face. The water shimmers. Out there, the horizon seems endless. Not even Michigan can take me away from how it feels.

"I don't think I like how things have turned out," I say.

Joe tosses a seashell toward the water. "Everything?"

"Dunno ..."

"You're not happy about the new fella are ya?"

Though my face is warm, it's tight, frowning. "I should be. I want her to be happy. And she seems happy."

"Maybe she is. Maybe she's better with him."

"What?"

"You took her for granted."

"Thanks for your support, pal."

"It's true, though, isn't it? You stuffed up. Forgot what you still had and now it seems like it's completely gone."

"Yeah, I did. But I thought as my friend you might offer me some more guidance or even just verbal support."

He shrugs. "Are you going to tell her this?"

"I dunno."

"Well, I can't help you. She's made a choice. Live with it."

"No ..." There's something hot inside my stomach. "Why are you getting at me like this?"

Joe tosses away a shell. "Because I've had to watch you lose the woman you love because you're too damn stubborn to let yourself be real and hurt. I had to watch the love of my life die. You chose to let yours die. Maybe that pisses me off and I don't want to hear you whining about it."

Awkward silence hangs between us.

"I'm sorry," I say.

Joe sighs and scoops up a handful of sand to play with now that the shells are gone. "You don't need to be sorry. I'm sorry for getting worked up. Was just trying to be real with you."

"It's all good."

One of the volleyball teams lets out a chorus of cheers. They must've just won.

"If there is something inside you," Joe says, "you need to let it out."

"It's hard to know what to actually do, though."

"Fight."

"What would you know about fighting? You're a harmless little hobbit."

"That's New Zealand, mate. Way off."

"Whatever."

"By that logic, you're Canadian. You're barely American, though. Barely anything."

"Are you done insulting me?"

"You called me a hobbit."

"Fair enough."

Joe stands and stretches. "I helped fight my government to recognize what they did to my people. I fought beside Rebecca when she was sick. Tried to fight death. Never gave up until it came. Then I had to fight wanting to die myself when she went. Had to fight wanting to believe I could be with her again with what I knew – that I was here … I've had to fight plenty, fella."

"Even if I wanted to fight. How am I meant to?"

"I have no idea, mate. I've only ever known how to not give up. How to hang on to hope."

Lake Michigan, lapping into the shore. Fooling me that's it's an ocean.

Let the water take me away.

Fool me.

Let me believe that's there's more than there might be. Believe. Can it be real if I believe it to be?

"Where do I start?" I ask.

"I guess the first thing you need to decide is whether you truly want to be with Isobel."

"I … I don't know."

"Then you're either lying or you don't want to be with her, mate."

What was like a shimmering blanket of gold before has dulled to a murky lake, pretending to be the ocean. The horizon has come forward and Michigan isn't that far away now. There's no endlessness, just a lake surrounded by sullied land and gray cities.

I consider it over and over again. Do I want to be with Isobel? Is there any point at even starting to fight for her?

"We can't be together." I eye Joe, and then peer around myself and my carriage. "Look at me."

"I see you, mate. But that's not the point. Love is about two hearts connecting, two souls meeting. You've still got a heart, and you've still got a soul."

"It's not that simple. My heart is torn, and my soul doesn't deserve to be connected."

He thinks for a while.

My head grows heavy; my eyes become sore.

"Just sounds like you're fighting yourself. I guess what you have to decide is whether the good part of you, the one that wants to be something better, can beat the sad sack you've become."

There's nothing for me to say. Just think.

Joe pats my shoulder. "Probably time to go."

He pushes me from the shore to the parking lot.

"Maybe we could all take a leaf from the kangaroo's book," Joe says, hitting the unlock button for the van.

I drive off the dolly and stop. The image of the smaller, more docile kangaroo comes to my mind. How it was dormant, still and unaffected, and how when it needed to, it fought.

How they always move forward.

Rotating my chair, I turn back to Lake Michigan.

It's somewhere between a muddy lake and an impression of endless beauty. Somewhere in the middle. It could really be either.

I wonder, can I beat the bigger part of me?

Is there enough inside me to fight?

Do I want to be with Isobel …? Is it too late?

My thoughts turn to Robert's office.

Blood clots.

Unknowns.

Still, I'm here. I'm not dead yet.

It's not too late.

Chapter 20

(THEN)

I waited eagerly in the living room, holding onto hope that this time it might be.

The toilet flushed and Isobel came in.

As soon as she looked up at me with eyes so fragile they could break, I knew the result. She shook her head and went into the bedroom.

I took a moment to gather myself. It was getting harder to hold on to hope. Each time the test came back negative, it hit my heart. I hated waiting for that second red line. Each failure bred life into a new fear that had risen. Maybe we wouldn't even get the chance to know whether we'd make good or bad parents. Maybe we just weren't meant to conceive.

I gulped down that fear, stood up and set myself to be the partner I had to be in this time. With everything weighing down on Isobel, I had to stay strong for her. For us.

She was sitting on the bed, her elbows pressed into her thighs, eyes somewhere between the threads of cream carpet.

I sat beside her, and put an arm around her. "Next time," I said.

Her muscles felt tight, her body rigid. Then she started to cry. "I'm sorry, Cody."

"Isobel, babe, you have nothing to be sorry about." I kissed her hair. "This is something we get through together. It'll happen."

After almost a year of failures, I'm not sure who I was trying to convince.

She brought her head up, her eyes bleary. "If I was sixteen and this was the last thing I wanted it'd probably happen like that," she clicked her fingers. "But now, when it's something I want more than anything, nothing."

"This sucks, baby. But we've just gotta keep trying."

She released a heavy, pent-up breath. "It sucks because of me."

"What are you talking about?"

"It's me, Cody. I'm the reason we can't have a baby."

"Don't say that, hon. We don't know that."

"We do."

I didn't say anything.

"You had the tests, Cody. We know it's not you."

"It might just take some time …"

"But we've done everything. We've both been doing everything we're meant to: we're healthy, doing it at the right time. The right positions. It's bullshit."

"I know. It's bullshit," I sighed, "but it's just something we're going to have to deal with."

"And how do we do that?"

"Well, firstly, you need to know that even if we can't …"

"Don't say that," Isobel said through gritted teeth, her voice fraught.

I knelt in front of her, took her hands and held them tight enough to let her know that this was real, and there was no way that she could slip away from me. "You need to know that even if we can't, it doesn't change anything between us."

"I've heard you. I know how much you want this."

"I do." I played with her wedding ring. "But you come first."

"And what if I've past my expiry date for having kids? What then?"

"You are my life, Isobel. And the only condition of our love is that it is unconditional. Kids, no kids, I'm still going to feel the same."

Isobel's distress was mollified, though her gaze fell to the floor. I brought her chin up with my forefinger.

She gulped, and then rubbed her eyes. She leaned forward and kissed me. "Thank you."

"Just know that we'll get through this."

We lay back on the bed and cuddled, Isobel's head resting on my chest. We stayed there for a long time, the only sound our breathing, and the beating of our hearts.

There was me, strong willed, determined. So assured in my words.

Inside, I was nervous. Tired. Afraid of so many different things.

A month later we sat anxiously in the doctor's office.

Scans, scans, tests and tests: laparoscopy, and a lot of other scopies. I lost track over the week they did it all in. They repeated my tests as well. And now we waited.

Although Isobel had retracted into her shell a little, sitting on her hands while she braced for the news, she still held hope in her eyes. I was so proud of her for this. Showing every part of her spectrum of human emotion.

It was getting harder for me, too, though I never showed it. At least she had the courage to be fragile and express her feelings. I was just a cliché male, an ignorant optimist. Her hope might have fitted with the logic that at least somebody wins the lotto most weeks, but at least she was honest with it.

Circling my thumb over the back of her hand, I wanted my touch to say the words my voice was too scared to say. *This is killing me, too.*

"It'll be okay," was what actually came out of my mouth. I had little belief in those words, but when she shone a smile at me, an impression of happiness, I garnered some hope from my own fake optimism. Maybe I could be genuinely sanguine, and not just a liar. Maybe things could be okay.

Dr Xui entered quietly, as if he didn't want to scare us with the noise of the door. He sat and opened a manila folder. "How are you doing today?"

The grip between our hands became sweaty.

I swallowed a tennis ball of anxiety. "We're doing fine."

"As we've spoken about, there are options," he began.

Tears were building in the corners of Isobel's eyes.

Dr Xui firmed his lips for a moment. "As we suspected from your ongoing light menstrual cycles, Isobel, you have difficulty ovulating. Due to a hormonal problem, the ovary is not releasing a mature egg. This is likely to be the main cause of your infertility."

Isobel retreated completely back into her shell now, burying her head in her hands.

"The other thing that we found is that you have a moderate case of endometriosis. This means the endometrial tissue is growing outside the uterus, as opposed to lining it from within. Even if you were producing mature eggs, they would have trouble sticking to the lining of the uterus. Combined, it is no wonder you have had trouble conceiving."

The words were like a punch combination from a heavyweight boxer. Left hook, right uppercut.

My mind went straight to the worst-case-scenario.

No kids.

We'd lived extraordinary lives, and now all we wanted was something so normal, so common, so ordinary and down to earth. Yet, we couldn't do it.

I found Isobel's hand and squeezed it.

"The first thing to do is treat the endometriosis," Dr Xui said. "This would require laparoscopic surgery to remove any abnormal tissue and clear any blockages in the fallopian tubes. Providing this procedure goes according to plan, the next step would be to treat the ovulation problem. The first option for this would be a course of medication aimed at stimulating ovulation."

"And what are the chances of conceiving after all of this?" Isobel was poking her head out of her shell.

Dr Xui closed the manila folder. "It is difficult to give a percentage, as every case is unique."

"Please, just be straight," she said. "What are our chances?"

"Given we are dealing with two separate conditions that are both affecting your fertility, it may be difficult to conceive naturally."

Isobel clenched her jaw, looking as though she could keep the tears in with pure will. "What if we can't?"

"There are numerous options: artificial insemination, IVF, or even adoption. They are all viable, provided you have the financial means."

We left the office with so much to consider.

I'd wanted to expand our family as eagerly as I'd wanted to see tomorrow. Now, I needed to consider how hard it would be, and if it could ever actually happen.

I felt Isobel's hand entwine in mine.

I thought about us, the life we'd lived together, what we'd been through and how far we'd come. What had always come out on top was us, our passion.

Walking with her hand in mine out of the hospital and into the sunshine of a Manhattan spring, I believed with all my heart that we could endure worlds falling.

That mattered more than anything. We mattered most of all.

We strolled through Central Park, still silent, but our connection was as strong as ever.

"There's hope, honey," I said as we passed a row of cherry blossoms.

A tired glow spread across her face. "We've got each other – there's always hope."

Chapter 21

(NOW)

"Isobel?"

She's sitting at the kitchen table, leaning her head on her hand, eyes out the window.

From the entrance to the hallway, it's just her profile I can see. The way her nose curves and points just a little. The rise of her upper lip, light shining in and glowing off her strawberry gloss. The small part of her eye that's visible is somewhere else.

"Isobel? What's up?"

"Nothing." She turns to me with a tired smile. "Just thinking."

"About?" I drive into the kitchen and park by her side.

Now her eyes find their way out the window, to where they were. "Just thinking about how things turned out. The decisions I made. The things I did to make it this way. Should I feel guilty for trying to be happy now?"

"Are you happy now?"

She shrugs. "I guess."

"If you are then just let yourself be. You have nothing to feel guilty about."

"If it wasn't for me then you …"

As fast as my hand can move, I push the stick forward and ram her chair.

"Hey!" she cries. "What was …"

"Don't ever say that, Isobel. Don't think it, either. Nothing is your fault."

She seems as though she wants to cry. "But … I …"

"No. I'm not hearing it."

Clouds are gathering rapidly outside the window, coating the sky in white.

The fucked-up thing right now is that this is the first time I've ever said this to her. When she suffered for so long thinking these things, drowning herself in guilt, all I did was let it be.

Here I am, though.

I can't take back the fact that I let her hurt, but maybe I can stop her hurting right now.

"You were an amazing wife to me." I raise my left hand as high as I can, reaching as far as I can toward her.

She sits up, shocked. And she reaches out, and takes my hand.

"You're still an amazing person, Isobel."

"Do you mean that?"

"I do."

We're entangled in this moment. This look.

Thoughts that have been whispering in the back of my mind amplify. Realization, loud, blasting to the front. Immediate.

Now.

"Do you really love him?" I ask.

Isobel stops moving completely, just sits there, frozen. Then she turns her eyes to me, a faraway look. "Why do you have to ask me that?"

"I want to know if he's the person you see yourself spending the rest of your life with."

She throws her arms up. "I don't know, Cody. I'm just taking everything one day at a time. And he's here. He's the person I've ended up with. That's how things went."

It feels as though I sink deeper into my chair. "He seems like he really cares for you, too."

"This is a strange, confusing situation," Isobel says. "I'm trying to make the best of how things turned out."

"And you're doing well." My gaze recedes, blurring. "You've found a guy that loves you."

Deafening quiet takes hold.

Everything is a blur.

But then I see something.

That photograph on the wall.

My vision clears. "But he'll never love you like I loved you. And that's the love that you deserve."

I reverse back and steer away.

✢

Isobel and Jake are in the bedroom talking soft enough for me not to hear.

He's the shoulder she leans on now.

I'm the one that has to lean on her.

A heavy weight.

But I'm lifting. Learning something about myself. I'm not dead yet.

The door opens and he comes out. Though my sensations are dull, I can feel discomfort when I see him.

He goes into the kitchen and then passes me with a rubbish bag.

"You should just stay out there with the rest of the rotten shit," I mutter to myself.

"Sorry? Did you say something, Cody?" Standing in the doorway with the trash in his hand, Jake is staring back at me.

For a moment, I'm about to say, "No, nothing," but without thinking I stop myself.

"I said you should stay out there with the rest of the trash."

He raises an eyebrow. "Good one."

I was always about peace in my twenties, but the urge to murder someone is dominating my present. The murdering thirties.

"I meant it."

The ten feet between us feels like a gulf.

"I know you did," Jake says. "Keep working on your comedy routine. You'll need it."

Isobel comes out of the bedroom. She is dressed up, and made up. She looks gorgeous.

Jake disappears out the front door.

"Why so dressed up?" I ask as she rummages through her bag on the kitchen table. "Where are you going?"

She finds her lip gloss and rolls it over her lips so that they are shining wet. "Why does it matter to you, Cody? Why do you care all of a sudden?"

Her words strike me like a lightning bolt. "No reason. Just curious."

I retract my finger from the joystick, and stay beside the sofa.

Jake comes inside and goes into the bedroom. What were they talking about? He's gotten into her head. He's telling her that I'm trouble. That I'm no good for them. That he's the only one for her now. He wants me gone, I know it, and he's got the inside edge.

Isobel stays at the kitchen table and stares straight at me. "It's not fair, you know. How you're being. I've moved on. I'm trying to make something work for me. I'm doing what you said." She says this so only I can hear.

Jake comes out of the bedroom. "You ready, Bel?"

She glances to him. "Yep."

"I'll just go to the bathroom and then we'll leave," Jake says.

It's just Isobel and me for a precious moment. "Cody, you've got to accept this."

"And what if I can't … what if I don't want to?"

There's sadness behind her makeup; deep within her eyes a reflection shines back. "It doesn't work like that."

Desperation jumps up my throat. "Maybe I've been wrong."

Isobel clenches her fists, frustration building. "You can't just take it all back, and pretend that this isn't what you've wanted."

"It isn't." I'm welling. "I know that now. I don't want someone else to have you."

"It's not enough to not want someone else to have me." She comes and sits on the sofa. "You need to want to have me."

In the hazel of her eyes, I see our life of adventure together. It flashes by at a pace as fast as my mind can gather thoughts. And it ends with how we came to be now. I can't say anything. My vocal chords just won't work.

"And even if you did," says Isobel. "It's not simple anymore. I've got Jake now."

She's always been one of those people so loyal and true to their word. Her loyalty lies with him now. It's written in her eyes, those beautiful gateways I learned to read a long time ago. Ones that I now know I can still read.

The toilet flushes and Isobel springs to her feet.

My voice has absconded. It feels as if it's permanent. I'll be a mute, speaking another thing added to my list of can't dos.

Jake sidles up to Isobel and wraps his arm around her, smiling victoriously. The doorbell rings. Jake opens the door for Joe, who waddles in with his backpack on. Isobel collects her coat and hand in hand she and Jake leave the house.

It's just me and Joe and a whole lot of words floating around in the air; a bundle of wished ones stuck in my throat.

We still haven't made it to the nursing home. Neither of us is in a hurry to get there. Instead we're uptown, atop Cricket Hill. There's a lacrosse game happening at the foot of the hill. Some families and young couples are picnicking, but other than that, it's relatively quiet.

Isobel and I would sometimes walk up here when we moved back from NYC. Strolling around the cities we lived in was one of my favorite things to do. Through Central Park in New York, Uptown, Brooklyn and Midtown. That was something I never thought I'd miss. Just walking about a place.

A call came about an hour ago. It was Jake. Now he's calling Joe about what is to happen with me. He must have been pleased to tell Joe they are going away for a couple of days.

"Summer's not long gone, but you can already feel that winter chill creeping in. Autumn seems like it's ready to pack up. Leaves falling quickly this year." Joe's eyes are cast to the line of trees that surround much of the grass expanse. "Skeletons getting ready to take over for a while. Christmas isn't close enough, though."

"Tell me about it," I say. "All I want for Christmas is an easy-fire weapon that can be attached to my chair."

Joe slaps a hand on my shoulder. "I'm thinking something similar, except I'd go a more traditional weapon."

"Who's got you in the mood for murder?"

"Work."

"What's happened? You sick of me?"

He blows air through his nose, releasing one of those laughs with no joy in it. "I've barely ever asked for a bloody day off the entire time I've worked there, but I do ask for the same one every year. But this time they aren't giving it to me."

"Why do you need a day off? Not like you've got a life."

He ruffles my hair. "They'll make a comedian of you yet, Codes … but you're right – it's not about having it off to go drink with the boys. Just a day I'd like to have off to remember when I had a life."

"What do you mean?"

"Three weeks from Thursday is Rebecca's anniversary. I like to take the time to focus on nothing else except our memories and life together."

There's an itchiness inside my throat. I cough. "More important things than work sometimes."

"People just need to pull the sticks out of their asses. See the bigger picture." Joe picks up a stick and throws it forcefully.

"Maybe we should just stay here all night. It's not snowing yet."

Joe flings another stick. "Not the worst option I've heard. But I'd probably still freeze. Easy for you, you don't feel the cold."

"Shut the fuck up, Joe."

"You're the one who claimed I have no life."

I beep my horn.

"What's that for?"

"Dunno. Just the best way I can think of to express my anger at you."

There's a few seconds of silence before we both start laughing. It begins as chuckles and then builds into a guffaw. It reaches the point where we are laughing so hard that it's become noiseless. Cramped, scrunched faces, tears of absolute amusement seeping from our eyes. Joe is crouched over, and I can feel my chair shaking.

Finally, we settle. Joe lets out that sweet post-laughter hoot. "This is ridiculous," he says, wiping his eyes.

"I know," I reply. "Look at us: an Australian Aboriginal so out of place, and a senseless cripple, on top of a hill, taking jabs at each other for no other reason than it's better than being at a nursing home, lamenting the women we've lost. You're right. This is ridiculous."

"A travesty to normality." Joe picks up another stick. Instead of throwing it away, he lifts his leg and snaps it on his thigh.

"So what are you going to do?" I ask.

He brings his hands up and wraps them behind his head. "That's the million-dollar question, fella. I'll probably get the boot if I don't show or call in sick. But I can't be there on that day. Never minded working this crappy-paying job while Rebecca was still here. Went to work happy every day, because I knew I had her to come home to. Didn't mind the hours because the wage helped make our life. I only wanted money to eat, pay rent and do fun things with her … not that we ever really needed cash to have fun, but still, iFly isn't free. But what now? What do I have to come home to? You're damn right. I have no life."

"Maybe you need to find a life, again."

He thinks about this, squinting and lost in the shedding skeletons of trees. "Maybe I do."

"Maybe I do, too," I say.

"Did you talk to Isobel?"

I beep my horn again. This time the frustration is at myself. "Yeah, I did. But I said more than I thought I had to say, and then wound up not saying all that I had to."

"You tell her you've had enough of this joker Jake?"

"Yeah, I did, and I let a lot of confusing thoughts out. I feel hungover about it. I'm not sure what I even really said, or if I even believe it."

"Fella, I think you know as well as I do that you believe it."

"How would you know? You don't even know what I said."

"Not word for word. But I can guess the general gist of it."

I peer at him, my head dipped, eyes looking up, skeptically. "Oh, really?"

"Yeah, I can picture it. You fumbling for words, trying to find the right way of letting your stupid guard down, and eventually telling her, in your own way, that you wish you had have appreciated what you still had with her sooner."

"You're a jerk sometimes."

"Am I wrong, though?"

I don't answer. There's no point telling him he's right – he already knows.

"So what are you going to do now?" Joe asks.

"Guess I'm in the same boat as you. No idea."

"Mine's just about a day off to remember the woman I love. Your situation, my friend, is about getting the woman you love back."

"I never said I loved her. I just want it back to her and me. No him."

Joe scoffs. "That's just semantics, mate."

"Stop telling me how I feel."

"I'm not, but maybe you should look inside yourself and come to terms with whatever you need to, and then pull out whatever feeling you have left from that vile, dark, deformed soul of yours, because the longer this goes on, the further she's getting away from you."

"So what do you suggest, smart guy?"

He shrugs. "Win her back."

Now I scoff. I think to beep my horn, but there's nothing funny here, and nothing I can be facetious about for any good. "And how the hell am I meant to do that?"

"How would I know?"

"You seem to know an awful lot."

"Maybe more than you, though that's not hard."

"Like I said, fuck you, Joe."

He reaches over and beeps my horn.

I slap his hand away.

Joe laughs at me, and sits on the ground beside my chair. "One thing you know more about than me is the one thing that is vital here. You know Isobel. More than anyone else in the world. *You* are the only person who knows how to get her back."

It seems as if more leaves have fallen from the trees in the time we've been here. Branches being revealed, appearing like black veins against the deep blue sky. Leaves blowing away, gust by gust. An augury.

Things moving further away. Further, further away.

The wind has grown colder, too. It's still September, but winter is in the air.

A lot is swirling inside me. Something is settling, though. It's what has always been pedantically annoying about these conversations, which in this moment is simply profound. Joe is absolutely right.

I know her better than anyone.

I still love her.

Chapter 22

(NOW)

Last night went as slowly as any night has ever gone. Sleep was scarce. I texted Isobel around midnight. Just to see how she was doing.

It wasn't until this morning that I got a message in return:

I'm doing fine. Sorry for the late change … Jake just wanted to have some time alone.

I haven't written back yet.

"Cody, darling, you're polluting this dance with your lack of movement."

Back in the room with a click of fingers in my face.

Sophie is standing in front of me with her hands on her hips. The recreation area in the nursing home is adorned with balloons and streamers, there's even some scattered confetti. The lights are dimmed and a disco ball is hanging from the light fixture. It's all a nice idea, but this dance looks exactly like what it is: a slapped-together Saturday night for old people and cripples in a second-rate nursing home in inner-city Chicago.

I guess it's better than watching *MASH* reruns.

This is all Joe's doing. I'm sure he actually wanted to do something fun for the residents. Partly, though, he's done it to shake things up. If word got back to Philomena, he might get in trouble. I'm not sure if he really cares, since he's still scheduled to work the day of Rebecca's anniversary.

"I'm not sure if you're aware, Sophie," I begin, sarcastically, "but I'm …"

"Oh, yes, pish-posh. I know you can't move out of that chair. Doesn't mean you can't dance. You can still steer that thing, can't you?"

"And do what? The four-wheeled cha-cha?"

"Or a two-step." She's gleaming. "Or if you want to tango, I can make two."

"I'll pass," I say and reverse back, bumping the chair behind me.

"Suit yourself."

She limps off back to Viktor, who is meant to be dancing, though it looks more like he is constantly checking to see if his fly is undone.

Most of the caregivers are sitting around drinking Coke and chomping on potato chips. The dancefloor is a thrift shop of hamburger hops and rock-and-roll dance halls. Johnny Cash and a whole bunch of music from the days of black-and-white television. It'd be nostalgic if I'd been born five decades earlier.

Pat Miller is doing the two-false-hips Charleston, while Maggie Santorini and Harold Brownfield are doing the awkward Sixth Grade shoulder-hold-hips-far-apart dance. You'd think by their age they'd just have the courage to come out and get it on. I guess flirting never gets easy for some people. And there's Joe, waltzing slowly with Fay Washington, a blind African-American woman who is unbeatable at chess.

People together. Dancing is absurd. Why do we dance?

There's so much laughter, so many smiles.

I guess dancing just feels good.

Any seated residents are one by one persuaded onto their feet and onto the dancefloor by Sophie.

Once she's done, she returns to Viktor and takes his hands. Two old fools who can barely walk, trying to attempt something of a tango.

They make me wonder what their lives were like before the home. Who their partners were. Who they loved enough to have families with. How hard it was for their families to put them in here. Or how easy? How can they be excited for life when they are so close to dying? How can they be happy knowing it's all going to end soon and they can't ever get back their youth? They can't take back anything they want to. They can't do it over. There's so little room left to make things right.

There they are, though, two old fools. Just dancing together. Smiling. Not missing their wonder years, but finding the wonder in their years.

I'm the only resident not on the dancefloor until a huge body throws itself onto the chair beside me. "I not keep up so good with young woman," says Viktor, slouched but pleased, looking half-drunk. "Not on dancefloor anyway." He winks at me, invoking a disturbing thought.

"You move fine, Vik. Like a man who used to know how to actually dance."

This makes him cock his head with a short, strong chuckle. "I once date dancer from Bolshoi Ballet. She teach me how to move."

Now, looking into his beady eyes under those bushy gray brows, I wonder just how crazy Viktor is.

"Really? I'd love to see what she taught you."

He leans in, grinning wryly. "I can only show some thing. Like American say, PG13." Another wink from Viktor and it is now absolutely assured I'll be traumatized. "But, this I do show."

With that, Viktor stands, staggers a few steps and then, miraculously, bounds once and leaps into the air, kicking his right leg back. His maneuver is met by collective applause and woops from residents and caregivers alike. Some call for an encore, Fay Washington asking what she missed, but Viktor waves them off and rejoins me.

"You believe me now?" he asks.

"Yeah. Maybe you're not as crazy as I thought."

"I not crazy at all, little Cody."

Viktor leans back so that he is hidden from the party. From the corner of my eye I see him take out a hipflask from his jacket pocket and have a swig.

"What have you got there, Vik?"

Still leaning back, he hisses at me, "What you think? I Russian – vodka, and if I tell you how I get, I have to kill you. You keep quiet, okay?"

"Only if you share it."

Viktor holds up the flask, darting his eyes around.

"Vik, you need to …"

"Oh, sorry."

He stands so that I'm shielded.

The vodka is cool as it hits my lips and then my tongue. It burns as it flows down my throat. I cough after I swallow and Viktor swiftly hides the hipflask back in his jacket.

It's been years since I've drunk alcohol. My belly is warm, and it feels good.

"You don't like it here, do you Vik?"

His head shakes fervently. "No. No freedom."

"Do you ever think about how you will get out of here, and what you'll do?"

It's stupid to provoke him … but it's interesting to hear people dream.

"When I get out, the first thing I do is take a car, so I can drive. Then maybe I come and get Sophie."

My left hand shoots up as high as it can, a finger pointed at Viktor. "See, I knew it. You have a thing for Sophie. It's about time you owned up."

"You keep mouth shut." Viktor points back. "None of your business."

"Okay, okay. Settle down. Give me another swig."

He stands and spins me around so that I'm facing the window, and then turns his seat. In the reflection, the geriatric dance party limps along.

We take turns sipping the vodka.

Minutes pass in scattered conversation. The alcohol begins to take effect.

I gaze at the old people trying to remember dances popular before I was born, and I feel good. It's all too stupid, those fading lights still trying to be bright. It's so special, too. Light never giving up. Never accepting the darkness until it is actually here.

These people have next to nothing: barely any family who visit, no friends outside of this hole, and the dawning contingency for most is the end of their life, yet here they are, squeezing ounces of fun and joy out of a Saturday night as if they are sixteen, as though life is eternal.

I roll my head to the side to Viktor. "So you'll just drive, hey?"

Viktor takes another swig and then gives me one. He gazes out the window as if he's seeing the open road right now. "Yes, I drive. With Sophie in front, wind going whoosh through her hair. Yes, that what I do. One day, I get out. One day I be free again."

"I hope you do, Vik."

His head dips and rises like a dashboard bobble-head when someone hits the brakes. "Yes. The only feeling better than freedom is love … True love makes you feel more free than anything."

This is the most profound thing Viktor has ever said.

That freedom. I want to feel it.

We share the view out the window for a while longer, taking turns with the vodka. Viktor is still here – his Alzheimer's hasn't subbed him out yet – and he's more here than I've ever seen him. Maybe all the old Russian fool needed to feel himself was a few sips of his motherland.

"Come on, little Cody, it's time to dance."

Objections come to the tip of my tongue, but that's where they stop.

The old folks cheer as I join them. I'm on the dancefloor.

"Good to see you found your dancing shoes, Codes," Joe says, twirling beside me with Fay Washington.

"What shoes does Cody have on?" she asks. "I do love shoes. I've got thirteen different pairs."

"He actually borrowed yours, Fay," Joe replies. "The ruby-red stilettos."

"They're not comfy," I add, "but they go with this shirt."

This brings an untamed smile to Joe's face. "Now you're getting it, fella."

The moment he twirls off, I'm joined by Sophie. The sneaky old tart. "My dear Cody, may I have this next dance?"

"Umm ..."

Before I can ask how, she takes my right hand and holds it. "It's not like you have a choice, young man. Now follow me and try to keep up."

Sophie trots around my chair, holding my arm up as if I have some control of what's going on. She starts to disappear into my periphery, so I steer to get her back in front of me.

"That's it, darling. Now you're getting it."

"That's the second time someone's said that to me in the last five minutes," I say.

"Well, then I guess it must be right ... Come on, keep up now."

I navigate my chair and follow her as she shuffles a circular path. Liquid courage is on my side. I can do anything.

It's my twenty-first birthday all over again, and I'm braving the dancefloor of an NYC nightspot. So convinced I look good. Ignorant of the fact that I really look like a dipshit. Not prepared for the reality check of the morning after.

Ha! Who cares for that? Not me, not now.

As the song changes, Sophie leaves me and ... I'm in the middle of a dance circle. Everybody is watching, cheering, clapping their wrinkly palms. The music takes me. Steer to the left, to the right. Forward, forward, and back. Now slide smoothly back, a crippled moonwalk. And now my climax – a speedy three-sixty.

The cheers ring out through the group.

The circle collapses in and I'm lost in there.

I slip out and make it to the window before anyone can really notice I'm gone.

From the deepening night sky, where hints of the galaxy shine shyly, I change my focus to the dance scene in the reflection of the glass. It's distorted. An impression still. Another impression. A different time and place. One I know. Where I can see those bodies moving on the dancefloor in a New York City bar, or even a Parisian jazz club. It's like a dream, like watching it all unfold through a camera lens.

There's a man, tall but not too tall, perhaps six-foot-two or so, with dark brown hair. His hands are holding the grooves of a woman's waist as if that's what they were made for. She's blonde, and tall, too, heels that make her legs look like they could hit the roof. They're dancing, they're laughing at a joke that nobody else in the room gets – they're not in the room, they are somewhere else, somewhere out in their own private cosmic bubble. They've got something that transcends space and time, life and death, heartache and being lost …

I'm waking up. I'm alive.

In a universe dominated by stars, even the brightest and biggest die eventually. Everything dies. One thing lives on, past all of the supernovas, deeper than any black hole. Bigger than life. Than the universe.

Love.

Chapter 23

(THEN)

The surgeries came and went. They hurt us both. Seeing the fear in Isobel's eyes before surgery, I wanted to take her place. Have my insides scraped. I'd have done it all awake, too, if that would make it so she didn't have to.

I wished there'd been another way. She endured so much.

Then came the medications. Clomid first, and then when that alone didn't work, injectable hormone treatments were added on top.

Eight months later, nothing had improved. We were no closer to creating a family.

What was meant to be a beautiful progression in our life together had turned to disappointment and stress.

We'd become mundane in the way we had sex; so concentrated on the destination we forgot the journey. Most of all, we'd become dull in ourselves and for each other.

The whole experience strained us.

Lost, deserted of a spark, I found myself in a position I'd never been in. Not scared of losing Isobel because of herself, or because she was too good for me, just drifting a little away from her myself. I was less sure of everything.

With the calendar for 2011 well expired, I tossed it in the trashcan, along with all the stupid dates marked off where this or that was meant to occur in Isobel's cycle.

"Maybe we need to start to consider those other options." Isobel was on the couch, hugging her legs, exhausted and withdrawn.

It was usually second nature to go and comfort her in these moments. Yet I stayed at the kitchen table. "Maybe we do."

The sounds of the city filtered in.

"And what if there's no way it can happen?"

"I don't know," I replied dolefully.

There was a chasm running through the middle of our apartment.

"Will it change anything between us?" The words came like a shot to my guts.

I glanced at Isobel, talking into her knees.

Car horns. Traffic. Gusting of wind.

Swallowing my own insecurity and anguish, with five steps I crossed the chasm and kneeled in front of her. "Baby," I said, bringing her arms out to hold mine. "It won't change a single thing between you and me."

"How do you know that, Cody?"

"Because I know us."

Despite attempting to assure her, my confidence was an imitation. Things inside me were held together with safety pins.

"Maybe it's just something we're not meant to do."

"I don't think that … you have to stay positive."

Isobel retracted her arms. "I'm not sure if I can keep going with this. Maybe it's just not for me."

"What are you saying?"

"Maybe I just want things to go back to how they were. When we were happy. Just the two of us. Not a hypothetical baby bringing us down."

With another five steps, I found myself back at the kitchen table.

"Be honest, Isobel. Is this something you want or not?"

"I don't know …" The words were choked with tears.

Suddenly the apartment felt huge; the chasm becoming a void.

My eyes wandered out the kitchen window, to the street below. Business people, buskers, tourists, café workers, families. Countless people with countless stories, countless challenges, countless missed opportunities to get what they wanted from life …

Promotions?

Holidays?

Homes?

Dreams they never had the courage to go after. Futures they never created.

Countless regrets accrued over years. Countless people dying never realizing how they could have truly lived.

Death-bed wisdom, the ending always the same. *It was right there in front of you all along.*

Countless missed opportunities for making the most of what they already had.

People.

Time.

That one person ... Isobel. Her beautifully flawed soul, her perfect heart.

I'd become so blinded by the desire to start a family that I'd been heedless of the family I already had. What lay right in front of me.

When I crossed the apartment this time, I didn't cross a chasm or fill a void, I stomped the idea with each step.

I slid my arms under Isobel's and pulled her to her feet. "As long as I have you I will be happy and fulfilled. I want you more than anything else in life."

She brought her eyes up, nervous yet hopeful. "Do you mean that?"

"I do. You are all I need, babe."

The smile she shone was water to my soul.

An idea came – an epiphany. "Stay here."

I went into the study, opened my laptop and with a few clicks had printed what I wanted.

Isobel was on the couch again when I came back out, though she was no longer completely closed off.

"You remember that time in Paris when we ran up to the top of Montmartre?" I sat beside her and held the paper out. "We've become oatmeal. We need to be Froot Loops again."

Isobel ran her eyes over the ticket in front of her. "Are you serious, Cody?"

"It's one of the last places on your list, isn't it?"

"You're really serious, aren't you?" she asked again, becoming excited.

"Yep."

She spear-tackled me onto my back. "Cody, you are truly amazing. I don't know what to say."

Gazing up into her eyes, the joy on the face of my beautiful wife, my excitement for life with her was reinvigorated. The love I felt for her was overwhelming.

So we kissed.

Long, slowly and deeply. Sinking into one another. Remembering the passion that we'd vowed never to forget.

We left for India two days later, and after a fifteen-hour flight arrived in New Delhi.

We explored, ate and drank, immersed ourselves in the culture and the experience. The climate was sweltering.

It was just the beginning of the heat, though, as meandering back through the Janpath Market, Isobel threw me a look that could've melted steel.

Entangled, we burst through the door to our hotel room with the urgency of a SWAT team, Isobel's legs wrapped around my waist. The dust that had gathered between us was being blown away with each second as we wrestled to be closer to each other.

Hands running over each other's skin, stripping away clothes and tearing down walls.

"Close your eyes and wait here." Isobel pushed me down and left me flustered. "Don't you dare open them!"

She knew the perfect amount of time to push me to the edge. I lay and waited. Throbbing, breathing heavily. Urgent to be with her.

Something light and leathery tickled my abdomen. I went to sit up, but she pushed me back down. "Keep your eyes closed."

Methodically, she kissed from my neck to my pectorals, biting my nipples before descending to my painfully hard dick, where she ran her tongue up and down the shaft, but avoided the head. Teasing, teasing and pushing me more.

"You can sit up but don't open your eyes until I say."

I obeyed, but couldn't help but start stroking myself.

"Hands off." Isobel slapped my wrist. "That's mine."

A tingling inside me added to the tension as she bit and nibbled on my lobe. She climbed onto the bed and ran her nails ran down my back, raising goosebumps along my spine, the coolness of the metal locket on her necklace tickling my skin.

Her lips soothed over my neck once more, her breath warm, and then she got off the bed. "Okay, you can open your eyes now."

She was wearing a belly dancing outfit she'd bought at the market. Beneath it was lace Agent Provocateur lingerie, the sheer set with ribbon crossing at the top of the front, meeting up perfectly at the top of the butt, open crotch.

In her hand was a whip, and on the bed beside me was rope. She handed me the whip.

The way she moved her hips was mesmerizing, swaying back and forth, circling and bumping.

When I tried getting up, she pushed me back down.

I had to wait, growing tenser and tenser with every angle she showed herself to me.

Isobel turned on the iPod. The song brought back memories of the runaway American youths we were … were still.

She positioned herself on all fours on the bed, handing over control to me. "You know what to do, baby."

I spanked her, first with my hand and then the whip, each spank bringing a gasp of pleasure. With my hand around her neck I brought her upright and kissed behind her ear. My hands now corseted her waist, her breathing deepened and she moved her body back against mine. I bent her over again, and traced my lips from the back of her neck, down her spine, her buttocks, calves and back up to her pussy, intermittently tickling her ass with my finger as I massaged her vulva and clitoris with my tongue.

Holding one leg in the air, and covering the small of her back with my palm, I entered her from behind. Rhythmically, I moved in and out of her, using only half of my dick, and massaged her lower back.

Isobel moaned, louder and louder until she was screaming and tightening around my girth as she climaxed. Each contraction of hers caused me to pulsate, my dick growing harder against her warm flesh.

She brought herself up, sighing with heavy relief and tremulous legs, and then turned to me, taking my head in her hands.

We kissed with flames too hot for CGI to imitate.

Then we relaxed, wrapped around each other, a gentle interlude.

Looking into her eyes, I wanted to cry, overwhelmed with emotional ecstasy. It felt as though every part of us was remembering the secret we'd almost lost.

Then a flare from her eyes and the fire roared again.

Isobel threw me onto my back and straddled me, pinning my hands and grinding me into another world of pleasure with her pelvic undulations. As she started to build toward orgasm she dropped down on top of me, still sliding up and down on me. I gripped her buttocks and forced her to continue through another climax. My hips moved in sync with hers. The room grew hotter, our breath fogged in the hazy light, steam rising as sweat evaporated.

With every thrust, we were waking up the whole of India, from Kolkata to Mumbai. Our pleasure thresholds were being broken, Isobel's eyes rolling back in her head, my jaw clenching.

We came together, longer and harder than we'd ever come before. We screamed and grappled with each other, Isobel hitting me, clawing me.

We lay there dizzy, and passed some considerable time with our eyes on the ceiling.

Eventually I broke the silence. "That was beyond anything I've ever experienced."

"I'm still not sure if it was real," Isobel replied.

"It feels good to be a Froot Loop again."

Isobel rolled over onto my chest, a sparkle in her eyes. "Let's never forget this again."

A week and a half later, the Holika bonfire crackled, sparks of confetti twirling through the air. Musicians played drums, plucked sitars and jingled bells while people danced and sang to kick off the start of Holi celebrations. Tomorrow would be the free-for-all carnival of colors.

We sat a short distance back from the revelry, Isobel leaning back on my chest, my arms blanketing her. The smell of smoke wafted through the air. I buried my nose into Isobel's neck to sniff her perfume. The smell of home.

"Where do you think we'll be in five years?" Isobel asked.

"I don't know. It's hard to imagine when you consider all that's happened in the last five years. Wouldn't have picked we'd be here."

"So you're clueless? Don't know a thing."

"We're all clueless about the future. Anyone who tries to say otherwise is just full of it. Economists, estate agents, fortune tellers: they're all in the same boat as you and me, and we have no idea where we're sailing."

"Yeah, but at least they have some fun trying to guess. It's not a deep question, Cody."

I started to tickle Isobel. "Are you trying to say an economist has more fun than me?"

She squirmed and giggled. "Stop. Stop! Okay, you're more fun." I let her go. "But I'm just saying at least they don't avoid the question of the future like you."

"Fair enough. I'll think it over. When I have a good answer I'll let you know."

"You do that Confucius. Just don't ponder too long." She stood and thrust her butt back into my face. "You never see it coming, anyway."

Off she went into the dancing crowd. I stayed and watched her for a quiet second, just to observe the best part of my life dancing as if she had never had a worry in the world.

When I joined her, our hands entwined, and we twirled around and around.

The sidelines weren't the place for me. The future wasn't something coming to think about. It was now. Now was all that mattered and all that ever could …

The next morning Isobel wasn't in bed.

On the bench in the kitchen of our hotel room was a paper bag. A trail of discarded cardboard packets led to the bathroom.

I knocked. "Hon?"

The door swung open. There was this unmistakable glow about her. Standing in a tank top and nanna undies, peering over one after the other …

"Isobel, what's going on?"

She handed them to me. "Look for yourself."

Like she'd just done, I looked over one after the other.

"But …" My eyes slowly rose to Isobel, radiating brighter than any star in the night sky. "But … we've stopped … the medication didn't … what's going on?"

Isobel took the tests from my hand while I stood there, gaping-mouthed. I didn't know where to look, how to move, what the hell to do … Isobel took care of that, though: she stood on her tiptoes and brought her lips to mine.

"Cody, we're pregnant."

She said it once, calmly, and then after I didn't respond, she stood back and screamed with her hands. "Cody, we're fucking pregnant!"

With a squeal of exultation, Isobel ran from the bathroom, collected a pair of shorts and bolted out of the hotel room. Dressing with hops and flailing arms, I pursued her.

Outside the world was a rainbow, paint and powder flying in every direction among the crowd like miniature fireworks.

Isobel was at the foot of the hotel steps, already covered head to toe. She was laughing, and waiting for me. I ran down and took her in my arms as paint and powder splattered on me.

"We're pregnant," she said, this time calmer.

Another glob of paint splattered on us. I laughed. "We're pregnant."

We shared but one fleeting kiss before Isobel broke away and hammered me with paint. And so we ran and danced and sang like maniacs.

That day of Holi was the brightest in my life, and it had very little to do with the paint.

Chapter 24

(NOW)

Bed time.

I'm bathed and my teeth are clean.

Bed time.

The final helpless event in my day.

It's early, but Isobel's turning in. Jake's out until late tomorrow. Stag weekend. He and his closest pals. He has another thing I never had …

Yet, I'm here with the one thing he has that I once had, and he's not.

Isobel's in the bathroom. Legs like totem poles in her night shorts. Youthful in that tank top. Hair free flowing. She takes off her makeup and washes her face. Brushes her teeth then gulps down her pills.

She closes the bathroom door and comes to me, a glass of water and my pills in her hand.

"Open up."

I shake my head. "I don't need them."

"Really?"

This is the first time I've said no to my night-time pills.

"Really."

Isobel stays in front of me for a moment, inspecting me. When she realizes I'm genuine, she ditches the pills.

"You ready for bed?" she asks.

Looking into the yellow light of my room, it feels like it will swallow me whole. Maybe it'll spit me back out without this chair. Maybe it won't regurgitate me at all. It's so empty in there, that murky bedroom, yellow light becoming sallow.

I drive in, and Isobel follows, ready to hoist me …

"Actually, I'm not tired," I say, looking up at her. "I might stay in the chair tonight."

"Really?" Isobel looks befuddled.

She releases the hoist. "Suit yourself. I'll be in my room if you need me."

"Thanks."

"Light on or off?"

The curtains are open enough for me to see the moon. "Off."

I turn to the window.

Isobel flicks the light switch. "Goodnight, Cody."

In the reflection of the window, I see her. She's there. "Goodnight, Isobel."

She dips her head momentarily, and brings it up with a nostalgic smile.

The doorway becomes vacant.

It's me and the moonlight. It's been such a companion to me. Nights on the street, it was the only thing bright. Nights in an orphanage, it filtered in and reminded me there was life outside the microcosm I was in. New York nights, cozy in my first home with Isobel, it watched over our life. It was there when we traveled, so many wild nights. There when we conceived …

And here.

A lifetime behind me. Existence now. What in front?

Who knows? But, there's something within me.

The white shine of the moonlight: somewhere in the world the sun is shining brightly. Somewhere it is raining, storming, windy, snowing, smoggy. Everything … the world can be nothing, but it will always be everything.

I navigate from my bedroom and whir next door, parking in Isobel's doorway.

She glances up from her phone. "Hey, what's up?"

"Can't sleep. Thought I'd see if you were still awake."

"Yeah, neither can I."

"Mind if I come in for a while?"

She locks her phone and concentrates on me. "Sure, come in. I'm not moving, though. I'm too comfy."

"You look it."

I reverse myself into the space beside the bed.

Isobel goes back to her phone.

"What are you looking at?" I ask.

She snickers. "Just memes. Facebook. Instagram. Usual stuff."

"Cool." I unlock my phone and pretend to play with it. It's a pretty vain effort. I have no social media anymore. Deleted everything a long time ago. "Are you missing Jake?"

Isobel glances up and shrugs. "A little. It's funny having the bed to myself again. He looks like he's having fun, though." She shows me a photo on Facebook of him and his friends.

"And look at us. In bed at ten on a Saturday."

"Yeah, we're old, Cody."

Funnily enough, right now I feel younger than I have for a long while. "Ancient."

She returns to her phone.

"Maybe we should send him back a selfie," I say.

She smirks. "Hash-tagging it awkward wouldn't do it justice."

"Is this awkward for you?"

Her brow raises. "Strangely enough it's not."

With her boyfriend, her lover, out of town, I'm here with her. Comfortable. But what am I to her? Only in name am I her husband. I'm not her platonic best friend. I'm not her lover. What am I?

Isobel's eyes are fading. She puts her phone on charge and then fluffs her pillow.

"I'm not going to be much company. I'm beat."

"That's fine," I reply. "I'll occupy myself."

"You can talk to me if you like. It'll send me to sleep."

"Am I that boring these days?"

"Yep."

The light in here is warm. Calming. Isobel's tired eyes struggling to stay open.

"What am I to you, Isobel?"

Her eyelids seesaw. She reaches out and touches the back of my left hand. "You're Cody," she says, groggily. "You've always been Cody."

I want to talk more, but her eyes are fully closed now. Her breathing deepens and within seconds she's sound asleep.

Without makeup, the lines around her eyes are noticeable.

She doesn't look old, though.

She appears raw. Real. Accomplished. A woman who's lived through so much, and is still here, still trying to be happy. Still her.

When she was like this, so unaffected, so untainted by the world, she was always her most beautiful.

I stay here and watch her sleep.

Her chest moves up and down. Her skin looks softer than clouds. Her lips so full and lovely.

She's older than ever, but she's so present.

She's Isobel. And she is more beautiful than she ever has been.

I'm here, too.

I'm Cody. Maybe more than just a vestige of the man I was. Maybe something greater.

The notification light on her phone flashes.

Jake. Away, drunk, but still here as well.

Three of us.

There has to be a fight.

How will I sleep by her side again?

⁂

In the morning, I rouse to the sound of birds outside the window. I'm still beside Isobel's bed; the sheets are rumpled.

She comes into the bedroom wearing just her small Paul Frank silk dressing gown.

She walks toward me.

Nervous energy rushes through me, my forearm raising for no purpose. Reaching?

I'm caught in another strand of time. The bow of the gown might be pulled seductively. She might coil herself around me. Naked. Soft warmth of skin on skin. The tickle of her hair in my face when she brings her head near mine.

"I was thinking of going to the mall."

My head jolts as I gasp.

"You okay?"

"Yeah, sorry. Just daydreaming."

"Do you want to come to the mall?"

"Sure. Getting anything in particular?"

"I've gotta top up on perfume, and I thought we could update your wardrobe."

I'm grinning. "So, you admit your fashion sense for me is terrible?"

"Watch it, or you'll find yourself in checkered shirts for the rest of your life."

In my bedroom, Isobel uses the pullies to transfer me from my electric chair to the commode chair.

Toileting isn't as painful as it used to be; now it's just something we do.

Showering, Isobel doesn't wear her usual uninspiring one-piece. Instead she dons a two-piece from a shoot in Barcelona in O-seven. My eyes meander around the paths of her body as she washes me, entranced by the stories that it tells. The bathroom fan just sounds normal, doing its job of keeping the steam from hiding what I want to see.

She finishes and dries me, and then herself.

She swallows her pills and feeds me mine. Rather than a ritual that reminds us of the deep cuts that caused our scars, it's simply something we're doing together, a commonality.

"I'll just go get some clothes," Isobel says, and leaves the bathroom.

My eyes are in line with her butt as it bounces side to side down the hall.

She disappears into my bedroom and then comes back out, crisscrossing her feet down the hallway in just that bikini, evocative of hot times in Barcelona.

"Plain white tee," she holds it up, "and dark blue chinos."

Isobel drops the clothes, slapping her hands to her cheek in astonishment. "Cody!"

"What?"

I follow her eyes. "Oh shit."

All I've had below my neck since That Sunday is use of my left forearm and hand – albeit with poor fine-motor skills – some internal feelings such as when I need to go to the toilet and, given the vagus nerve remained intact and my hormones unaltered, something else, too. Including an incident in my teens that involved Janine's mother, a *Playboy* and a surprise visit, this is the most awkward erection I've ever had.

It's there, standing tall and aimed at Isobel like a canon.

Shit.

For a short time after I became quadriplegic, we had sex, but it was mechanical and mundane, lifeless. Soon, we stopped completely, and the passion of sex became a distant memory to me. Morning glories never disappeared. But this is the first time since ... well, since I told Isobel to move on, that it's sexual ... because of Isobel. Goddamn bikinis.

"Umm ..." She doesn't know where to look. At least her hands have lowered from her face.

"If only my right hand still worked."

The dirty, immature part of my mind has woken from its slumber, along with my dick. I'm thankful for it because a smile is working its way across Isobel's face.

Fanning herself with her hand, she breaks into nervous laughter, continuing to avert her eyes from my dick.

"Well it's good to see you've found Jake's Viagra stash."

"He needs Viagra?"

"Sometimes. Shit I shouldn't have said that. Just trying to push the awkward elephant out of the room. Please don't say anything."

And just like that, I've discovered a flaw in the perfect man that is Jake Townsend. Of all the pills I take, that's not one I need. He seemed like someone who could conquer anything he wanted to in life … but even the Roman Empire disappeared into oblivion.

Everyone can be beaten.

"I won't. I'd rather not talk to him at all to be honest."

Isobel sits on the edge of the bath, now at ease with my boner. It's amazing just how quickly we humans adapt. Or our ability to ignore the bleatingly obvious. "Cody. If we're all going to work in this house, we've all gotta work."

I hmm to this. "It'd work better without him here."

"Do we have to have this conversation again, really?"

I try to work my left arm toward my erection. It flails feebly for a brief moment but it doesn't make it. I can't even touch my dick. Not even a stroke, let alone jerk off.

"No. It's okay. I get it."

Isobel entwines her hands together and hugs them in between her knees. "I know it's a strange situation. Trust me, I feel it too."

"What do you mean?"

She spends several drawn-out seconds staring at the tiles. "Nothing. I'm just moving forward, Cody. Like you said. It's strange that we're sitting here talking about it."

I gulp. I'm getting sick of swallowing stones.

"Yeah, you're right. That's what I said. I'll leave it … you seem like you enjoy it. The Viagra must work just fine."

"I thought you said you were leaving it."

"Okay, sorry. But just answer me this … Does he make you feel how I did? Do the two of you make love like we used to?"

This makes Isobel stand swiftly. "Maybe today isn't the day to go shopping."

She dresses me hurriedly and then pushes me down the hall back to my bedroom. Into the harness, and back into my electric chair.

Not a word is said the whole time.

On her way out, she stops in the door. "No, we don't, but neither do you and I."

Chapter 25

(NOW)

"Hey …" I say, parking at the kitchen table, "I'm sorry."

Isobel drops the dishcloth in the sink and leans on her palms, her eyes lost in foam.

"I shouldn't have asked you that before, and you're right – I need to stop being so abrasive toward him. It's your choice and my opinion doesn't matter."

She stays at the sink.

"Cody." Her mascara is moist when she turns, but she's not sobbing – I don't think she'll let me see her like that anymore. "Things are so fucked up."

I steer around the table, right up to her. "I see the reason for that, too, when I look in the mirror."

She inhales a breath as if the air can heal her heart. "I just don't know where the hell my feet have landed. I just need to do something that isn't part of my life now."

"Well how about we go shopping then, like you wanted?"

"I'm not so sure."

I beep at her. "Come on. I promise not to be a dick if you promise not to get me any more terrible shirts."

Isobel snickers. "I won't get you crappy shirts, but it's easier said than done for you not to be a dick."

"Try me."

She puts a pan in the drying rack and sighs. "It won't be awkward?"

"It won't … Let's not just go for me. Let's go for the both of us. I think we both need it."

Scanning her eyes over me, a smirk forms on Isobel's face. "You do look terrible in those shirts. I don't know what I was thinking."

❦

The lights of Water Tower Place are bright, mesmerizing. They remind me of the times I came here as a lost youth. Drifting, far away from the girl who changed my childhood, not yet in sight of the woman who'd change my adult life. Not yet found by a man who changed the direction of my life.

I'd come here and lift paper for my Polaroid. Scavenge leftovers. Toilet and shower. It was a place where I didn't feel homeless for a time during the day. Somewhere I could sit and watch the people go by. The kids, the teenagers, the adults. The moms and dads. The families. I could get close enough to hear what they were talking about and imagine that I was the child that was being asked what they'd like for dinner, what they might want for their birthday. I liked to even imagine I was the one being told off. That lady's voice was talking to me, and it was me saying "Sorry, Mom."

Back here, my old halfway house.

And I'm drifting again. Imagining I'm someone else to the woman who's walking in front of me.

I'm not even in my chair right now. What chair?

Her butt is in line with my eyes.

It sways.

Her hips narrate the action.

Above them her waist watches over it all.

I'm jealous of her red dress. It knows what panties she has on.

"Cody."

There's a song playing.

Something is humming, sweetly.

In the afternoon …

"Cody."

The light is pale white.

Things have stopped.

This sweet humming, wind blowing in through an open window.

Warm air. Steam on the glass.

A back to mine.

The light catches shades of muscle tone.

Shadow is cast onto the sheets, a shadow of true sensuality.

The dip of the small in her back. The arc of her butt.

"Cody!"

My head jolts. The airy bedroom is gone. Mall lights, splash.

Oh, *this* chair.

"Have you heard a word I've said?" Isobel is standing over me, her hands on her hips.

"Umm."

"What were you doing?"

Caught. My head wants my hands to fumble. "Just thought it was easier trailing, crowds and all."

Her brow creases skeptically. "Right … Well, do you want to go in here?"

Topless men, six packs on show, tans from a bottle. "I'm not sure that I'll pull off the Abercrombie and Fitch look. I'm a touch pale."

"Your hair is on point, though."

"And don't forget what I'm packing beneath this shirt."

The humor in this day, this frivolous time, is here again.

Like a dog trots beside its owner, I drive into the store with Isobel. She points at tees, pants and jackets and I respond with a "Yep", or a "No way", or a "Maybe …" and soon she has her arms full with clothes and I'm loaded up to my chin.

"Ah, excuse me," says the change-room assistant as we go to pass, "our policy only allows five items …"

"I know, but you see," Isobel interjects, "my husband is in a hurry, and we don't have the time go back and forth. And I don't have the space to hide anything, and my husband, well, he just wouldn't."

The assistant is taken aback, singing a silent opera with her gaping mouth.

I'm trying not lose it.

"Umm … It's store policy." The poor girl doesn't know the woman she's dealing with right now.

"We can go back and drop some of this stuff off." Isobel lowers her voice. "But you'll have to explain to his squash partner why he's late."

The girl darts her eyes between me and Isobel, a quizzical expression creasing her forehead.

Isobel is absolutely messing with her. What a rambunctious little shit. She could be twenty-one right now.

"Umm," the assistant fumbles, "I guess it'll be fine."

We enter the change room.

Isobel closes the door and dumps the stack of clothes. She leans down to pick up the ones on my lap.

"Well that was quite a strange interaction," I say.

She looks up, her eyes in line with mine, and smirks. "Sometimes it's just interesting to confuse people."

"You certainly boggled her mind." Then I think of something as she stands. "Did you really mean what you said?"

"No, I don't think you're going to make your squash partner late. You'll be perfectly on time."

"Glad to see you've found your facetiousness. Where's it been hiding?"

"Same place as my sarcasm."

"No, but really Isobel, did you mean what you said, about me being your husband."

She leans down again, and then glances up at me. "Cody, shut the fuck up."

Then she pulls my tee up and over my head.

Nothing else is said about it as piece by piece Isobel tries the tops on me. There's far more than vestiges left in her – she's someone else, someone new. It's inspiring.

"That's it, baby," I say as Isobel takes my pants off, her head not far from my crotch.

"What happened to not being a dick?"

"My dick became too self-interested."

She throws a baleful glance at me. It's thrilling – she might actually harm me. Those resplendent eyes lit with fire, reminiscent of a time when she'd use her nails and a whip to damage me perfectly then rebuild me better than before.

I can't help myself. I want to push her more. "Honestly, it' so exciting, I can feel one of my legs again."

"Do you want to find out if you can still feel your nuts, too?" She rips the pants from my feet.

I've never known a bad day in my life. It's all too fun.

"Seriously, say something." Isobel glares. "I dare you."

It's exhilarating to be at risk. To *have* something to risk.

The dull roar of the store fills our change room: house music playing loud enough to drown out objections and second thoughts.

We leave A & F with practically a new wardrobe for me, including a black brushed twill cap, which now sits atop my head.

"Where do you want to go next?" Isobel's fingers are red, wrapping around the handle of the shopping bags.

"I dunno … maybe we could do some shopping for you."

This surprises her, pleasantly. "Well, I don't really need anything."

"Some would disagree."

Now that pleasant surprise turns to playful disdain. "Oh, really? Get a couple of new tees and pants and think you're cool, huh?"

"Just saying."

Isobel dumps the bags on me. "You know what? Stuff you, Cody. I *am* going to go shopping for me, and you're going to help me, regardless of how long I take."

Every man has his threshold for shopping. I'm keen to push mine right now.

The first half an hour Isobel spends leading me to a bunch of stores, in which she finds absolutely nothing of interest, not even trying one thing on except a floppy spring hat in Hollister. The escape plans that used to come when shopping aren't present in my mind. I'm here, and it feels good.

In Forever 21 she finds items worth trying on – two skirts and a top. She takes them to the change room and I wait patiently outside, parked out of the way.

Minutes later she comes out. "What do you think?"

She's got on a tight gray skirt and white top that hugs her body. A stranger wouldn't be able to guess she's thirty-two: she looks barely a day over … twenty-one, I guess. Even I'm fooled. With all the books I've read, all the newspaper articles, all the things about language Larry wanted instilled in me, all I come out with is, "Hot."

A slow, sarcastic clap sounds in my mind. *Bravo, Wordsworth.*

"You think?" Isobel rotates her hips side to side. "Not too tight?"

"Tight has always suited you."

She plays with a lock of hair. "I don't have the figure I used to."

"Some would disagree."

Shyly, she smiles and looks away, blushing, before she returns to the change room.

I stay where I am.

Then I hear Isobel's voice. "Cody." She appears in the doorway, her shoulder bare aside from the black strap of her bra. "Come in, I need your advice."

I knock several items off their coat hangers on the way in. We barely fit in the cubical.

She slips on another top, a black one with sequins. "What about this one?"

"I like the white one better with the gray skirt."

Now she reaches behind her back and unzips the skirt. Wriggling her hips side to side she works off the skirt.

My breathing increases as I gaze upon Isobel, only a foot away, her waist and hips and the lacy panties right in my face. Their intricacy swallows me: the sewn patterns, the transparent parts on either side of her crotch, the shine of the silk bands that arc around her hips. In the mirror, I can see them connect at the back, under which the material narrows into a thong.

I want my lips on her butt. My tongue sliding under the straps. My teeth pulling at the elastic and then letting it go to slap against her skin. To hear her breathe with pleasure at the sensation.

She hasn't put anything on yet. And now she takes her top off as well.

"You're beautiful." It leaps from my mouth without intention. A thought that was too strong, too big, to stay hidden inside.

"Do you really mean that?"

Our eyes meet. I trek my gaze from her eyes to her shoulders, her collarbone, the thin valleys on either side of her abdomen, the shallow V that points to her pussy. The lace panties, the gap between her thighs. Her soft, supple skin.

"I do," I croak, nervously, "you could still model if you wanted to."

Her hand touches the top of my left. Softly, she holds it and brings it up to her stomach. The sensation under my fingertips is like coming home.

Our eyes meet again. In hers, I see the same tears ready to spill as I can feel in mine. Isobel closes her eyes and a tear does breaks free. I close mine and release one, too.

As glorious as the sight of her is, it's the presence of her in my heart right now that is the most profound thing of all.

Seeing her.

Feeling her.

I spread my fingers as wide as I can, trying to take in every inch of her as she smooths my hand around her body. Down the side of her hip and onto her thigh. And then up toward ...

"Excuse me," says the change-room assistant, "do you need any help with sizes."

Isobel jumps and lets my hand flop. "Ah, oh, sorry. Yes, I mean, no. We're fine in here."

She quickly dresses while I sit, my hand trembling.

Something has just come out of me.

I'm scared. Afraid of something … afraid of being truly hurt.

⚹

Isobel leads me into the house, and goes into her room to dump the bags.

I steer after her and stop at the door. I feel like suggesting something. Something naughty. Something kinky. For a moment, I almost believe that I can stand and straddle her from behind. Wrap my hands around her waist, and kiss her neck, peel the shoulder down on her top. Exhale a hot breath of air onto her skin.

The front door opens. She turns to the noise, and then notices me. "What are you doing, Cody?"

"Ah … nothing."

The floorboards creak behind me. "What's going on?"

I'm sandwiched between Jake and Isobel.

"Just went shopping." Isobel comes over and stops in front of me. There's not enough room for her to get to Jake. I'm the blockade between them.

"Ah …"

"Umm …"

They mumble awkwardly.

I'm an elephant on four wheels. Who'd have guessed being this obtrusive would ever be of benefit.

For a fleeting moment I'm preventing them being together. No puckering of lips. No sweet caressing of the cheeks. Nothing for them.

The elephant has entered the ring.

And it's hilarious.

So, here I am laughing, fighting. Bellicose in the most abstract of ways.

"Ah … what's so funny?" Jake asks.

Though I can't wipe the tears from my eyes, feeling them form is exhilarating.

"You know that old Stealers Wheel song?"

Isobel snorts with laughter, and sits back on the bed. "You're an idiot, Cody."

What a wonderful insult, spoken with a smile.

"I don't get it." Jake's confused.

I navigate my chair around so I'm facing him. "What you don't get could fill Soldier Field."

"Really, what's the joke?" He raises his arms and then slaps his palms on his thighs.

There's no joke to get, just awkwardness. But he doesn't get it, and so he's become the butt of it.

"Cody's just being a clown or a joker, that's all." Isobel stands and steers me out of the doorway so she can pass. "Come on, let's relax. Tell me about your weekend."

She takes Jake by the hand and leads him into the lounge room, leaving me with my shallow little triumph.

Shallow.

But, still, something.

By the entrance to the hallway I stop and look in on them like an oversized fly on the wall. They're cozied up together, facing the television with their backs to me. I can hear they're happy, though – Jake chortling away about the stag weekend, Isobel listening quietly, giggling intermittently.

Seeing her comfortable in his arms tears shreds of hope from me. Hearing them fuck later will hurt.

I can still laugh with her, make her smile, still touch her, still feel her (the change room …?) but he can sweep in and have her back in his arms at any moment. He can walk in, and walk out with her. They can run together.

My motor will never keep up.

"We went shopping," I hear Isobel say.

"Oh, really?"

"Yeah, needed to update Cody's wardrobe. I've been dressing him horribly. Didn't realize until he told me."

Jake doesn't reply.

"Something the matter?" Isobel asks.

He shrugs. "It's just a bit strange, you taking him out shopping."

"I'm still his caregiver, Jake. I need to look after him."

That hits me in the chest.

Swallow that pill, fly.

Jake takes his time to respond. I need to see the insecurity in his face right now. See this self-assured Romeo come down to my level. Know he's not so different from me.

"And what was the deal before with that joke? I don't get it."

"What's your problem?" Isobel shifts away from him. "You're acting strange."

His body closes off to her. "It just doesn't sit well. The way you two are sometimes."

Her words stung. His words splash water onto my face.

"One minute you're telling me about all the fun you had and the next you're getting upset over me taking Cody shopping." Isobel stands.

"Because it's weird … this whole situation … it's just strange. I want to be with you. Not with you and him."

Isobel shakes her head. "Are you really jealous?"

"I'm not jealous. I just …" He trails off, like a little boy telling a fib.

There's some seconds of nothing.

"I'm taking a shower," Isobel says.

I steer hurriedly into my room.

Isobel flashes past my door.

The bathroom fan turns on. That sound. It's somewhere between two polarities of what it has been.

I'm stuck in the middle of them. Moving away from one, do I want to be the other that I can never be again? Chasing the past, so uselessly … or is there another part of this sound that I can attach to. A new one?

A wedge sits out on the couch.

One I let in.

I drive out of my room.

He's still sitting there, staring into the black screen of the television.

"Have a good weekend?" I ask as I drive into the lounge room. "Seemed like it."

Jake glances up. "What do you want, Cody?"

"Was just asking about your weekend. Making conversation."

"Bullshit. You're never just doing anything. There's always an agenda."

This is more pugnacious than Jake's been.

The more flawless someone is, the more room they have for new flaws. Jake's cracking.

"Don't get shitty at me because you and Isobel had a fight."

He throws me a baleful glare. "You're at the middle of every issue we have. If you weren't here, things would be perfect."

"Well I am here and I'm not going anywhere. Get that through your skull."

"I don't think I've ever met such a pathetic human being." His eyes, painted with disdain, won't leave me. "I tried to get along with you and like you, I really did. But I can't. I detest you, Cody."

"The feeling's mutual, jerk-off. If I could swing a punch, I'd smack you right between your pretty eyes."

This makes him chuckle malevolently. "But you can't, can you? You can't do a thing. If your chair ran out of battery, I could screw Isobel right in front and you couldn't do a thing except beep your horn. Pathetic." He shakes his head and peers out the window dismissively.

"That's if you could even screw her in the first place."

His eyes dart back to me. "What?"

"My limbs mightn't work but at least my dick does."

Jake's face becomes florid, jaw tight, fists gripped.

"How the hell … have you been snooping through my stuff?"

"How would I do that? I can't do a thing."

"Isobel told you?"

I don't need to say a thing. I've played my trump card, though with it I feel a profound emptiness. There's no victory in my quarrel with Jake. He's still her boyfriend, whether I make underhanded jokes or not. If I one-up him in a verbal joust, nothing changes …

I go to drive away.

Jake steps in front of me. "You didn't answer me."

"Get the fuck out of my way, Jake."

He stays like a concrete statue, quietly glaring at me.

"What do you want me to say? I'm Isobel's husband and you're her boyfriend, how are we ever going to get along? Words get said, but we can co-exist." It's hard to believe I'm trying to placate him. Yet, in this moment, I'm thinking of Isobel. She doesn't need this. And yeah, it's my fault, I didn't need to come out of my room, but I'm trying to leave.

"What did Isobel say? Tell me you fucking rat."

A few months ago, when I first saw this man's pearly white smile and endearing manner, I wouldn't have pictured him being so belligerent. Have I pushed him to this? Has my burden led him to a new side of himself, or is this just him showing a side he'd rather have kept to himself?

"She didn't say anything." I push the joystick forward. He doesn't budge. "Seriously, Jake. I just went snooping."

"Bullshit. You just said you didn't."

"I lied."

He stays.

I beep the horn. What else can I do?

He still doesn't move and so I go to beep it again, but Jake slaps my hand away.

"Shut the hell up and just answer me."

"Why do you care so much?"

"I need to know if I can trust her."

I raise my brow. "If you're questioning that, you're the one who's pathetic."

Pushing my hands down, he leans in so that we're almost face to face. "I can't take it here with you anymore."

"Then how about you leave," I growl.

"You're gone, Cody. You'll be a lonely cripple in a home. You'll be nothing more than a memory to Isobel. Those shitty photo albums of yours will get thrown out when we move from here to somewhere you don't know. You'll be forgotten."

I snap.

My head slams forward into his chin, connecting with a sting in the top of my skull.

Jake stumbles back.

The chair whirs as I take off and ram him into the wall.

"Argh!" he cries.

Smack. His fist hits me in between my eyes. Then my chair reverses, Jake pushing the joystick back.

My vision blurs. I try to shake it off.

Clearing, I see Jake. I push the joystick forward and go at him again. Jake slides back and slaps my hand away from the joystick. He takes hold of my hand and twists it. A sharp pain stings in my wrist. Then he pins my hand on the rest, pounding the back of it punch after punch.

"You're a cunt, Jake." I'm panting, wincing in pain, trying to break my hand free. "You're fucking worthless. You can attack a cripple but you can't fuck a beautiful woman."

He lets my hand go and chokes me. "Shut up!"

I gag, gasping for breath. My hand aches as I bring it up to the joystick.

I push it forward, full throttle, and ram him against the wall again. He lets go of my neck, screaming in pain as I try to crush his legs. He hits me in the face again, but I don't stop.

I want to destroy him.

"What the hell is going on?!"

I reverse and release Jake.

Isobel is standing in the archway in a towel, hair dripping wet.

The bathroom fan has turned off.

"Nothing," Jake says, rubbing his shins. "We're just sorting some things out."

My breathing is deep and heavy. As I calm, I notice the path of destruction I've mowed. It's as though we've been robbed.

The coffee table has tipped over. A vase is smashed in the kitchen. Chairs flipped over. The couch out of place.

Isobel scans the room. "This is getting silly."

"Yeah …" is all I add.

She sits on the couch and thinks for a time.

"We need to find a way for this to work, otherwise something's going to have to change."

"You're right." Jakes sits beside Isobel and covers her hands, turning on his ingratiating manner. "We can't keep doing this to you. You deserve better."

"I don't know …" Isobel switches her eyes between Jake and me. "Maybe the three of us can't live together."

"It won't come to that," Jake replies.

"I hope not." Isobel gets up and leaves us alone.

Jake looks at me smugly. "One step closer to the door."

"I'm not going anywhere." I reverse back into my spot beside the sofa, switching off from Jake's snide remarks.

Though my words are resolute, inside I'm fragile.

I'm stuck between two hopeless choices. Continue to battle him and risk losing Isobel completely; accept the situation and confine myself to being a spectator to her happiness.

Be angry, what I've become; or be nothing, what I've been.

What other alternative is there? Be … what can I be?

Chapter 26

(THEN)

At the twelve-week mark, we broke the news. Our friends were excited in their own way. My parents were ecstatic. I called Isobel's dad, too. It sounded like he choked up on the phone, but he said very little before he hung up.

We moved back to Chicago soon after. It made sense to be near my family. My parents were there anytime, practically on call.

Pregnancy suited Isobel. It was as though there was sunshine following her wherever she went, her skin glowing.

When we made love, it was slow and sensual, and even as her belly ballooned during the second trimester, she turned me on, if not more than ever. I'd never understood how people found pregnancy attractive before I experienced Isobel's. She redefined how profound I thought beautiful could be. Isobel, with our growing child inside – there was nothing more amazing.

Time flew by and my career rolled on: a bevy of high-paying shoots ensured our baby would have an easy trip through school and university. Eighteen weeks in, unable to contain our curiosity, we made a trip to the hospital.

"Cody, are you coming in?" The nurse's voice was soft and reassuring.

I was sitting outside the room, charging my phone. I'd forgotten my camera, and this was a moment I needed a photo of, albeit a terrible phone snap.

"You're going to miss it, you big goof," Isobel called.

She was lying down, the technician moving the ultrasound wand through the goop on her belly. She was gazing at a black and white screen with numbers and a blurred image.

"Smile," I said, holding up my phone.

Isobel turned and poked her tongue out for the photo. "So, that's what you were doing."

Then I noticed what was on the screen. With a tremulous hand, I pointed. "Is that …?"

The technician laughed, as did Isobel.

"Cody, come here." Isobel's eyes returned to the screen. I followed her instruction and came over to the bed.

"You can see the head here," the technician said. "Here are the hands and feet."

They were there. Few moments had inspired so much awe inside me as this did. "And if you look here, you can see her heartbeat."

Isobel turned to me, beaming peacefully. "Say hi to our daughter, Cody."

It felt as though I was in the middle of a vacuum, everything drawing into me. "We're having a girl?"

"We're having a baby girl." Isobel took my hand.

First steps, first words, first day of school; first fight about a party, about a boy, about the door staying open. It all flashed through my mind like rapidly flicking through a photo album.

On the screen the small blob of life that was our daughter moved.

My mind had never been so clear; my heart filled with pride and security it had never known before.

Chapter 27

(THEN)

Sun shone off the pavement making the gray concrete appear a bright, light yellow as we strolled from our apartment toward Lincoln Park. If the streets could have smiled, they would have been beaming at us. With the trees along the sidewalks whispering in the gentle summer breeze, the city was calm. Bright summer clothes, rumbles and chimes of laughter forming a melody from cafés and bars, even the taxicabs didn't sound annoyed.

With our hands entwined, soaked head to toe in sunshine, every step forward felt salubrious. My travel camera was around my neck, like it often was on walks. We went on quietly for some time, a comfortable silence that I could only share with Isobel.

Passing the conservatory, she gazed into the distance. "It's getting very real."

"It is," I said, glancing to her belly.

A glimpse of North Pond appeared through the forest. We crossed West Fullerton and started on the track into the Nature Sanctuary.

"We've been coming here our whole lives." Isobel stopped.

Without thinking we'd made our way to the seat where we used to meet as teenagers.

She surveyed the area with a faraway look in her eyes. "It all seems so much smaller now, doesn't it?"

"Everything does." I took her hand and helped her sit, then sat beside her, my arm wrapped around her.

"Are you scared at all, Cody?"

"I'm excited, and I guess a little nervous. I don't know if I'm scared, though."

Isobel held her belly. "I am."

"What scares you?"

"That I won't know how to be the mother I want to be."

The father I never knew came into my mind. A flicker of a face I couldn't remember properly. And then Larry, the man who became my father. What did I know about being a father? I could read a million books about it, but what could I really know until I felt the touch of my child?

"I guess when I think about it, I'm a little bit scared, too."

"It fills me with joy to think that I'll be meeting the person that you and I created soon … but it scares me, too, that she is mine."

"I'm confident that you'll be the best mother to our child. I'm not so sure about my own abilities, but I care so much about you and our daughter that I'll figure things out."

Isobel became reserved, gripping her wrists. "And what if I get bad again?"

It'd been so long since she had. In my mind, it was something of the past. Now, it was obvious that it wasn't for Isobel.

"What if I'm not fit to be a mother? I've barely been able to take care of myself – how will I take care of another person? And what if I pass this stupid head onto our child?"

Weaving my fingers between her hands, I broke into her reservation. After everything we'd endured and experienced together, the battles we'd fought within ourselves and each other, with our love expanding into a family, there was no way I could let us revert to yesterday's afflictions.

With my free hand, I soothed my palm over her cheek. "This head, with all its darkness, is still the brightest, most beautiful mind I've ever known."

Her eyes smiled in a way that could make everything else in the world invisible.

"I'm going to be there every step of the way," I continued. "If anything happens, I'll be there to take care of you and our child. We're a team and we're always going to be one."

Isobel squeezed my hand. "I trust you, Cody."

"Trust us, babe. We're strong. Together we can do anything. We can beat anything. We can have the happiness we deserve."

I rode through this moment presenting an assured picture of us. But all my affirmations couldn't remove the nagging fear I had inside. Isobel had showed me hers, and it had reignited mine. After all of our growth, we could still just be two fragile little children pretending to be adults.

Maybe this was how we were always going to be. Maybe all I could hope for was that our daughter would grow up to be the human being we had both wanted to be. With any turn of luck, she'd just inherit the good parts of us. She wouldn't know what it was like to worry about losing someone they love, to live with the fear of being alone.

It had to be that way. We had to make it so.

I gazed at Isobel, her eyes following the flight of birds from the water into the sky.

I had to make sure she was always here …

I had to believe that there were two truly secure people inside of us, who would emerge and blossom once we were responsible for another life.

"Come on." I stood and offered my hand. "Let's keep moving."

We continued along the trail, deeper into the heart of the sanctuary.

"Wait here," I said.

I jogged to the edge of the shrubbery, knelt and turned on my camera.

"What are you doing, Cody?" Isobel raised her arms.

"Smile."

"My back is sore, I feel like a slob, my hair is messed up and I have barely any makeup on."

"And that's why I want a photo of you."

"Do I look like I'm ready for a photo?"

"Absolutely not. But that's why it's perfect. You're just you. Natural. Raw. In a place where we came to know each other for the first time. Now we're here and our daughter is growing inside you. There's never been a moment more perfect for a photo. You've never been so beautiful."

She blushed and went quiet, her cheeks dimpled in a shy smile.

With the trees in the background, through them the water of the pond that had watched us grow, I focused on Isobel, cradling her tummy, our baby girl, in her hands.

I snapped her fervently, as if this were a shoot. I looked over the photos for a second and then returned my sight to the viewfinder. When I focused again, the image I saw shot fireworks of joy off inside me. Standing on the path, one hand still cupped under her belly, Isobel stood holding her middle finger up to me, like she'd always do when we shot.

I broke into laughter, dropping to my butt on the grass, and every time I looked back to her, still with the bird cocked, I was set off again.

Wiping a tear from my eye as I calmed, I saw her again, white sunlight hitting the side of her face.

The day had become so bright.

In that moment, I believed with conviction that we could do this. That we could be those happy, secure parents for our daughter.

Walking toward her felt like a movie. Like this was the moment we'd been working to get to, something solved within it.

I ran my hands along her cheek where the sunlight held. "There doesn't seem like there are any words that could really do justice to how strongly I feel for you right now, so I guess I love you with every part of me will have to do."

That kiss, with our baby sandwiched between us, was one I sealed in a special place in my heart. Nothing had ever felt so real. I decided that if any doubt ever crept into my consciousness, I would access the memory of this kiss and dispel it immediately.

"We're going to be alright, aren't we?" The hope in Isobel's eyes was contagious.

"We are, baby."

Through the look we shared, we told each other so much. *I'm scared. I know nothing. But I'm here, and I always will be.*

"Just one more photo, okay?" I said, and then jogged back to my camera.

I set the timer and ran back to Isobel.

The beeps counted down and then the camera clicked.

When I looked at the screen, I saw a family photo that made me tingle with excitement. One that I knew had to always be on show. I would print one to put up in the kitchen, where we'd see it every day, and a tiny one for Isobel to keep in her locket, where it would always be close to her heart.

I couldn't wait to see our daughter, to hold her, talk to her, watch her grow. Be a family.

"So, I've been thinking," Isobel said as we continued. "And I might have something …"

"You're talking names again, aren't you?"

We'd been through thousands – what seemed like every name in at least three different languages. Our maybe list might have been a dozen at best, but none stood out.

"I am, and I think I have the one."

"If you say Michaela again, I'll tear my hair out."

Isobel giggled. "No not Michaela. This one's perfect for us … H, O, L, I." She beamed. "Holi. That's where we made her."

The little girl in my imagination beamed, too. "It's perfect."

Chapter 28

(NOW)

I'm parked in the social area of the home, the same as yesterday and the day before, watching the patches of sunlight on the grass in the courtyard change as clouds move across the sky. The light's always changing. Everything moves and moves on. Nothing stays lit forever.

We could all do with a few days off.

That's what Isobel said, which means that Jake convinced her that it's better to put me in the home for a few days so they can have the house to themselves.

It's fair enough. Maybe I'd do the same thing in his position.

I'm not in his position, though. I'm in mine. And I'm being left behind. The better part of me knows I should let them be happy. Give her no stress, no obligation. But the selfish side of me can't let Isobel go completely. It took me so long to realize that I still love her, and now all I want is to capture something with her before it's too late.

What can I give her, though? Not what he can … but I can't believe anyone else will ever love her like I did … do.

He's there, though. With Isobel. I'm here.

Maybe the strongest love isn't always the one that makes us happiest. Love matters too much to never hurt. Ours hurt so much that dying inside was easier than living through the pain.

My eyes wander from the courtyard. Viktor is slouched on an armchair beside me, flicking through channels on the television.

"You ever had an enemy, Vik?"

"Nothing good on television," he grumbles to himself.

"Vik?"

He grunts and sits up. "What?"

"I asked if you'd ever had an enemy."

This makes him chortle. He switches off the television. "Oh, little Cody. I from Russia. Everybody have enemy."

"What did you do when your enemy got in your way?"

"I stay away from enemy as much as I can. Who wants to be around someone they don't like?"

"What if your enemy was with someone you wanted to be around?"

He raises his brow and strokes his gray stubble. "Well, that is harder. I guess you have to make enemy go away."

"And how would you do that?"

Viktor ponders. "Everybody have a weakness, Cody. If you want someone gone you need to know this and use it."

Store fronts roll by as we crawl through traffic. Signs advertising things people think they need, things to be gained for a price.

What's to be gained for me when I get home? A pleasant Sunday night being the third wheel. I'm sure Jake will be thrilled to see me roll back in after three days of having Isobel to himself. How will she feel?

"I'm hungry," I say.

Joe peers back at me in the rear-view mirror, his forehead crinkled. "You ate like an hour ago. Used to be a pain to get you to eat. Now you're like a fifteen-year-old boy."

"Isn't that a good thing?"

He grumbles. "Do you really need to? Traffic's terrible."

"That's why I need something to eat. It's taking forever to get home."

"You could've told me before we left the home."

"Who's got a stick up your butt?"

Joe sighs deeply. "Sorry … It's work. Still won't give me the day off on Thursday. I'm at a loss. Thinking I might just pack it in and quit."

My eyes leave the street. I'm nowhere except the van. "Don't do that."

"Don't what?"

"Don't quit."

"Why not? They deserve it. I've been good to them."

"Yeah, but …"

Joe swerves into a park. "What are you saying, Codes? That you'd miss me?"

When I look up, he's turned his head to me, a cheeky smile painted across his face.

"Nah … Never," I say. "Just like having you around. I don't feel as short as I normally do."

"We'll just see what happens, ay … What do you want to eat?"

"I dunno. Just snacks."

Joe climbs out of the van and waddles into a 7-Eleven.

It's quiet in here. Car horns, conversations, wind: it's all muffled. Just me. Is there a van I can drive myself? One I can sit in and not feel like this? Are there jokes I can tell myself and laugh at? Is there a part of me I can tease, who'll return fire with a better jibe?

The van door slides open and the noise outside floods in.

Joe leans in. "Got you some chips."

He holds up a bag of Lays.

"And," he reaches into the plastic bag, grinning, "some of these babies."

Now he holds up a jumbo bag of Reese's Peanut Butter Cups.

"You're a genius."

"I know, right."

He opens the bag and stuffs one in my mouth, before munching down one himself.

"Are you really going to quit?" I ask between mouthfuls of chewy peanut butter.

He shrugs and swallows. "Maybe. Or just not come in. That'll probably get me night shift for the rest of my life, or fired. Think I rub some people there up the wrong way."

"How could *you* bother anyone?"

"Maybe I will just quit." He takes out another cup and holds it up to me, before tossing it into his own gob. "Might become homeless, but at least I won't have to put up with your sarcasm."

We share a wry smile.

Joe leans in the van doorway, gazing out to the street moving by. We pass minutes in silence, munching on salt and vinegar potato chips and Reese's.

"I'm full now," I say.

Joe places two more cups on my tray, and winks. "For later."

When we get home, Isobel and Jake are still out.

"They won't be too long, mate," Joe says, looking at his phone. "Have just been shopping."

Shopping?

His idea, I'm sure.

Isobel and I did it. He can't just let me have one thing. He needs to take over that, too.

What's he got? What's she got?

Have they found their way into the change room together? Him, standing there, Isobel stripped down to her panties to try on a new skirt and top. Him, standing there, able to direct his hand onto her body. Wherever he wants to. On her smooth skin. His head above hers. Able to lower his lips onto hers. Breathe hot breath onto her neck. Hold her hands. Be on the same level as her. Able to look her in her eyes. Make her feel wanted. Good enough.

Leave it!

I steer back into my spot beside the sofa.

Don't let him sully those moments you had.

Joe sits on the couch and plays on his phone.

I stew.

Bubble.

Want to boil.

"I just need to make a call, mate," he says. "Beep if you need me."

He makes his call.

I wait.

Frustrated. Stuck wondering about the day Isobel and Jake had.

I wait.

My hand jerks and knocks the camera, my phone and the peanut butter cups. I muster the effort to get my hand to my mouth.

I chew – sweet, salty, sweet. Chew more. Swallow. Savor the lingering taste. And wait.

For what …?

The other cup finds its way into my hand.

Then Viktor comes into my mind. Enemies … What do you do to those who stand in your way?

Joe glances to me as I drive out of my spot. I go into the kitchen and over to the pantry. I work the door open with my chair.

On the second shelf at my eye level there's a bunch of snack boxes. Mostly the things I used to eat, which are unopened, a few things Isobel will occasionally munch on, and some new ones – gluten-free this, paleo that – Jake's.

I scan through them, looking for the right one. There's a Tupperware container on the left side. The lid is ajar. The protein balls he eats all day.

The Reese's Peanut Butter Cup rolls around my tray, becoming a ball beneath my palm.

I drive right into the pantry until the container is in reach. The new protein ball drops in with the rest. I reach in and move it around until its gathered enough coconut to be at least a little disguised.

Back out in the living room Joe is still on the phone, arguing with someone from the home. He hangs up and releases a frustrated grunt.

"Still no luck?"

He shakes his head.

I reverse into my spot, anxiously waiting for Isobel and Jake to return.

Joe remains on the couch, dejected.

"Least you'll get to spend another day with me," I say.

He feigns a laugh, his head low.

The awkwardness is broken by a key in the front door.

Jake bustles in first, leading Isobel by the hand. They're laughing, beaming. She's in the middle of something special with him. Not just this moment, either.

"Hey!"

"Hey!"

"How ya going?"

A muffled greeting.

Isobel bounces into the bedroom. Jake thanks Joe.

"See ya, Codes."

A muffled goodbye.

What am I doing? This is ridiculous.

Isobel comes out of the bedroom. She looks weightless, so free. It's as though she's aging in reverse, so young and unburdened. He's emancipated her from all the heartache we found. It's gone. In their holidays, their laughs, their new love. It's all gone.

Jake comes to her and takes her in his arms again.

Muffled hopes.

He smirks over Isobel's shoulder at me, his eyes taunting me. *She's loving me, now. She's close to me, now. You're gone.*

Fuck him.

"What are we doing for dinner?" Jake asks Isobel as they release.

She shrugs. "Hadn't thought about it."

He goes into the pantry.

A rush of adrenalin shoots through me as he comes out, shoving a protein ball into his mouth …

Chew, chew … Nothing.

He eats another.

Nothing.

"Do you feel like anything in particular?" Isobel asks me.

I shake my head. "Nothing, really."

Time recedes into a stream of forgettable observations.

Isobel tidying.

Jake reading.

The two of them embracing.

Isobel on the phone.

Jake watching television.

Isobel pouring drinks.

Them, cuddled-up watching television.

A knock at the door.

Isobel collecting the takeaway.

Mouth open. Food in.

Isobel feeding herself.

This is life, remember?

Get used to it, again.

Mouth open. Food in.

Dinner over.

Back to the television.

Back to my spot beside the sofa.

This is life. Movement everywhere, but nothing moving to any effect. Me, observing it all, but seeing nothing. Figures in the distance. Crawling … wheeling back into the abyss I tried to get out of. No sounds to get me from there. No bathroom fan.

Get used to it. This is all I can have.

What was I ever fighting for? I wasn't even in the ring with anyone. Just swinging into thin air. For what? For a part of the past I'll never be able to live again. For someone I pushed away because I was too afraid of more pain? And it gets me here. Still observing. Still a spectator …

"Oh my god!" Isobel screams and leaps from the couch.

Jake stumbles back into the living room, clutching his throat. He drops half a protein ball. My concoction plops onto the floorboards.

His hands clasp at his throat as he tries to wheeze in air. His face becomes florid, deepening red by the second as he chokes.

Chokes.

Choking.

He stumbles forward, struggling to stand, leaning on the couch for support. He slaps his pockets searchingly. For just a moment his eyes find me. Me, no longer observing, not just a spectator, a player in this moment. Now I'm the one who's smirking … his eyes flare, and he points to me.

Isobel gets his attention. "Jake! What do I do?"

He tries to speak, but nothing comes.

He's helpless.

Isobel is panicking, shaky and white as a ghost. Jake reaches for her, his face like beetroot. He points to his pocket and then drops to his knees.

Isobel reaches in and withdraws his EpiPen. Jake moves her hand to his thigh, trembling.

Isobel pushes the injector into his thigh.

Seconds of silence … and then a loud gasp comes.

Choking, gasping, sucking in air desperately, but more easily with each gasp. Jake's face becomes less florid and begins to return to normal.

Isobel holds him.

It takes several long minutes for him to recover completely. My disappointment grows as he gains strength. Gaining control.

Eventually he stands up and then takes a seat on the couch.

Isobel sits beside him. "What the hell happened?"

Jake gathers his thoughts, his eyes pinned to the floorboards, and then stares across at me. He stands and goes over to where the half-eaten Reese's Peanut Butter protein ball landed. Kneeling, he examines it without touching it.

"I think you should ask your husband." He glances to Isobel and then focuses on me. "He might be able to tell you."

"What do you mean?"

"Well, somehow a peanut butter cup found its way into my protein balls. You used to love these, didn't you Cody?"

Isobel gets up and goes over to the dirty weapon. "Cody?" The look she throws me is heartbreaking, pleading for it not to be true. "You didn't do this, did you?"

For everything I had, everything I lost, everything that could be said, done, faked, hidden, and everything in between, I never could lie to Isobel. Looking at her beautiful eyes of glass that look ready to shatter, I still can't.

All I do is gulp, no reply.

She knows me well enough to know.

"Oh, Cody. Why?"

My jaw clenches. "Because I …" Now I'm the one who's choking. "Because I want you, I want us, and I can't have you if he's here."

The world's frozen for a moment.

In the middle of it all, Isobel and I are together sharing pain.

"What are we going to do?" Jake's voice is croaky. "Call the police and have him arrested?"

Isobel turns her head to him. "No, Jake, don't be ridiculous."

Now her eyes fall to the floor.

She takes her time, silence filling the house to the point where it's hard to breathe.

"I had hoped that I wasn't right … We all can't live here." Her stare meets mine. "I wanted to make this work, really. But it's clear that it can't … I think it's best if you move to the home permanently, Cody."

Chapter 29

(NOW)

Joe fills the armchair. "You look about as happy as me."

Mulling repeatedly about my choices, I've barely moved since the home became my home. With one thought, I question how I could do something so egregious, and in the next I try to conjure another reality.

"Yeah," I grunt. "I lost."

"I'm sorry, fella. It makes me sad."

"What's sad is that I couldn't think of a better way to win my wife back than murdering her boyfriend."

Joe chuckles, and then sighs. "I didn't think much of him – bit boring for Isobel – but probably doesn't deserve to die."

I laugh. "Maybe not."

"Least he's not going to press charges," Joe says. "You're too pretty for jail."

"Don't think they have a prison gang for cripples, either."

For a fleeting moment, he brings me out of desolation. But our jokes subside and the feeling of defeat returns. Murmurs from the television fill the void in our conversation.

Joe slouches lower and dejectedly flicks through something on his phone.

"And what's got you so down?" I ask.

"I lost too … It's Rebecca's anniversary and here I am working."

"Why don't we just leave for the day?"

Joe claps his hands together. "I wish it were that easy. We're short staffed. They won't let us leave. I need to be here."

We're both miserable. Stuck here when we want to be anywhere else. So, we sit and mope, two sad sacks lamenting what they miss. Rebecca's dead. Joe can do nothing about that. Partly, I envy his ease of choices. Mostly, though, I have sympathy for my friend. He has no choice.

Isobel's alive. With Jake. There's nothing I can do about that. What choice do I have?

There's musk in the air. Old people. Death. Nothingness.

Sunlight moves about the courtyard as clouds drift across the sky. The light is always moving. Always changing. The light, *outside.*

Viktor and Sophie stroll by ... two old people, staring death and nothingness right in the face. Sophie's hand slides into Viktor's. His eyes move from the world over the fence to her. Two old fools, so close to the end, yet still clinging to the hope of something new.

As long as you're alive there's hope.

Joe's words. Joe's philosophy. Joe's demeanor ...

Yet, the same man, whose optimism rings loudly in my ear, is as dejected as me.

We all lose, eventually.

The ridiculousness of life floods over me. How I cared about so much, how I came to care about nothing, how I've come out of that abyss to care about something. How it all means nothing. I'll be gone and there'll be nothing but a few old pictures to let the world know I was ever here. Who'll look at them?

My breath gets shorter and then it comes. My head shakes. I start coughing.

Gulping, gulping. Wheezing. Thin air.

"Cody?" Joe jumps up and rushes me to the exit.

Philomena comes out of her office. "What's going on?"

"Cody's having an attack."

"It's okay," I wheeze. "I'll be fine."

"Is it urgent?" she asks. "Should we call an ambulance?"

"No time. He's wheezing. If I don't take him to the hospital now, we risk him drowning in his own lungs!"

"Okay. Go! Quickly."

Joe rushes me outside.

A chilly gust of wind slaps me right in the face.

My breathing calms. Fresh air does a world of good.

"You can relax," I say. "I'm fine."

"We've gotta get you checked out, mate." Joe opens the van door and lowers the hydraulics. "You know the deal. Attacks need to be monitored."

"I'm sure the doctors have more important things to monitor than a cripple impersonating an attack."

He stops and stares at me curiously. "What are you talking about?"

I feel a stupid grin forming on my face. "Perhaps it's not too late for my acting career. Had you all fooled."

"You cheeky bugger."

"You don't want to be in there," I point my head, "and neither do I. You can have your day as you'd like. Just park me somewhere nice."

Joe beams at me. "You're a lifesaver, mate."

I drive onto the lift. Joe buckles me into place and loads me into the van.

"Take your time," I say. "I feel like this attack could last a while …"

He slaps the top of my hand and then closes the door.

"So what do you usually do on these days?" I ask as we drive.

Jo glances to me in the rear-view mirror. "Lots of little things, stuff we'd do together."

"As long as you keep your hands to yourself."

"Don't flatter yourself, mate. Not my type."

The first stop we make is a pancake parlor uptown. It's got the feel of a fifties diner: booth seats along the walls, napkin dispensers on every table, red and white pinstriped uniforms.

"We'd always sit in that booth," Joe says, pointing to the corner. "Every Saturday morning."

He stops at a free-standing table and pulls out a chair to make room for me.

"If that's where you normally sit then go sit there, I'll be fine here."

"Are you sure, mate?"

I nod and he waddles off to his booth and slides in.

For just an instant I stare out the window and see a short, Australian-Aboriginal man with an Asian-American woman, moseying down the street about to enter their favorite weekend breakfast spot.

"It's too weird." Joe startles me, now standing beside my table. "If I look over and see your fat head, I'll feel like I'm being stalked."

He takes hold of my chair and drives me over to the booth. Before I can ask how, he is unbuckling me, lifting me and then tossing me onto the leather seats.

"How am I meant to sit here?" I ask, as he jams me into the corner and fixes me in place. "What are you missing, seriously?"

"You'll be fine there, Codes," he says as he steers my chair out of sight. "Use your imagination."

Out the corner of my eye I can see myself in reflection: a doll that's been stuffed into the seat. "You're ridiculous, you know that, right?"

"Life's ridiculous." Joe slides in opposite me. "For one, you're meant to be at the hospital."

"And you're meant to be at the home."

"Guess we're both stuffed then, ay." Joe opens up a menu in front of me, but not for himself.

"Let me guess," I say. "You get the same thing every time you come here. How romantic."

"Waitress should know my order by now. And watch the sarcasm, fella. You're not spoiling my day."

"You wouldn't have a day if it wasn't for me and my sublime acting."

He huffs and puffs for a moment, and then finds himself with a smirk. "Settle down – you're not winning any awards. What are you getting?"

"Probably lemon and sugar crepes."

"Good choice. Bit of sweet and sour."

"Yeah. Something like that. It's what I'd always order when I went out for crepes with Isobel."

"Well, we're not so unalike then. I'm getting the strawberry and ice-cream stack. Same thing Rebecca and me would get and share – too big for one person." He pauses. "Now I just let half of it sit there and go to waste. Such a waste …"

People pass by the window, flashes of pastel color, vibrant color, hats, hair and shoes. Every one of them with a face I'll never remember, but one I could attach to at any moment and wonder where they are going. Strange to be so close to someone – only a matter of feet – but living completely different lives.

This table is a marsh of regrets. It's depressing. The two of us: sad old losers who have lost the one thing that made them whole. Trying to clutch at humor to forget that.

"You know what, I'm going to get banana and Nutella instead," I say, my eyes still attached to the people outside. "About time for different choices."

It's silent for a moment, then I hear Joe slide the menu across the table. I look over to see him running through the selection of pancakes with intense concentration. I've never seen someone so serious about food.

Maybe this isn't about which topping.

A waitress comes to take our orders.

"Nutella and banana, please," I say.

Joe slaps the menu closed. "And I'll have the bloody lemon and sugar!" An insane laugh leaps from his lips. "Yep. I'll have the lemon and sugar."

The waitress eyes Joe quizzically, and then collects our menus and leaves.

"We're fucking sad, aren't we?" I say.

Joe grips his hands and nods fervently. "Yep, absolutely pathetic."

"You ever wonder how you wound up here?"

"That's the million-dollar question." He leaves his stare somewhere between Australia and the table of a Chicago pancake parlor. "Guess you get hurt. No matter how good something is, you'll get hurt. Everything in life ends with heartbreak. Even a friendship or a relationship that works still ends in heartbreak. One of you has to leave first, right? Everything has a hello, and a goodbye."

"And is where you ended up somewhere after that goodbye?"

"I think it's hard to really pay much attention to anything after some goodbyes."

Our pancakes come. Joe alternates between eating his and feeding me.

"These are pretty good," he says. "Been a long time since I've had anything but the strawberry stack."

"Been a long time since I've had pancakes," I reply. "But why do I get the feeling we're not talking about pancakes?"

"Of course we're talking about pancakes, fella. We're sitting here whining about them. Because pancakes are just shit if you don't have a beautiful woman to share them with. Sweet breakfasts are meant for sweethearts."

"Yeah, I guess they are." I accept another fork of pancake and chow it down.

We finish with coffee, no straw in sight.

At his apartment in Roscoe Village, which he claims is not usually like this, Joe takes me through photo albums of him and Rebecca. The place is covered with photos of them.

"You are a terrible photographer," I tell him.

"It's what's in the photo that matters, mate. Not the clown behind the lens."

"She was beautiful," I say, looking upon the sweet Asian-American woman with olive skin and happy eyes. "Far too good for you."

"Yep. Too right. Way too good for a fella like me. Always knew that. But I just figured that maybe I could fill her heart with my character, not my boyish good looks, or lack thereof."

"That's what it's always about isn't it?"

"Yeah, it is." Joe closes the photo album. "You can lust after any woman for a while, but you need to love a woman to lust after her forever. To have that insatiable appetite for her."

"Always thought I could have that for Isobel. Be that man."

I left traces of myself with every woman I was with before Isobel, but my entire heart got left with her. She has it. She'll always have it.

"Do you believe in soul mates, Joe?"

"Dunno. Don't think it really matters to be honest. Maybe it just matters that you meet someone who you believe could be yours. To have something that profound."

"Do you think you could ever find something with someone else like you had with Rebecca?"

"No," he answers immediately. "Maybe something's possible, but I'll never love anyone like I loved Rebecca. Could you?"

"Who's going to love me?"

"No one, but that's not the point. You don't choose who you love, and sometimes you don't get it returned."

"Yeah … you don't choose, do you …?"

My eyes wander around his apartment walls, the scrapbook of their life together. My mind turns to the townhouse, the one photo that clings to the wall with a slipping grip of the life Isobel and I had together.

"Do you think Isobel feels for him what she felt for me?"

As I ask it, I beg another question in mind – *what did she feel for me?*

"I don't know, mate, but I guess if you believe like I do that one person will always fill more of your heart than anyone else, there's a chance that you filled enough of Isobel's … there's a chance she'll remember that."

"I tried to fight for her, and I lost. What now?"

Joe closes the photo album. "You fought, mate, but what fight did you fight?"

In front of me I see Jake. Holding Isobel, kissing Isobel, loving Isobel. Jake. I fought Jake. He slips away, and all that remains is Isobel.

These are streets I haven't ventured along in what seems a lifetime. It was another lifetime.

Up North Ashland Avenue, and then right at West Irving Park Road.

It hadn't yet occurred to me where we might eventually go today.

The trees line the side of the road as I remember. The city falls behind us. I see it directly if I look back, like I did in a side mirror in that other life.

It's sunny today. Blue skies above.

It rained that day. Bruised black skies.

As Joe parks, the sound of the handbrake is déjà vu.

My heart becomes curious to be hurt.

He turns to me. "Well, this is the last stop. Rebecca's last stop."

Graceland Cemetery is a paradox. A beautiful place of death. Peace in every heartache. Fondness in regret.

Looking out the front window I look through the lines of trees. "Where is she buried?"

"About two blocks in." Joe's eyes are now cast toward the forest of tombstones. "She faces south, and a little east … You might find it a bit freaky, but I chose the nicest place where she'd be facing our apartment window. So I know when I stare out of it, we'll be looking at each other. Silly, I know, but it makes me smile sometimes when I do."

"Do you talk to her much?"

He takes a long time to answer.

"Still say goodnight and tell her I love her every night from that window."

I let my head hang and inspect the putrid dullness of the van's floor. "You go in," I say, the floor disappearing below me. "I might just stay here. Give you some time."

"Thanks, mate."

Joe leaves the van.

There's no right place to look. Eyes open and I'm here, at the edge of the cemetery, sheltered by green leaves that turn yellow and orange before they fall. It's in there … I've never been back, but I know I'm just a periscope away from it. Eyes closed, and I see the path that leads there. A winding track of years, a palace of prosperity burned down in a matter of months to nothing but crumbled vestiges in memory.

Inhale and try to suck in something sweet from the air.

Exhale and try to release something abrasive from inside.

Get stuck. Stuck between breaths.

I raise my head and look out of the van's windshield, through the forest, through a tunnel, to the exact place. There's Joe stooped over in front of a gravestone. He kneels and places the bouquet of flowers. The corner of his mouth is moving. I can only imagine what he is saying …

I find myself speaking words of my own.

"What we could have been.

"What we could have been, if only …

"What our life could have been.

"Could have been.

"Could have been.

"Could have …

"Could be."

I can't be here anymore. Not in this moment. Not in this mind.

With a tremulous finger, I push the button to rotate my chair. I need to get out of here. The motor of my chair whirs as I push the joystick forward as far as it will go and hold it there. The straps that hold me in place stretch, but don't budge.

"Let me go!" I cry, as though the nylon, plastic and metal is conscious.

The straps don't listen

They can't hear me.

It's not them I'm talking to.

There's an ache behind my retinas, a stinging on their surface. My lap is gathering moisture – it looks like I've pissed my pants. My body shakes and quivers with each blunt wound of a memory.

The hospital floor. The corridor. The smell of sterility. The passing of the trolleys and white coats and patients. The look of the doctor. The words that ripped shreds from my soul.

Fuck that day! Fuck that moment!

The door opens, and shocks me back into reality like a defibrillator.

All that remains in front of my eyes is Isobel. She is everything that needs to matter. What we had matters. What we tried to do. The love that brought us together and the love that tore us apart. The same love.

The pain matters. We can still survive it.

The regret I've created can't matter. Jake can't matter. He is nothing to me.

I've been fighting the wrong fight.

What we can *have* matters.

Isobel, and me.

Us.

Chapter 30

(THEN)

Feeling the SoCal sunshine, I wondered how I could ever live anywhere else, how those northern winters were bearable, let alone enjoyable. The warmth and bright light of day, the pastels of dusk, were so connected to happy memories. Why leave?

But then I looked across to Isobel, sitting beside me on the back deck, twenty-two weeks pregnant, and remembered that it was never where we were that mattered. It was who we were together that made memories in the heat, in the cold, anywhere.

Larry and Janine were skiing in Vancouver for the week, and had urged us to get away.

This was our last trip before we were to meet Holi. Before I could put my finger in her tiny palm and feel her grip. Before I could admire Isobel holding her, the two loves of my life.

The sunset was a rich aura of red, orange and pink.

"I see Larry hasn't fixed the handrail yet." Isobel nodded toward the loose, rotted wooden handrail at the back step, grinning. "It's never getting done, is it?"

I took a pull of my cider. "Actually, Janine texted and asked me to do it. Tired of nagging the old guy. Suppose it's the least I can do while we're here."

"Can't imagine you using tools."

"I'll have you know I'm quite the handyman."

"I've got more confidence with a leaky pipe than you."

"Whatever, I was an orphan, you were a private-school girl."

"All you did was pick tomatoes and chase girls."

"Doesn't sound too bad now I come to think of it. Why did I even run away?"

"Who knows, Cody? You could've really made it had you stayed."

"I know, and here I am, talking about fixing a handrail."

Isobel relaxed back in her chair. "No way it's getting fixed."

"Nope."

We both chuckled.

"This is perfect." Isobel sipped on her mocktail. "Sunshine, my baby and my overgrown baby."

"The best thing is that in a few months we're going to find a new level of perfect."

"It's crazy to think that things could be even better."

I held up my glass. "It's scary, too."

"It is, but I'm more excited than scared now." Isobel clinked hers on mine.

"So you're feeling good?"

She nodded. "I'm great."

"Not letting anything creep in?"

"Nope."

"Are you sure?"

Isobel laid down her drink and then picked up the iPod. She settled on a song, docked the iPod and then leaned back.

Don Henley's smooth voice came over the sweet acoustic guitar. Isobel cocked her head back, opened her mouth and belted out the chorus of "Take It Easy".

"Yeah, okay, you're fine."

We sipped on drinks until the sky became dark, and then we held each other under the glow of the stars. Pointing to the constellations, the moon and what we thought might be planets, we showed our daughter, who couldn't yet see them, the wonders of the universe we see from earth.

It was dawn when I awoke alone. I trudged into the living room, a hint of a headache and a touch of cottonmouth for the five or so ciders I'd had. Long gone were my party days of countless drinks.

Isobel was at the kitchen sink filling a drink bottle. She was wearing tiny little running shorts, a tank top and Nikes. Her legs looked a mile high.

"Morning," she chimed, turning to me. "I didn't wake you, did I?"

I rubbed my eyes. "No, you're fine. What are you doing?"

"Just going for a quick walk."

"Hold on, I'm coming." I ran back into the room.

"I'll meet you on the beach," she called on her way out. "They could build Rome again in the time you take dawdling."

I splashed water on my face in the bathroom, ruffled my hair and threw on some shorts and a tee.

When I came back into the living room I could see Isobel through the kitchen window, surveying the shoreline. I smiled and bent down to do up my shoelaces.

Two ticks of the clock.

And then a scream sounded.

I shot up like a prairie dog. Isobel wasn't in the window anymore.

Rushing out of the house, I stopped on the back deck. The handrail had given way.

Isobel lay at the bottom of the steps on her side.

My heart froze. Life stood still.

"Isobel!"

I was at her side. She was breathing frantically and grimacing.

I pulled her to her feet.

"Cody …"

She bent over, holding her stomach.

"Are you okay?"

"Cody."

I wanted to vomit. Scared to breathe, scared to talk, scared to move … No idea what to do.

"Hon, we're going to the hospital."

I took her by the hand and went to walk, but Isobel didn't move.

"Cody …"

The look in her eyes made me wish the world would just die. Everything else just fucking die.

I followed her eyes. A line of blood ran down her leg like an elongated teardrop. At her feet was a small pool of blood.

"It hurts."

My mouth quivered but no words came.

The sweat between our palms made it hard to hold on.

The blood ran down my arms and into my palms as I carried Isobel from the backyard and into the car. Cherry-stained hands slipped on the wheel as I drove to the hospital. I wiped my left, my right, my left, my right, but it just wouldn't disappear, no matter how many times I wiped them on my shorts. That blood was tattooed.

The world was spinning. Nothing seemed real. It was a nightmare.

Wake! I blinked. Blinked over and over, my eyes burning. Peeled awake. Nowhere close to asleep. Everything real.

We rushed through emergency and Isobel was taken into a room. She disappeared through those doors … I stood there, alone.

In the waiting room, I paced back and forth. My emotions spewed out and I kicked the shit out of a vending machine.

Maybe the receptionists, the doctors and nurses, the security, maybe they all knew why I was so angry. What those tears meant.

It had never stung so much to cry before those tormenting minutes I spent sobbing and beating my head.

A doctor in a surgical gown appeared. He slid off his gloves and pulled down his duckbill mask as he approached. When he stopped in front of me with a face painted in sorrow, I knew what he was about to say.

I'd heard the words so many times in life, but when the doctor looked me in the eyes and said, "I'm sorry …" I found out what sorry truly meant.

The light was soft. Machines with black screens and green-lit numbers beeped intermittently.

I stood at the doorway and stared at Isobel lying in the bed. She rolled her head over.

We stayed like this for some time, not a word being said. The talk through our eyes was mute. A million thoughts spun around my head, and I knew nothing of what went through hers.

Eventually I went and sat by her bedside.

When I gripped her hand, there was something missing.

With all the ebbs and flows of our life together, the fear, insecurity of losing, I never thought loss could feel like this … Despite it all, I'd never felt so far away from her.

From myself.

From us.

The day our baby died was when we started to too.

Chapter 31

(NOW)

A week's passed since the home became my home.

Maybe I can breathe more freely now, maybe I can cry with conviction, but maybe the means that brought me to this confusing place was all just a mix-up in my head. Perhaps I'll look back on this time, when my marriage was really ending, and see that I was just blind to what was happening. There were remnants in certain moments, which I tried to grab at, but they were just leftovers – nothing new to be found or built upon.

Isobel hasn't called; nor have I called her.

Had I known what I came to know in the van last week, maybe I could've salvaged something with her instead of concentrating on him. I have the knowledge, but where are my means now? Stuck here in a place where people come to die.

The fund that pays for me to be here will run out eventually. If I make it that long. If I do, I guess I'll get to be that crippled bum on the corner, begging for anything. What a turn it would be, back on the streets again. I'm not sure if people will toss as many coins in my hat these days. My photos are non-existent, let alone good.

It was hard to imagine having nothing when it felt like I had everything. And when I had nothing, it was just as hard to imagine having everything. Now I sit in purgatory, somewhere between the two. With something – a desire, an urge – but not what I ultimately desire.

Staring out of my bedroom window into the courtyard, I can imagine anything. Nothing, everything, anything in between. With each passing minute, the sun is fading, the day slipping away. Another one has passed with no movement.

I unlock my phone and open Messages. There's a long line of unsent drafts. They take me several minutes to write: those one-hundred-and-forty-character sentiments are a novel to me. They all say the same thing in different ways. They're all addressed to Isobel. They remain unsent.

A knock sounds at the door. In the faint reflection of the window I see Joe enter and then sit on my bed.

"Thanks for the other day, mate," he says.

"Not a problem."

"You were out of sorts when I came back to the van."

"Just cemeteries …"

"Who's there?"

I gulp, but don't respond.

A blast of Californian sunshine pervades my mind. The sunshine that felt so attached to beautiful memories … the sunshine that is forever entrenched into the most painful memory. I never saw Isobel fall through the handrail that Larry was meant to fix. That I was meant to fix.

I've pictured it a million times, though. Isobel, the woman I've loved since I was a boy, shining brighter than that sunshine, falling literally and in every sense: from a woman with everything in front of her, to a grieving mother, a battered soul with everything behind her.

But that's not her … that became me.

"The ashes of my baby girl," I say. "Isobel was twenty-two weeks pregnant when it happened."

It hurts with relief to say it aloud.

"I'm sorry to hear that," Joe says. "Truly."

"You've always wondered why we fell apart … that's what started it. Losing Holi."

It's been an age since I've spoken my baby's name. It whispers in the back of my thoughts every day, but I try not to listen, try to dull the whisper. I can't bear the excruciating regret that comes with it.

The dusk outside feels heavy. I feel heavy, my head weighted.

In this moment there's nothing dull about my baby's memory. It hurts and I'm glad it does. Because it should. Because I feel human.

I feel like a father.

"I can't imagine it." Joe shuffles from the end of the bed and slides next to me. "Something I always wanted, kids. Just never got the chance."

A heavy sigh exits my lungs. "Neither did I."

"You know if you ever want to go there to visit your little girl, I'll take you. Anytime, mate." He pats my hand. "It's the least I can do after the other day."

"Thanks."

The bell for lunch begins to ring.

"Slops about to be served," Joe says.

"I'm not hungry."

"Nor am I."

So we stay in my room and talk about the remnants of a summertime that are stuck in a rear-view mirror.

Dinner could've gone better. Well, the actual dinner went perfectly fine, but the result could've been better.

Perhaps I was just delirious after skipping lunch. Or maybe I just needed some fun after the tests this afternoon. It doesn't matter now. I'm here, with these thoughts, regardless of what led me here.

It all started with Maryann Bellow being down. Her son's ex-wife is taking the kid to Cleveland. No more visits from little George. This prompted Carl Ainsworth to tell everybody about how he used to always start food fights at school, and then when he was in the military.

"Nothing brings joy to any situation better than spaghetti flying through the air and landing on someone's face," he said, and chuckled.

Joe was feeding me and was ready with another forkful of fried rice.

"Can I try and do it myself?" I asked.

"Of course."

He placed the fork in my left hand, holding the plate of rice and teriyaki beef close for me to scoop. Carl continued telling the table about one time in Vietnam when he planted a meatball on his sergeant's forehead.

It just happened without much thought. I worked a piece of food onto my fork, and then exerted every bit of force I could muster. A pathetic effort, but it made it.

The way the slice of chewy, salt-soaked beef hit Carl's forehead must have been at least a little serendipitous for him. He sat frozen in stone for a moment, his hands halfway through a sentence, his expression of shock caught in perfect suspended animation.

Everyone froze.

And then splat, an entire plate of food was smooshed in my face the way a clown gets cream-pied.

"War is declared!" bellowed Viktor as he stood, raising his arms in triumph.

Sophie burst into a fit of laughter before she was hammered by flying pellets of rice. Carl was laughing. From there, it snowballed ... meat-balled. The dining area transformed into a high-school cafeteria with the alumni of the *Happy Days* era chortling and soaking anything in sight with shitty Chinese food. I swear even the caregivers joined in at one point.

"What in high hell is happening?!" I'd never heard Philomena shriek like that, not even that time I broke a vase by knocking it with my chair.

Every single person resumed their game of statues. The party was over.

"The place is a mess ... can someone please tell me what's going on?"

The group of seniors looked like frightened school children. And then all eyes fell upon me.

"Cody," Philomena said, "can you tell me what happened?"

It all felt more serious than it should have been. "We just did what should be done with this food. I mean seriously, is it even meat?"

"These people need to eat, Cody! They need their nutrition."

"They need some fun."

"This can't keep happening."

Bang!

Philomena turned to the sound, as did everyone. Viktor's fists were clenched and planted firmly on the table. "You leave little Cody alone."

"Viktor, please calm down."

He was breathing heavily, huffing and puffing and bubbling.

"Viktor ...?"

"Argh!" he screamed and then began to hurl plates and cutlery through the air. "We need to be out of here!"

Philomena summoned Allan and Julian. They came over with Viktor's kit. Sedatives and tranquilizers. Capsicum spray.

Viktor stood and swung his arm, clobbering Julian as he tried to prepare a needle. Sophie cheered, but it was a short-lived victory. Allan had prepared one, too.

The fork was still in my hand ...

The piece of teriyaki beef didn't hit Philomena in the face like I'd hoped, but it plopped nicely on her skeletal chest. She turned to me, exasperated. The meat slid down her uniform and Viktor laughed as he drifted off into a sedative haze.

Philomena's brow crinkled. "I think we need to talk."

I followed her into her office.

She sat at her desk and clasped her hands together. "What are we going to do, Cody?"

"What do you mean?"

"This just isn't acceptable. Not here. This is meant to be a peaceful place. It's for people to retire to … You're young. I know it can be hard being in this environment."

"What do you know, huh?"

"There's no reason to talk to me like that."

"And there's no reason to take this all so seriously."

Philomena turned her chair and browsed through her shelf. She slid the brochures onto the table. "There are other options for you, you know."

A strange feeling came over me. "I don't want to leave here."

"I know this is the only care facility you've been in since your accident, and it's close to your home, but if you're going to be somewhere permanently, there might be better options for you. A place where there are younger people. Somewhere where you can make friends."

I thought of Joe, Viktor, and Sophie. "I have friends here."

She closed the brochure. "Then perhaps you should start to think about what might be best for them. Do you think it's good for Viktor to be riled up like he was? To have to be sedated because he's been triggered?"

It hadn't occurred to me how selfish I might have been.

"I'm not going to ask you to leave, yet, but I am putting you on notice, Cody."

People called out to me, but I didn't talk to anyone on my way out. In my bedroom, I parked at the window and gazed out at the light of the stars. The dead ones, the living ones, and the ones somewhere in between. All the different lights. Everywhere and nowhere all at once.

I fell into myself, into what my life was really like, a matter of only a few years ago.

This one life I've had, with what feels like numerous lifetimes within it. The different people I've been. The happy little boy, the orphan boy, the scared boy, the homeless boy. Transient youth, apprentice photographer, successful artist. Playboy with a supermodel wife. Dad-to-be, with everything to look forward to. The breaking man. The broken man. The apathetic cripple. And now …?

The man who wants to feel the love of his wife again. The man who loves his wife.

I unlock my phone and scroll through those unsent drafts.

I write another.

I hit Send.

❦

A creak wakes me. Someone is opening my door. A dark figure stands beside my bed, silhouetted in the moonlight.

"Cody?"

The whispered voice is so familiar, but it can't be. This must be a dream.

"Isobel?"

She lies down next to me and her face appears in the moonlight, her cheek resting in the palm of her hand, her elbow in the pillow. Her eyes are tired and worn, bordered by yesterday's eyeliner.

"I'm dreaming, right?"

Then I feel her fingers run over the back of my left hand. "No. This is real. I'm sorry to just show up so late. It's just been one long day and night, and I needed to … I needed to see someone who knows me … and then I got your text."

"It's been an interesting night here, too."

"What happened?"

My eyes gravitate to the splinters of moonlight splayed across the ceiling. "Nothing to worry about." I roll my head back toward Isobel. "Are you okay?"

She relaxes her arm and rests her head on the pillow so our eyes are level, closer than they've been since another lifetime some lifetimes ago.

"I don't know." A deep, cathartic breath leaves her lungs. She stares into the linen. "I got a call this evening from my father's attorney. He died this morning."

"I'm sorry."

"He had a heart attack while he was eating his oatmeal. There was no one there to call the ambulance. His cleaner found him with his head in the bowl."

"You're not bringing yourself into it, are you?"

"I'm just thinking about how life turned out for me and him. It makes me sad that he died alone. And now I'm thinking about the relationship we never really had, and how I've always wished we did. Now we'll never get to have it. Don't really know what to feel."

"Have you talked to Jake about it?"

"I tried but … it's tricky."

There's a carousel of questions spinning in my mind. I want her to see that we have more than they do, that there are ways that I'm more to her than him … but Isobel needs me. Me. Not some yearning, jealous cripple.

"How did you get in this late?" I ask.

"I sent Joe a text, hoping he was on tonight. Got lucky and he let me in."

"I'm glad he did."

Isobel raises a smile momentarily. "So am I. There's no one else who'd really get it."

An urge to wrap Isobel up in my arms rises in me so fast that my left forearm tries to move to do so. I graze her thigh with my hand, but that's it. That's all the consoling I can do.

"Sorry," I say. "I just wanted to give you a hug … seems the like the thing to do. Forgot for a moment that I can't."

Isobel cozies up to me. She takes my arm and puts it around her waist and then hers around mine. "You can still hug, Cody."

Last time we lay like this all I could think of was how I couldn't feel her anymore – couldn't feel her heart. Now that I literally can't feel her, I can feel her heart closer than ever.

In her arms, that seemingly delusional hope I've been clinging to doesn't feel so ludicrous.

We stay like this, talking at times, reminiscing at others, or just lying in silence, until the morning birds start their sweet wake-up symphony.

With Isobel's head resting on my chest, her arm draped around me, we fall asleep on my bed in the nursing home.

When I wake, Isobel has gone.

I'm alone.

Sunlight is blaring in through the curtains.

I'm alone.

Did I dream last night?

A food fight.

My last warning.

Isobel sneaking in.

It seems like a dream.

But there's a note on the pillow next to me. It's not long: just two words and a letter.

Thank you x.

She was here.

Here more than she's been in this lifetime.

And I am too.

More than I have been since That Sunday.

Chapter 32

(THEN)

We held a private burial at Graceland Cemetery, just Isobel, me and the cremated ashes of our child who never got the chance to live.

I held the box in my hand for some moments, struggling to let go of it and give it to the eulogist. It was as if I was letting go of something that had a heartbeat, a personality, as if I was letting go of an actual baby, not just the dusty remains of ours.

Eventually I passed it over. Such a tiny box. She placed it into position, beneath where the plaque would sit.

What do you write on a plaque for a child you never got to see? How do you end a story when it never got to start?

You write a name.

Holi Foreman.

Not even a birthdate. Just the date of death.

We left the cemetery holding hands. Together. We had to be. I would have fallen to pieces completely without something to hold onto.

Sitting in separate seats in the car felt worlds apart.

Words came on the ride home like water comes to a desert.

"I always worried about how I'd be as a mother," Isobel said. "Whether I'd be good enough to take care of a baby. Whether I could be here long enough to see my daughter grow up. Whether I'd just turn into my mother. I was so worried."

"I was scared too."

"And look how it turned out. I wasn't even a good enough mother to bring a child into the world."

I turned into our street. "It wasn't your fault, Isobel."

The handrail came to my mind. All those times it was meant to be fixed. By Larry. By me. And then the scream. The collapsed handrail. Isobel on her side. Helpless and in pain.

"It wasn't anyone's fault. You need to know that."

Rubbing the back of her hand, I didn't know who I was consoling more. It was more my fault than hers.

My parents were waiting for us back at our apartment. We hadn't seen them since it happened. Hadn't seen anyone. People tried, but it was just too hard – we weren't there. Just two shells of people, breathing, barely eating and sleeping. Doing nothing but hurting.

"It's probably better that it happened now. It would've only been worse if we'd brought her into the world. I'd just have hurt us more."

I parked and wrenched the handbrake back violently. "Don't say that!"

Isobel was unmoved. She stared blankly through the windshield for a moment, and then got out of the car.

Alone in the car, the silence was deafening. Then I burst. I cursed and screamed and belted the steering wheel until my palms felt bruised. It did nothing to placate me.

Larry and Janine were on the couch and Isobel was curled up on the armchair when I walked in. Janine was leaning over with a hand on Isobel's arm, trying to console her.

Larry came to me and gripped the side of my shoulder. When I was younger, longing for a family in the orphanage and then on the street, I always dreamed of a reassuring touch from a parent. Larry and Janine had given it to me. But in this moment, I hated his hand being on me.

Anger pulsated through my veins. I tried to remind myself of everything I had with these people. All that I ended up seeing was what I'd lost. And why I'd lost it.

"Kid, I'm so sorry." He let go of my shoulder and hugged me. I didn't return the hug. "How're you holding up?"

I shrugged. "We're just getting through each day. Waking up and forgetting all the shit that's happened and then going through it all over again before we don't eat breakfast."

"Honey …" Pity oozed from Janine's eyes. "I haven't stopped thinking about the two of you. We wanted to be there for you right away …"

"We needed space."

She nodded. "I understand. But please know that we are here anytime you need us."

"Come, sit for a bit, kid." Larry escorted me to the couch.

Isobel's eyes remained out the window.

The quiet hum of the city occupied the airwaves for some time.

"Is there anything we can do for you?" Larry asked.

Janine tried to grip Isobel's hand. "I can help out around here. Cook, clean, whatever you need."

"It's okay," Isobel replied, keeping her hands to herself.

My stomach felt sick. The room was stuffy. Boiling.

That handrail. It had been broken for years. Fifteen goddamn minutes is all it would have taken to fix it!

Larry's hand again rested on my shoulder. "And if there's anything I can do …"

"The only thing you could have done is fix that fucking handrail before my pregnant wife fell through it."

Larry and Janine looked as if they had been hit with a Taser.

He gawked at me with sorrow in his big brown eyes.

Janine stammered, "Cody, I know you're upset …"

"You don't know shit."

She wasn't my mother. She was just a pathetic lady, so desperate to have a child, because she couldn't conceive herself, that she'd adopted a homeless, scummy kid right off the street.

"And why, after so many fucking years of demanding and nagging him to do it – why didn't you just hire someone to fix it? It was obvious he wasn't going to do it."

They didn't even know me. I could have been anything – a murderer, rapist, thief – and they took me in.

"I'm not sure that this is the time to be breaking apart, Cody," Janine said. "We need to all come together. We're a family."

Larry's eyes were buried in the rug.

"No, we don't," I said, standing. "We're not a family, so why don't you just get the fuck out of here!"

Janine started to cry.

Larry stood. "I'm so sorry, kid."

His eyes pleaded for forgiveness. He raised his hand and tried to touch my shoulder, but I swatted it away.

"You're not my father, and I don't want your damn apologies."

"Cody, please," Janine blubbered.

Now I pointed in her face. "And you're not my mother. So just shut the fuck up and get out of my house."

Larry pushed my arm down. "Kid ..."

That was as far as he got.

I swung with every bit of force I had in me and connected with his jaw.

The man who had found me on the street and given me a home. The man who had taught me how to photograph properly. The man who was the reason I found Isobel again.

The man who saved my life.

I leaped on top of him the moment he hit the couch and pummeled him fist after fist, letting out every bit of blame onto the man I'd called Dad. I tried to leave it all on him – every bit of anger and grief I felt.

He didn't resist. Just lay there and took every punch I had in me.

His face was bumped and bloody when I finally tired.

Janine helped him up from the sofa.

I breathed heavily, simmering.

Nothing else was said as they limped out of the apartment. At the door, Larry turned back to me with that same regretful gaze, his mouth ajar as if he was about to speak. But he didn't – he just dropped his head, his eye now covered over, and walked away.

The door closed and the room became cold. A sickly cold against my sweaty skin that made me want to vomit.

I looked across to Isobel. She hadn't moved an inch, still staring out the window. For the first time, I noticed she wasn't wearing her silver necklace with pictures of us in it.

I considered going to her and holding her. Touching her. Being together. But I didn't.

I just sat on the couch, yards away but worlds apart.

Chapter 33

(THEN)

We sank into a hole so deep that there was no escaping it.

Larry and Janine tried tirelessly to apologize, but all I did was grow to despise them more. I lumped the blame with them, distracting myself from what I truly felt.

At times I tried to be there for Isobel. I'd tell her it was going to be okay, and that we'd get through it. Mostly, though, we hurt alone beside one another. Scattered conversation about nothing.

It was a cold Sunday morning in early December when I sat at the kitchen counter, watching coffee evaporate under my nose. Isobel was on the couch, in the same spot she occupied nearly every waking hour, staring out the window. Her hair was messed, her makeup was from the day before, which might have been from the day before that, too. Shadows were collecting under her eyes as the weeks passed. I don't know if she was sleeping at all. We slept on opposite sides of the bed, and if I ever tried spooning her, it just didn't fit like it used to.

Isobel's phone went off. Surprisingly, she read the message.

"It's Kate. She and Tania are in town with a few of the old crew. They're having a get-together tonight."

I mumbled a response.

"Babe." Isobel stood and came to me. "I think we should go. Get out for a while. It'll be good."

She was warm, hopeful, in a way she hadn't been since it happened.

"I don't know if I can."

Isobel took my hands. "We have to get out; we have to keep living."

It was relieving to see Isobel like this. I became light like a feather. The breeze took me. "Okay. Let's go."

"Great." Our hug was stiff, two mannequins embracing. "Is it okay if you run ahead? I just want to relax for a little while. I'll meet you there."

"I can wait. I'm in no hurry."

She held my head in her hands. "You need to get out, Cody. Go have some fun."

"Okay, okay …" In a cold, dark winter, there was a thin needle of light. "Hey, do you remember when we were in Munich a few years ago – at the beer hall?"

For the first time in what seemed forever, Isobel smiled. "You're going to remind me of the man with the sausages, aren't you?"

"Yeah, I was." I smiled back. "Das wiener is tasty!" I chortled in my best German accent. "Taste the wiener."

This made her laugh. "Thank you."

We lapped up minutes in the afterglow of laughter. Remembering what it was to be happy together.

On the wall near the refrigerator, my eyes wandered to a photo. The same photo that I'd come to find so often in the townhouse we'd end up in.

"We'll get through this, baby," I said.

She nodded, and then seemed to swallow a golf ball. "It'll be okay, Cody."

The next embrace felt genuine, like something we used to do.

"I love you," she said.

"I love you, too."

"Now go and get ready. The party starts soon."

She kissed me once more, and it felt as though things might actually be okay …

The apartment was adorned in Christmas decorations, a plastic tree lit with colorful globes, the obligatory mistletoe. The party was packed. Most people I didn't know, but there were some old acquaintances.

I texted Isobel, prompting her to get here.

Despite everything I'd lived through, and the ways I'd grown, there I was, alone in a room filled with people, unable to connect with anyone.

No idea how to stand, what to say, where to look. It was a police station, an orphanage, a cold Chicago street. And I was waiting for her.

My eyes darted to different people and I wondered whether they knew … conversation … social media. They'd know.

The drinks started to disappear. Glass after glass, until I'd lost count and the room felt just that little bit warmer, until I was just there in the yellow lights and fluffy carpet, the decorations, the hubbub of the party. I was there, nowhere else.

"Cody!"

Arms wrapped around me. It was Kate. She looked the same as she always did, grinning as though she knew something you didn't.

"Where's Isobel?"

"She's coming."

She topped up my drink, glanced around and then took me by the hand, led me down the hallway and into a bedroom.

She set down her drink on the mantelpiece, opened a drawer and took out a small bag of blow. She sat on the bed and racked up three lines.

"Come here, babe," she said, and then snorted a line. "I think you need to smile a little bit."

I was the feather, taken by any gust.

I snorted a line. My nose burned and twitched. It had been years.

"I hope you're not planning on taking my share." Tania was leaning seductively on the doorframe of the bathroom, stripped down to her black lingerie.

She came over and kissed Kate, then took the note from my hand and vacuumed a line.

The girls kissed, tongues flailing over one another, and then turned their attention to me.

Molly took hold. The room floating, my mind absorbed in every word, every movement, every smell.

Then I was naked, the moment arising as if I'd just woken up to it, Kate's lips caressing my body, Tania's wrapped around the head of my cock. I looked down at them, immersed in this moment, taken by pleasure.

I felt nothing.

The molly was doing everything – the jaw contractions, sweat, buzzing in my muscles – everything except bringing euphoria. My mind and my body were disconnected, a polarity: the commotion of reality in front of me, and the still emptiness inside me.

Two beautiful women kissing, caressing and sucking me.

Who gives a shit?

Then they were on top of me. Kate riding me, Tania sitting on my face. Me, a toy, a dummy, a blow-up doll. Their noises were echoes of pleasure, something that once seemed like it meant something. To please a woman, to be emancipated by raw sexuality.

The sounds were torturous.

One bent over, eating the other out.

My eyes, avoiding them. A painting on the wall.

Their sounds.

Isobel, sitting at home, alone on the couch. My wife, the love of my life who I no longer knew. I felt like crying.

I had to get out of there.

"Cody, where are you going, babe?"

Dressed, and walking out the door. Down the hall. Out of the apartment and up the stairwell to the roof. Out into the icy December night.

The moon was hidden by whispers of cloud, pollution.

On the roof, I paced.

The cold was something to me. It was home. It was where I was meant to be in that moment.

I found myself sitting on the edge of the roof, my butt soaked. Looking ten stories down at the street below, I wondered about the people passing by. Whether they could have some part of my life. Did they know what had happened? Little tufts, moving up and down. Going somewhere to see someone. Not worried. Not hurting. Living their lives like they meant something. Not aware how much it can hurt to live.

I wanted to the be the man in the parka, walking hand in hand with his child and wife. Going shopping for the Christmas ham.

I wanted to be the man in the black duffle, old and gray with his arm wrapped around his wife. Going to see their children now grown up who had given them grandchildren.

I wanted to be the children … any child.

But I was me. A lost man on an icy Chicago roof.

I thought of Isobel. Sitting at home on that couch, alone. Just two blocks over and a million miles away.

I wanted to be me, the man who loved her.

My eyes burned with tears, the world became blurry.

Then my phone rang. Reality hit, how freezing it was, and I began to shake. It dawned on me how drunk and high I was. Everything I'd come to forget flooded over me.

"Where are you?" I answered the call from Isobel.

"Cody ..." her voice trailed off drowsily.

"Isobel, where are you?"

"The bath ..."

"Isobel, what's going on?"

"I've done something ..."

"What have you done?"

She didn't answer.

"Talk to me!"

"It's too hard, Cody ... too hard. I need to rest."

My heart tried to punch its way out of my chest.

"Stay on the phone," my voice trembled, "stay with me, don't stop talking."

"I'm sorry, Cody ... I'm sorry."

I went to stand and push off ... stopped by the slate on the roof's edge ...

The slip.

The rush of cold air over my skin.

An endless sky above. Stars among the blackness.

Freefalling.

Blackness.

⚭

I sucked in the world with a gasp as I woke.

My breathing took some moments to settle.

The beep of machines became audible. The light was white, airy, flowers by my bed, the smell of fresh chrysanthemums.

A nurse in blue scrubs was adjusting something on a machine beside me.

"Isobel," I croaked, rolling my head over to her. "Where's Isobel?"

Her eyes grew wide when she realized I was awake. "I'll be back in a moment."

She hurried from the room.

I went to sit, but the only thing that moved was my neck.

"Isobel. Where is she?"

My arms were lying atop the blanket. I tried to move them.

Nothing.

My arms, my legs, why won't they move?!

Nothing.

I stared at my limbs, instructing them to move. *Roll over, raise your arm, bend your leg, wiggle your toes, tense your stomach. Do something!*

Panic filled me. But all that happened was my neck wrenching up and my head rolling side to side as I called for Isobel.

She was dead, and I'd let her die while I fucked her friends.

I deserved to die.

A doctor came into the room. "Cody, you need to relax," she said.

"Where's Isobel?!" My voice was little more than air. "Where?!"

Tears running down my face: the only sensation.

"Isobel is okay. She is in recovery and she's going to be fine."

"I want to see her."

My neck continued to jerk up as I repeatedly tried to sit. My head bounced side to side on the pillow whenever I tried to move some part of my body.

She signaled and the nurse injected something into a line that was attached into my right hand.

The tears wouldn't stop.

"Why can't I move?"

"Cody, you need to listen to me."

"Why can't I move?!"

Eyes burning. Tears on my cheek, my neck.

All that I was.

"Three days ago, you fell from a rooftop. The fall fractured your spine."

I stopped crying. This couldn't be real. It was just a horrible dream. I was going to wake up and go home.

There was a heaviness in the air that I knew, though. It had been in that police station when I was a child, when another doctor told us that we couldn't conceive, when an ER surgeon said that he was sorry my unborn child had died …

"I know this is difficult to hear," the doctor said, "but our team will be with you every step of the way."

"What's going to happen …?"

The nurse and doctor exchanged a solemn look.

"Cody, it is unlikely that you will be able to walk again," the doctor said. "You are going to have to be in hospital for some time. Rehabilitation and adjusting take time."

The heaviness returned, the heaviness that had been there on a rooftop when Isobel called me to say goodbye, when she tried to kill herself.

This was real.

"Isobel." I groaned and started crying again. "I want to see Isobel."

She nodded to the nurse, who then pumped more drugs into me.

I called for Isobel until I had no voice. I cried until every tear I had inside me had been cried.

Scared. Alone.

There was no escaping what I was destined to be.

Nowhere to run to. No running at all.

Stuck.

In that bed, unable to feel the sheets, no feeling below my neck.

And all I wanted more than anything was to see Isobel. My wife who had tried to kill herself with sleeping pills. To be there for her like I'd promised to be. To not be alone.

I couldn't be, though. I had no choice but to hurt alone …

In that bed, I started to fade toward numbness.

Nothingness.

Nothing cannot be alone.

Nothing.

The only way it wouldn't hurt.

Chapter 34

(NOW)

"Cody, can I talk to you?" Sophie has taken a seat beside where I'm parked in the recreation room.

"Of course."

"It's Viktor." She dips her head. "I'm worried about him. They've had to change his medication again."

He tried to escape again this morning. He was so angry he had to be sedated.

"It must be hard for him."

"It's hard for anyone, darling, to depend on other people to live. But here we all are, and it's what we've got." She drops her head solemnly. "I just wish he'd see what he has here."

"Maybe you need to tell him that."

"Maybe I do …" Sophie stops and then snickers to herself. "It's so silly. I feel like such a schoolgirl around him. So young and naïve, not sure what to do sometimes."

"I'd have thought you'd have a handle on things at your age."

She rests her hand on my left. "Cody, if I've learnt anything in all my years on earth, it's that love never gets easier."

"You can say that."

"Oh, honey, you're still a baby. There's so much more for you in this life."

I wonder about this. I consider it. I hope.

Viktor is wheeled out into the recreation space in a chair. He looks braindead. His lips drooping, saliva dangling from them, his eyes darkened by drug-induced numbness. Sophie gasps, clapping her hands to her cheeks.

"He looks terrible now," I say, "but maybe the new meds will work."

Sophie gets up and hurries to him.

Drowsily, he responds to her by touching her face, smiling a drug-induced smile. Sophie wipes a tear from her eye.

It's so stupid for me to care. Five years ago I would have passed these people on the street and not said a word to them. The closest I would have got to them is sitting at a café watching them pass by the window, wondering for no more than a moment about the lives they live.

It's not five years ago, though. It's now, and they are my friends.

We all have more experiences to go: Viktor, Sophie, Joe and I.

There's no abyss for me, no loneliness. There's an open plain. Freedom for my friends and me.

Five years ago, I think again.

The prime of my life.

Was it, though?

"Cody." Caren is standing in front of me. "You're needed in the care room. Doc's come to visit."

It's such a stale room for a space that's meant to be about care. Plain, plastic furniture from Walmart that makes me glad I'm stuck in my chair.

The impressionist painting on the wall must be fake, or a massive score from a pawn shop.

Robert enters the room.

He says hello, and then shuffles around me and onto the chair behind the desk.

"How are you feeling, Cody?"

"Grand," I reply. "Never better."

"Glad to hear it."

"You don't seem quite so peachy, doc."

He sighs. "Last week's scan results came back." His fingers entwine, and a moment of silence ensues.

"And …?"

"Clots have reformed in your legs."

Slap. The words collect my cheek.

"So, what now?" I can hear myself. I sound timid.

"In a small percentage of people none of the medication works."

"And I'm in that small percentage."

He nods, and then opens his folder. "We have also found two small pulmonary embolisms. Clots in your lungs." He slides a scan of my lungs across the table to me.

Smack. Those words hit right between my eyes.

"You said those new drugs would clear them."

"The Warfarin and Heparin cleared the original clots in your legs. But unfortunately the drugs have been unable to prevent further clots. You've been dealt a crappy hand, Cody. Your blood clots faster and is less responsive to medication."

"So there's nothing you can do?"

"We continue with the medication to slow the clotting and prevent further clots as much as possible. They are small right now. With any luck, we can keep them that way."

I reverse my chair back. "So some meds that didn't do shit, and what?"

"I'm afraid that's all we can do, Cody." He takes back the scans. "I have to be honest with you. Given what we have observed and where the clots have now formed …"

Now I drive forward. My head is swaying like I'm drunk. "What are you saying?"

"I'm saying that it is only a matter of time until these clots become fatal."

The air becomes heavy. It weighs a ton. I know this feeling.

My lips are dry as I go to talk. "How long …?"

"You could live for years with them … but it might be months, even weeks."

I laugh. What a ridiculous thing to do right now. But I do. "Life's kind of funny, isn't it?"

He gives me a sorry look. "Along with your caregivers and nurses we will put in place a care plan. There will be palliative caregivers and chaplains who will work with you, and everyone around, to make this time as comfortable as possible."

A plan to die … it seems wrong.

Shouldn't I fight this? Struggle and scream and bite until the bitter end? Hell, even shine on brightly with a rainbow coming out of my ass, pretending like this isn't it, or that there's something else to come. Be ignorant of life, or ignorant of death, something, surely? But a plan to die. I don't get it.

"Is there anything in particular you would like me to do, or to organize at this point?" I've never had a doctor ask me this. "The chaplain is a wonderful lady. I highly recommend talking to her as soon as possible."

"I'll consider it." A lifetime of thoughts sweeps through my mind. In the middle of them, one pounding heartbeat. "I'd prefer that you don't tell my wife, that no one talks to her about my care plan … I'll tell her when I feel right about it."

The floor is a funny color. I've never noticed it before. Not quite purple, not quite blue, almost aqua, something like teal. It's just something I can't figure out.

Isobel is at home, a home that used to be mine. She's there with Jake. But the other night, when she needed someone the most, she was here with me.

She doesn't need to know what's going on with me. She just needs to feel happy again.

I just want her to feel happy again.

She can't know about the clots.

I just need to make her smile again.

To make her feel at home.

I want to be home.

Home isn't that townhouse. It's not an apartment in NYC, or Chicago. It's not an orphanage or a house in the north. It's comfort, a place where I can be myself.

Home … It's the same place it's always been, where it always will be.

With Isobel.

Chapter 35

(NOW)

I'm sitting up on my bed on top of the sheet, with pillows stuffed behind my back. It's something I used to do when I was waiting for Isobel to come to bed. Those silly nights when Isobel would still clean her teeth in the door to the bathroom and fill her mouth with enough foam to make a beard, and then ask, "Is there something on my face?"

I messaged her during the week, asking if she feels like coming around again. She's been busy, though. It happens. That's life, hey. We get busy.

My chair is beside the bed. The camera Joe had fixed to it is staring at me.

I regret that I didn't fill the last few years with something more than apathy, anger … and regret. It's a cycle, isn't it?

I could have had a whole collection of photographs to look back on and smile at.

The last photo I have of us together is the one taken in Lincoln Park, just by North Pond, Isobel pregnant with Holi. Her bump, my hand, us. The perfect photo.

I wonder if it is still in the kitchen, or if Jake's taken it down, or worse yet, if Isobel has taken it down.

The noise from the bedroom light sounds loud. Buzzing, right in my ear. Buzzing until I let the thought emanate enough to be heard fully. I wish that I had had the courage to fight past the pain and get to a place where we could still be happy together, instead of just refusing to let it in by blocking everything out. I wish I'd had the courage to open my eyes enough to see that she was still there for me. To realize that I still loved her.

It's never too late, they say, but what if it is – then what do you do?

She's with Jake now.

I'm not her man.

I'm dying.

And I still love her. More than ever.

There's a knock, then Joe peeps around the door. "Always have to knock first, never know what cheeky business you'll be up to in here, fella."

"You were two minutes too late."

He enters and sits on the side of the bed. "I heard you were always two minutes too early."

"Funny. Heard you never even arrived."

"You wouldn't know where to go, mate."

I find myself smiling. "I've never met a bigger smartass, ya know."

"Guess you've never been to Australia, have ya?"

"I don't think I want to if it's full of people like you."

With a big grin across his fat lips Joe turns to me. "You'll fit right in."

We pause momentarily.

"I guess you've heard by now," I say.

Joe nods. "Talked to the doc earlier. Thought I'd give you some space."

"I appreciate it."

The wind picks up outside and whooshes through the trees, becoming another voice in the quiet.

"Are you going to talk to the chaplain?"

"What will she tell me?"

"Dunno," he shrugs, "I've never been told I'm dying."

"Neither have I."

Joe rolls his thumbs over one another. "Well I guess we know as much as each other. I've only had one real experience with death, and I don't think blowing a kiss goodnight to your dead wife from your window every night is a healthy way of dealing with it."

"Hypothetically, though, what would *you* do?"

"Hard to know …"

"That's not overly helpful."

"Maybe I'd just do whatever I felt like."

"Again, not helpful, when I can't."

"I thought we were talking about me?"

I sigh. "Yeah, right."

"Seriously, though, I think I'd just let go …"

"And what about fighting? You're the one who's always tried to make me fight for something."

"I don't mean give up. I mean let go of all the little shit that people spend so much time worrying about. Let go of the regret. You've created enough, don't create more by regretting the fact that you have regrets. Just let go. You're dying. What's there to worry about?"

"I'm dying …" I trail off.

"We're all going to die one day, mate."

"We're going to die," I say, and then for some strange reason I start laughing.

Joe peers at me curiously, and then his expression turns from quizzical to humored. He joins me, chuckling. "We're going to die, Codes."

"We're going to die."

Our laughter turns to guffaws.

"We're going to die!" Joe hoots.

"Poof! We'll be gone."

"Dead." Joe wipes a tear from his eye. "How is that even remotely funny?"

"Because life's a joke."

Joe points at me. "And at the end of any good joke there's laughter."

Calming, my mind wanders to an inevitable thought. "Should I believe that I'm going somewhere after I die?"

"Depends what it gives you while you're here." Joe lies back on my bed, not far from my feet. "I guess for all we know, and I mean know, not believe, or want, this is all we have. Maybe there's more, and maybe you can make a bargain, make your peace when you're close … but maybe there's not. On the chance that this is all we have, we better make the most of it. Live like tomorrow will never come."

There's a ball gathering in my throat. It needs to be swallowed soon. Any day. The lump is big, and as I gulp I realize its true enormity.

It gets stuck in my throat.

Tomorrow might not come.

"It's funny, you know. All I tried to do for so long was get to nothingness. If I felt nothing, then I couldn't hurt. Now all I fear is nothingness."

"Does it scare you, dying?"

There's a traffic jam of leaves piled up outside the window. Every few seconds one finds a break on a breeze and flies free. Many stay stuck in a pile, jammed in a rat race that is ultimately going nowhere. We're all fallen leaves, being taken by the breeze.

"I don't think it's the nothing that might come after I die that I fear, it's the nothing that can come in life. I don't ever want to feel that again."

In the quiet of night, we lie for some moments, the sound of the wind coming in through the window.

"Think it's time to turn in," Joe says.

He gets up and puts me to bed. He goes to leave, but stops at the window. He stares out at the courtyard, and then into the ever-expanding depth of the universe.

"Someone forgot to lock your window." He flicks the clip, turns and walks to my door. "Thanks, fella."

"For what?"

"The talk."

"What do you mean? You were the one giving out guidance."

"Maybe …" He holds the door handle for a moment longer. "Anyway, goodnight, Codes. Sleep well, mate."

He closes the door, and I'm alone again.

A noise wakes me. Was it in my dream, or did something hit the window?

The red blur of the electric alarm clock clears to show 10:14 pm.

Another noise at the window. Rattling. In the moonlight, I catch sight of a silhouetted hand. Someone's breaking in!

It's happened before – they took every bit of Fay Washington's antique jewelry, and the only thing that kept her sane, and from totally losing hope, was that they missed her heirloom chess pieces, which she's had in a safe ever since. And now my room – what the hell is in my room?!

The window is opening.

I can't move to get up and run, or fight. I'm stuck.

What are they going to do to me?!

My breathing is shallow and rapid, my heartbeat flirting with the minute mile. I go to call out to Joe – he's still around isn't he? I go to scream, but I'm short of breath and nothing but a dry, meager wheeze comes out.

A leg comes in.

It's long and skinny.

Then a head.

The person stands and steps toward me.

In the moonlight long, flowing, sandy-blonde hair appears, hair that looks like it was made for hands to run through. Isobel's smile is the next thing I see.

"Surprise!"

I feel a tear press at my eye, a salty drop of anxiety, relief and happiness. "Hi," I say.

She's in Converse, yoga pants and a hooded sweatshirt.

"I thought you were a burglar."

"Well, I kind of am." Isobel comes to the opposite side of my bed and turns on my chair. "I'm stealing you."

"Pardon me?"

She holds her forefinger to her lips. "Shhh. Not so loud. Sneaking out isn't something you announce."

Before I can question her again, she's wrapping her arms around me, lifting me with the hoists, dressing me, and lowering me into my chair. My heart is fluttering again, this time with excitement and anticipation.

On the way out of the home, doors clipping closed gently behind me, I feel life flood back into me. "Where the hell are we going?"

"We're going for a little adventure," Isobel replies.

The cityscape at night is no less magical than it was when we were kids. The streets are busy with all types of people. Buskers filling the air around them with tunes, families finishing their fall outing with ice-cream; cafés, bars and nightspots brimming. The city is alive.

Everything is alive.

There are couples, too. Everywhere I look. As we go along side by side, I fall into the experience enough to feel like this is just another stroll around our city. Like we always used to.

"Been a while since I've done this," I say.

"It has." Isobel stops and reaches into her coat. She opens the small five-by-eight photo booklet onto my lap.

"God, it's almost been just as long since I've looked at these."

The collection is small, built up over years. Some pictures are newer, of the city almost as it is today, and some are old, of the city that I knew as a kid, and everything in between, of the city as it grew and grew. A timeline of my city in a Walmart display booklet.

"I don't know why I never got a better album for these. It could be really cool."

"You were too busy putting other stuff in the good albums."

Isobel sits on a bench and I park beside it.

"Was probably filling them with pictures of you."

She shakes her head, and then gazes up to the building. "You definitely got your placement mixed up then. The city grew prettier as time went by."

"I don't think I had things mixed up at all. You made this city as great as it was for us."

"You ever wish you could have a remote control for life, Cody?"

Through the buildings, the night sky is a deep blue. No stars are visible. "I'm still waiting for someone to fix one to my chair."

"It never stops, does it?" Isobel searches the night sky, gazing around the city. She looks so young, the wonder of a child in her eyes.

Life carries on for the world, but it ends for everyone. We're all going to die. I'm going to die.

"I've missed you, Isobel."

She glances at me with those gorgeous eyes. A thought goes to leap from her mind to her mouth. Her lips open, but it stops short of entering the atmosphere of the undeletable.

"Come on," she says and stands. "We're being far too serious."

We roam the streets, every corner and landmark a vestige of our years together. We're fireflies with faded bulbs, but we're still alight. We're still here.

I'm jabbering on about the time we spent in Berlin. Two nights straight in Berghain. No sleep. One of the stupid times we grew out of, but one of the reckless times we survived and that serves as a great memory.

"All I wanted to do was go to sleep when we walked into the apartment the next morning, but you …" I stop when I realize where she's led me.

Isobel turns and leans on the wire fence of St Madeline's.

"You used to look so cute in your overalls on the other side of this fence," she says. "Dirt on your hands and face. Picking tomatoes."

I steer close to the fence and look at the dark, haunting buildings of the orphanage. "Used to eat them like apples."

"It's so funny how well I remember it. Being young and shy and scared of the world. And then you came along right here with your camera."

Through the wire fence the concrete walls of the orphanage hide in the dark of night. I wonder which sisters are still there, wonder about the children who are sleeping there, the people they lost. What they'll find in life beyond these fences. "You gave me a reason to leave my comfort zone, to find something more."

"Why do we have to stop being like that?" she asks.

"Are you asking when we stopped?"

"I don't know …"

"I stopped being young when I thought of it as something to do with age, or another time of life outside of the present. I'm the oldest I've ever been today, but I feel younger than I have for some time. How does that work?"

Isobel pushes leaves around with her feet. "I guess that maybe youth can be a way of life, not just a part of it. I used to always think about growing up and getting myself sorted. Getting everything settled. Finally figuring things out … but what was I figuring out?"

"I don't know, babe. All I know is that we had something special."

She's beaming at me. "You haven't called me that for a long time."

"Oh …" I realize my slip of the tongue. "Didn't mean to."

"Sounded nice."

Isobel turns and grips her fingers through the wire. With the blink of a star in the night sky, I'm taken back to another time. When I had everything because I had her.

I want to know what's inside her head, like I always have. All those pretty little fucked-up thoughts running around and colliding in rainbows and train wrecks every second she ponders.

"There was this crazy woman who used to take me on joy rides so high, and then to some scary, dark places really low. She was everything to me. I miss her. I miss knowing her so well that she feels like a part of me …"

The fence shakes for a moment as Isobel pushes off the wire. She comes over to me, and then, like that crazy woman I used to know, she plonks down on my lap, her legs dangled over the side of my right arm rest. She unbuckles my left arm from the rest, and takes my hand from the joystick. Her skin under mine is one of the most exhilarating things I've ever felt. Just the touch of her hand, how I used to take this for granted. Guess sometimes you need to get lost in a desert before you really appreciate water.

Isobel cradles my head in her arms and rests hers on top. "She's still crazy, Cody."

"But is she happy?"

"What kind of question is that?" She takes her head off mine. "I'm human. I can call myself happy and I can feel it. But we're human. We're everything. Not just happy."

"You know what I mean. You're not happy with him."

She gets off my lap. "Why do you have to bring that up? Just leave it, Cody!"

"No." Annoyance is building in me. At myself, at the situation. It builds, bubbles and pushes at me, and then … it bursts … "I won't just leave it. Maybe I'm too damn late, maybe I pushed you so far away that you found something else. I know it's my fault. We're here, though – you're here, not with him, and you need to know what you deserve. I'm probably not it. But is he? Do you love him like you loved me?"

She paces, clutching her hands, scrunching and releasing. "I've been happy all night just doing the same crap we used to when we were young and in love. But you go and spoil it. Why?"

Do I tell her about the clots? That I could die any day.

"Because … I'm older than ever, but I can't be old. I'm crippled, but sick of being useless. I need to be young again. I need to have whatever I can have with you. We're not going to live the life we used to, but we can still find happiness with each other …"

Smack. She slaps me across the face.

The blood flows to my left cheek and warms it with a flush. What was anger and then desperation inside me has now become exhilaration.

"Fuck you, Cody. You're a jerk. You've got your voice back now, and you're just a damn jerk." She is scowling at me, her forefingers stabbing the air as she speaks. "I told you that very same thing over and over for eighteen months and all you did was push me away. I've spent so long hating myself for what I did. I've blamed myself for our daughter's death. I've blamed myself for you being in that chair. I've blamed myself for our lives turning out like this. Every day I wish that I'd never let you go alone to that party, that I never had the idea to take those pills … I wish that I never tried to kill myself … but every day I wish that I had succeeded, too.

"Despite those wishes, I've hung onto hope, tried to find some small happiness in life. I always thought that was with you – I truly believed that we could be something like the people we were before all of this. I was always willing to be your wife, to be there for you – to love you. But you made me feel like nothing. I've never stopped hurting about everything, and all you've done is turn away from it. I leave all of it behind for a night, for some time with you to just be us, and you throw it back at me. How can I just turn around and say it's all okay now, just because you've woken up?"

That exhilaration has gone, and a strange feeling takes hold of me. One where my hand shakes, my heart speeds and weakness flows through my veins.

"Okay." For all she just said to me, that is all I have. Okay.

"Maybe it's time we head home," Isobel says. "It's getting late."

She starts to walk, but I stay parked.

Leaves are shadowed in the glow of moonlight, dead and decomposing on the ground. "I'm late, and maybe I'm too late. Maybe Jake is the man for you. Only you know that … For what it's worth, Isobel, I'm sorry. For everything."

She comes back to me and kisses my forehead. The smell of her perfume is just hers, the sweet Chanel scent I would wake up from a night of dreams to, only to fall into another with the thought of her and the night before.

"So am I, Cody."

Like she used to do, she grazes her hand over the back of my left as she stands straight.

The feeling of her fingertips sliding over my knuckles replays as we move away from the fence where we first met over twenty years ago.

Behind me, two kids from different worlds are saying their first nervous words to each other. A shy private-school girl, a scared orphan boy. The boy who saw her for who she truly was: beautiful. The girl who took the time to know him, help him grow. Lead him through life. They are there, and they always will be.

Leaves crunch beneath my tires as I roll away.

That hazel-eyed girl is beside me. The woman she's become. And I'm here, the man I turned out to be.

Chapter 36

(THEN)

Six months in hospital, rehabbing physically. Day in, day out. Failing and failing. The only movement I got back – my left forearm and hand.

Six months for Isobel, rehabbing mentally. Day in, day out. Medications and medications. The only thing that carried on was a shell of herself.

Those six months away from each other. Trying to mold ourselves into some sort of being that could keep going with life. Connected by daily phone calls alone. Calls punctuated by silence. Scattered conversation. Nothing.

The van parked.

Isobel lowered me out of the back for the first time.

"Everything is ready," she said. "Just need to get a railing put on the ramp."

Railing. That handrail. No handrails. Why did it matter? What damage could be done that hadn't already been done?

I stared at it. Our new home. The shitty townhouse, modified to accommodate my carriage. The ramp out the front, fresh gray concrete.

Isobel toileted me for the first time alone that afternoon. Wiping my butt as I tried to die enough inside to not hate everything.

In the lounge room, I found the only place I seemed to fit, beside the sofa like a second armchair.

The doorbell rang.

Isobel got up to get it. "Must be the caregiver from the home."

I dreaded meeting the stranger who I would come to rely on.

She opened the door and a small, hobbit-like man waddled through.

"Name's Joe." He sat on the couch next to me.

I glared at him. "Don't talk to me."

Isobel looked nervous for a moment, and then went into the bedroom and closed the door. I knew she'd be crying. She only ever closed the door when she cried.

"No problem," Joe replied, turning on the television. "I've never minded talking to myself. Call me crazy, but it can be interesting."

Looking at him as he smiled and laughed at the television, I wondered how long he would last. Whether he'd break the one-month record my in-hospital caregiver set for staying with me.

Then I switched my attention to the abyss I'd been building, trying to ignore the tears I knew Isobel was shedding, trying not to shed my own. Trying to forget baby Holi, trying to forget that I'd ever had legs to walk on, that I'd ever had love in my heart.

Forget everything that made me feel.

I had nothing.

Just a strange man beside me named Joe.

Chapter 37

(NOW)

Air shoots into my throat as I wake with a gasp.

I'm in my bed, my chair is beside me, my hand within reach of the call button, just the way I've always been put to bed here.

The calendar on the wall seems to jump at me. It's standard issue in the home, like a pair of socks for a soldier. I've never really looked at it, or touched it, but it's on the right month. Someone's keeping it up to date for me. I roll my eyes over the numbers one by one and then the number twenty-seven whacks me in the face. I've been wondering how it would feel this time around.

Joe knows it. He's standing at the door, leaning in. "Morning, fella. What time you wanna go?"

I look back at the calendar and then roll my head out the window. Sun pierces through the canopy of gray and white. "Maybe we can get ready now?"

I'm somewhere else while he gets me ready for the day.

It's an autopilot kind of morning all the way until we park. I've lived this day twice before, and I remember both times the way you remember your first visit to the dentist. There are images and feelings – fear mostly, and pain – but I'm not quite sure if I lived them, aside from the fact that I must have.

"You want to go solo from this point, Codes?" Joe asks as the lift lowers from the van.

The aisles of green are ahead of me. It's more frightening than I thought – to do this alone. Can I park in front of it … her? Can I look down and talk to her? Tell her what? Say sorry? Can I answer the questions that may resonate from the ground?

"You think you could come?"

"Of course, mate."

I steer toward the green aisles. As I enter the first block of stones, I look around, immersed in the cemetery, lost in a city with no directions home. The gravestones rise like skyscrapers, the mounds and plaques like train stations and taxi ranks. It's alive in its own way. Every one of the dead commuters moving and going somewhere. They've all got their own story to tell, a place to be in yesteryear, forever stuck in fading photos.

My stop is approaching.

An array of emotions wants to break free from me, but my jaw is a steel cage, holding it all in. With each rotation of my wheels I move closer to the tiny gravestone. The steel cage doesn't feel so strong … but I grip my jaw tight, keeping it in.

I park in front of the gravestone. Don't let it out, I tell myself. Not like this. Not around Joe. Not around anyone. Not my baby.

"Holi's a beautiful name," Joe says as he stands beside me.

At the sound of her name, the steel cage shatters. Everything breaks free.

Joe puts a hand on my shoulder as I weep and shake and he leaves it there until I start to settle. Joe wipes my face: the tears and the snot.

"We put everything we had, every part of ourselves into having a child. She would've been loved and cared for with every part of our hearts and souls."

"You would've made a great dad."

"I couldn't even be a good enough husband to get to being that dad. I didn't take care of my wife. My child. And I paid for it." Another wave of razor-blade tears explodes out of me. "I lost everything, and I deserved to."

Once more Joe pats me on the shoulder. "You can blame yourself all that you want, mate. But eventually you need to realize that it wasn't your fault. I didn't know you back then, but I don't see how you could've caused this. I'm sure you cared about Isobel and Holi like nothing else in life."

"I did. But I could've stopped this from happening." I look up at him. "I didn't fix the handrail like I was meant to, and that's what Isobel fell through. One lean and it collapsed."

"I can't tell you how to stop feeling pain, mate. But all I know is that it wasn't your fault."

He pats my shoulder once more, and then leaves me.

Alone.

Alone with my unborn child.

With Isobel's belly, the bump that would've been Holi. Our greatest creation.

Alone.

With regret and wishing and broken promises and failed dreams and useless apologies, all running so fast from my mind to the grave.

"I'm sorry, Holi," I say, gulping, scared that she can't hear me. "I'm sorry," I repeat, and as I picture Isobel's eyes, the bump in her belly, and the glow about her that shone so brightly in those months, I realize I'm apologizing to Isobel. "I'm sorry, babe. I'm sorry."

Those words continue to fall from my mouth, as if eventually one might catch the wind and get taken to Isobel. To her now, or even maybe all the way back to those six months when she went from wanting to create life to wanting to take her own.

I jolt in my chair as a hand grips my shoulder. Isobel is beside me.

"How long have you been there?"

She shrugs. "Not long. Me and Joe have swapped cars. I'll take you back."

She sits down beside my chair and grips her hands around her knees, her eyes forward and lost in the sliding doors behind the grave.

"Three years," I say.

"I still come here most weeks. Usually just sit here and think about stuff. It's as close as I get to being back then. It's comforting. I kind of get to forget for some time. It's hard leaving."

I've wished every moment of every day since I've been a quadriplegic that I could move again. I've never wished as much as I do right now. To be able to reach down to Isobel and put my arm around her, hold her, bring her in close and make her feel secure.

"It was my fault that it happened."

She looks up at me. "No, it wasn't."

"Yeah, it was. And it was yours, and it was Larry's, and it was Janine's. And it was no one's fault, too. Everything could have been different, but it wasn't – things turned out the way they did and I can't change that. I can only change what is yet to happen."

"And what is to happen?"

A crow squawks from two rows over and then flies high into the air, soon becoming a distant speck of black against the overcast sky.

"I don't know … All I know is that I'm still in love with you, Isobel."

Her head gets lost between her knees. She looks back up, her eyes now bleary, though she says nothing in return. Her jaw clenches, the same steel cage mine had been.

"I want to have whatever time I have left with you. We'll never be what we were, but we can be something new. We'll never get our yesterday back, but we can have a tomorrow."

"This is a confusing time, Cody. You have to understand that."

"I know, and that's because of me. But what do you want?"

"Does it really matter?"

"It does, Isobel. You need to know that."

Picking blades of grass as if one could hold the right answer, Isobel takes her time to respond.

"All I want right now is to sit with my daughter, and my husband."

And that's what we do.

No words. No concern for anything or anyone else. No regret, no wishing.

Nothing except this moment.

Nothing except us.

Chapter 38

(NOW)

Second thoughts shoot through my mind.

Turn back.

Turn back.

Leave it be.

Yet I don't stop driving up the front path I used to walk up every day.

Another attack yesterday.

Would I be doing this if I didn't know I was dying? I don't know. It doesn't matter, though, because that's how things are, and this is where I am.

I steer up the ramp. Joe closes the van door and meets me on the front step. He rings the doorbell and we wait. The dull thud of footsteps on floorboards comes closer. The door opens.

Janine's hands cover her mouth. "Oh my god. Cody."

She's not shocked because I'm in the chair – she's seen me this way – it's because I'm here.

They really never stopped trying until I made Isobel shut them out. I made sure she never gave them our address; I blocked their numbers from calling me and asked Isobel to do the same. It was a fucked-up time in my life. I was totally focused on laying blame and shutting out the ache inside my heart.

Eventually, she moves her hand from her mouth to her chest. "Come in, the both of you."

In the living room, Joe sits on the recliner and I park beside him. Janine fetches a plate of snacks from the kitchen and drinks for us all, then sits opposite. I introduce them, Janine nodding a nervous hello and Joe tipping an invisible hat.

My eyes survey the room. This was my home, where we used to play board games, where we'd have family meetings, where I'd shake and handle presents leading up to Christmas and wonder what I was getting … where I first felt like I had a family.

"Is Larry at work?"

Janine dips her head, and the old grandfather clock in the hall dominates the airwaves for some moments. "I'm not sure, Cody."

"What do you mean?"

The clock ticks and ticks. Her hands wrap around her teacup, veins protruding with deep blue and green. I used to love the smell of tea on her breath when she'd kiss me on the cheek.

"We separated, darling. A while ago now."

"Why?"

"Things just …" Janine gathers herself. "Things just changed after it all happened."

It. Everything that happened. It didn't just break Isobel and me, it broke them too.

"Was it because of me?" I ask.

"It wasn't you, honey. Larry just wasn't himself, and I couldn't do anything for him …"

Isobel always used to fear becoming her mother. She nearly did. But did I become my father?

"It's so good to see you, Cody … Please don't take this the wrong way, but why now? Is there something wrong? Is Isobel okay?"

"Everything's fine." For a second I feel like blurting it out, letting someone know what's going on. But I can't, there's no need to make her worry. "Everything's great, actually."

A smile spreads across Janine's face. "I'm glad you came. I've missed you."

"I've missed you too …" It's liberating to admit. "I kind of wish we'd spoken."

"We could have, Cody, but you made a choice to shut us out. That's what you wanted."

"I know …"

"Whenever I've spoken to Isobel, I've always hoped she'd tell me that you wanted to talk."

"What do you mean?"

"Isobel and I have kept in touch. I thought you knew? I mean, we didn't for a while, but after some time she started to talk to me again. Larry, too. I presume they still talk. She was the closest I could get to you …"

It's as though a blindfold is pulled from my eyes. How much have I missed? "It was hard for me."

Janine drops her eyes to the rug. "It was hard for me being hated by my son."

Moments pass in heavy silence.

"You didn't deserve to be treated how I treated you," I say. "I'm sorry."

She looks up with a forced, sympathetic smile. "It's okay, honey. We all hurt in our own way."

"Do you still talk to Larry?"

Janine takes one last gulp of tea and then puts the cup down on a doily she crocheted when I was a teenager. Her eyes become glazed with happy-sad. "Sometimes …"

"How is he?"

That happy-sad loses its happy. Her head drops into her hands and a deep sob escapes. Without thought I push my joystick and whir around the coffee table over to her. I raise my left hand as far as it will go. In my mind, it's reaching out to rub her shoulder.

Janine brings her head up, eyes frosted with pain. She takes my hand and holds it. "It's okay, honey. It's not your fault."

If I wasn't still afraid to hurt right now, I'd let her know that it is my fault.

On the mantelpiece there's a photo of the three of us. It was always my favorite. It was taken at Disneyland when I was sixteen – the first family holiday we went on. I'd been homeless only a year before, but on that holiday I truly felt the beauty of childhood sunshine, when summers feel as though they'll last forever, and that growing old and making stupid mistakes is something that just couldn't happen …

"We talk every now and again, Cody." She wipes away the residual wetness from her eyes. "But it breaks my heart every time."

Her hand now feels like the one I'd cling to when I screwed up as a teenager, when I'd done something dumb and thought I'd risked losing their love and everything they'd given me.

"Why?"

She sighs. "He's just not the same person, Cody. I tried to help him, I really did."

"I don't understand …"

"He's often in the city … he sits and he waits in a spot. Isobel knows where. She said it's a place where you'd know. He's just not the same person …"

Now she does break.

I try to squeeze her hand the best I can. "Hey." I nod my head up to the photo on the mantelpiece. "I see you've still got that up there."

Her sobbing calms, and she wipes her nose. "We were so excited to take you there."

"I couldn't sit still the whole way. I remember you wanted to fly, but Larry was all about taking me on a road trip. It was long but it was worth it."

"Motel beds got pretty tiresome after four days on the road."

"I don't think I slept, so I wouldn't know."

"You were full of beans, weren't you? You and your father playing that ridiculous game spotting stuff on the road – what was it again?"

"Dead animal. We had to spot roadkill."

"That's right."

Our eyes meet, somewhere between this living room and an open highway half my life ago.

It's cozy here, comforting. I've missed my mom.

For the rest of the morning we go through albums of family photos and relive the stories behind them, with laughter and more than a few sighs. We turn the pages of some of Larry's more notable work, and even find some of my early shots that I'd forgotten about.

I never chose to lose my first mom.

I chose to lose the second.

Right now, though, it feels that I never truly lost her.

Every so often I ask to touch the photos, and Janine brings the pages up, or takes a photo out and hands it to me. I run my fingers over the surface and close my eyes and remember.

The light of all those memories.

Mom and Dad. My family.

Soon, the morning has disappeared, and I'm parked on the step saying goodbye.

"It's been wonderful, Cody," says Janine. "Please come back again."

The goodbye is sweet, like it's a beginning rather than an end.

"I'll come back again sometime soon." I lie.

She waves to me, glowing, excited for something that will never come. She has hope.

I begin to drive away, but then my hand stops. "Mom," I say, "thank you for everything."

※

There's an acoustic guitarist playing. It won't be long until someone calls the cops. Buskers have been banned for nearly a decade along North Michigan Avenue. The guitarist bends and then rises with the notes he's singing.

At the lights I wait with a small crowd for the signal.

"How do you know this is the place?" Joe asks.

"I just do."

On the garden beds near the Best Western there's a man. It's too far to see his face, but I know the posture. As we get closer, Joe leaves me to go ahead alone.

The jacket he's wearing I remember him buying in New York, but now it is ragged and used up. His hair is longer than he ever wore it, and his beard patchy and gray. There are photographs and albums at his feet. He's wearing dirty white sneakers with holes in their toes.

And, lying on the ground with scattered coins in it, an old gray Nike hat.

He's here, the place where he found me selling photographs for change, nearly two decades ago.

Maybe we become our parents, and maybe our parents live long enough to become us again. Maybe people are all the same.

"It's kind of funny, isn't it?" I stop near him. "What a cycle."

With squinted eyes, he looks up from the ground. "Huh?".

"I think I used to make more money selling Polaroids."

His eyes spark with recognition. "Is it really you …?"

"It is."

Larry bursts off the seat and clings to me.

My jaw grips, trying to be that steel cage again.

His pungent stench soaks into my nostrils. A once-proud man, elite photographer – my father – a bum. It's impossible not to well up.

"It's so great you came," he says gruffly in my ear, his head still pressed into my shoulder. "I knew you'd come, Rich. I'm sorry to see you like this, though."

Rich was a photographer who Larry had a business with when he was coming up. He died in a car crash when I was seventeen.

Larry stands and looks deep into my eyes. Whatever he is seeing isn't what's here. He sits back on the garden bed and takes a bottle in a brown paper bag from under the bench.

Seeing him like this … it kills. Every wince of pain I need to live through.

The collections he has at his feet would have once sold for thousands to galleries or private buyers, back when his name meant something. Celebrities, events, landscapes. Work that I could never emulate.

"You sell many photos?"

"Get a few people interested. You know, the ones who see real potential. Missed you last week at the launch, though. I'm going to get people interested in my work, you know."

"You will," I say. "Your stuff is good."

A wave of confusion flows over his face. "Who, who did you say you were again?"

"It's …"

I stop. His mind is gone. What's the point?

Some men in business suits walk past, their shoes shiny enough to be mirrors. One scoffs as he looks down at Larry and his photos. "Bum – a fall collection," he jibes. His two friends snicker.

"There was a time," I try to shout as they walk away, but other than a glance back with a self-assured smirk from one of the suits they ignore me. I turn my head to Larry, who is staring at the sidewalk. "There was a time when you were the most incredible photographer. You were the biggest name in the business and you taught me all that I know."

"You're nice to say that." He points to the camera on my tray table. "You take photos too, do you?"

"Not anymore. Just decoration these days."

For an instant, he looks like the guy I used to call Dad, as he sits up straight and raises his finger. "Photographs are life, kid. Cameras are the portal to them."

This brings a smile to my face that makes me want to cry.

"You know, you're right."

He squints at me, as if he's trying to make out a magic eye. "Something seems real familiar about you."

"We used to work together."

He slaps his knee and laughs. "I worked with so many photographers. Sorry, takes me a moment to recognize everyone at times. Remind me."

"Name's Cody."

Larry nods, but the searching look in his eyes makes it clear that I'm not in whatever memories he is stuck in. "Yeah, yeah. I think I remember. We did the Spring Fashion in NYC one year, right?"

"We did."

"Say, what do you say we go take a couple of shots for old time's sake?"

I stare at the shitty digital camera that's locked in place on my tray table. "I don't …" I pause. My eyes meet his, so full of hope, so naïve and happy for it. "Sure thing. I'm rusty, so you might have to take the lead."

"Don't worry, so am I."

"How about we head to Oak Street Beach?"

"Deal!"

I text Joe.

On the way, we are immersed in conversation about who we are and what we do. He doesn't know me, and I don't know him. Two strangers who were father and son.

When we arrive, Joe is waiting with the platform dolly. He introduces himself to Larry, as I reverse onto the dolly. Joe fixes my chair in place, wheels me onto the sand, and then leaves us.

"So, I was thinking," Larry says as he unclips the camera from my tray, "that maybe we can do some shots from right down on the sand, you know, like with the camera flat, looking up."

"The way a baby would look up at the world on their first trip to the beach," I say.

A look of surprise hits his face. "Yes, exactly. Great minds think alike."

This was the first shoot that I ever did with him. He was teaching me how to create a mood and a story, how to capture light from the viewer's perspective. That was when I started to appreciate the depth of the art. Its power to take you away to somewhere new. Somewhere gone. Somewhere that'll never be. To make you feel.

The child's eye, he called this idea – recreating the feeling of seeing one of the wonders of life for the first time.

The first time is special, but forgotten.

Dreamed about, but realized in a photograph.

Our first shoot together … relived and realized now.

Like he did so many years ago, Larry talks me through every aspect of it, every shot he takes lying prone on the sand in his grubby, tattered clothing, his bourbon bottle in a paper bag beside him, focused and without a lick of care for the sand that'll eat up his crotch.

One thought about rainbows from a mind of nothing but gray, matter, it did not.

It was a caption Larry wrote for a photograph. One of the few that stuck with me.

Larry shuffles to his feet and brings the camera to me, flicking through the photos he's just taken. "You like?"

For every poorly framed, out-of-focus shot he shows nothing but wonder. When we first shot this, the photos were beautiful, balanced, framed perfectly. But these, right here in this moment, make me feel the wonder that they are meant to. It warms my heart and breaks it.

"You haven't lost your touch." He has, though, yet he's taken some of the best photos of his life. "These are brilliant."

He stands tall, smiling with pride, and then he leans over and fixes the camera back onto my tray table. "Your turn. Show me what you've got."

I stare at the camera. I'm nervous. "It's been a long time."

"Like riding a bicycle," Larry says, waving it off. "Come on, kid."

My eyes find his and it looks as if he's truly here, now. Kid, the word echoes in my head, reverberating with a cascade of memories.

On the screen of the camera there's an unbalanced scene with poor juxtaposition. I tilt and rotate the camera up and down, side to side as I try to find a picture in the lens that I want to snap.

Nothing. I can't beat the shots Larry got … never could.

"Hey, Larry, can you do me a favor, for the photo?"

"Sure thing."

"Just sit down and look out to the ocean. Look out and see everything you want to see."

While Larry sits on the sand, I play with the aperture, ISO and zoom. I'm not riding a bicycle, but as I press my finger halfway down to focus, and then all the way down to capture, I'm photographing again.

An old, lost man, who so many people loved, sitting on the sand in bare feet, staring out to the water. An old, lost soul, who doesn't know he is anything – a son, a husband, a friend, a father, a hero.

It's there on the screen. My new first photograph.

As I continue to marvel at it, I breathe in the beach air and forget there's a city behind me, that there's anyone else around except me and this old man.

He stands and walks to the water to dip his feet in. I snap that too. And I don't stop, my finger like a pulse.

This old man, once strong and noble, now wrapped up in a ragged jacket, the vestige of his former self, staring out on the fading horizon from his withered, bearded face. Seeing everything he wants to see. Everything that he can see.

I hope he is seeing all of the beautiful things that once filled his life. I hope he is feeling them.

✢

The afternoon fades, night-time cold permeating the air. We sit on the beach, me in the chair, Larry with his arms wrapped around his legs, and we stare out to the water. Michigan can't take this from us. It's endless, I know, as much as I know it can't be.

"This was great," I say. "Like old times."

Larry chuckles. "Sure was." He pauses and I look down at him. "Who ... what was your name again?"

"Cody."

"Had a son called Cody. Not my birth kid, but my kid through life, you know ... I, I, I can't really remember him being older than ... I don't know what happened to him." Confusion, fear and panic beset him. His eyes are looking around, trying to find the memories. "I'm sorry ... I just don't know."

"It's okay, Larry."

He starts to fidget and gibber. "Like, I always keep forgetting to fix up the handrail for the back stairs at the holiday house. Janine tells me, but it just goes straight out."

There's my heart, palpitating furiously. It's as if the gentle ebb of the water rises high and crashes down on me when the thought comes to mind. I realize that every lens I've looked through in the last few years was the wrong one. I never knew. Janine never knew. Isobel never knew. His mind has been going for so long. The occasional wrong name, the wrong number of candles on a birthday cake ... The handrail.

"You don't need to worry about that stuff now."

"I just wish I could ..." He drops his head into his knees and sobs. "I just don't know where everybody is now."

Six months ago, I was an implacable, small shell of a man. I feel tall right now, out of my chair and with a straight back. "Wherever they are, Larry, I'm sure they love you and want the best for you."

He smiles at me dreamily, as if he's seeing a picture of his future so full of color and wonder that my words are a painting.

"Most of all," I pause and allow the fusillade of thoughts and feelings to flow through me, "I'm sure that your son is thankful for everything you did for him. You're still his father. And he still loves you."

Chapter 39

(NOW)

A party hat and a sash.

Thirty-three today.

If I'd known that this was likely to be my last birthday maybe I'd have drunk more, danced more and reveled more in being the center of attention on this day previously.

"Blow out the candles," Sophie encourages me.

I manage two out of thirty-three.

There's not meant to be alcohol in the home, but Joe and Caren are on tonight, so there is, and in good supply. Most of the residents are gathered around.

Viktor puts down his glass of vodka and brings the cake under my nose. I try again and manage another five. Three breaths later and I get it, resisting the offers for help.

"Now make a wish," Sophie says. "And if Viktor touches the bottom when he cuts the cake, you have to kiss the closest girl."

The youngest woman here is Caren and she's in her forties. Other than that, I could pucker up for Fay Washington.

"What you wish for?" Viktor asks.

Sophie slaps his wrist. "He can't tell you, Viktor. It won't come true."

As Viktor cuts through the chocolate mud, I think for a second that I see a blonde wave of hair out of the corner of my eye. I dart my eyes around and hope to see her, moving closer – close enough to be the closest girl.

The room reverts to reality. The television is playing something from the Space Age, I'm surrounded by old people, and there's no Isobel anywhere.

"Uh oh," Joe says. "Looks like Viktor hit the bottom."

The wooing and whistles make me laugh. Sophie is closest, so she bends down and plants her cherry red lips smack bang on my cheek.

Caren slices the cake and portions it out for the residents. They disperse and form small circles as though this were just any other party they've been to, and the people some they haven't caught up with for a while.

Joe sits and feeds me. "Thirty-three years young, big fella."

"That's it," I reply, swallowing cake. "Needs to be. I can't grow older now."

We sit here and talk, about nothing really, though it feels like a deep and meaningful, while the other residents continue to mingle.

After some time, Sophie calls them in.

Then come the games: Mr Wolf, pass-the-parcel (which I'm terrible at) and musical chairs (which I'm exceptionally good at).

I'm grinning while Viktor tells an old story about life in Russia when I see something out of the corner of my eye – again. I glance to the blonde bob, but this time it doesn't fade with the movement of my head.

Isobel is standing across the room, gleaming at the party, and at me. In her hand is a brown paper bag and a wrapped box.

I sneak away and meet her halfway. "You've become the queen of surprises."

"Wasn't I always your queen?"

"Always."

The gold wrapping on the present is something Isobel always used to do. Gold is my least favorite color. Isobel is being her usual smart-ass self.

"I see you haven't forgotten how much I love gold."

She grins cheekily.

We remain here for a moment, closer to the young lovers we were than the distant couple we became. That's gone. We're just who we are. All of it.

"I came to celebrate your birthday, but it looks like you've got that sorted."

"Wouldn't be much of a celebration without you."

We blend into the outskirts of the party.

Isobel places the present on my lap, before unwrapping the wrapping she'd just wrapped. "Hope you like it."

It's a photo album. Isobel opens it. To my surprise, there are photos in it. "I tried my best to create a story with the album, like you used to. I don't think I did quite as good a job as you, but still …"

One by one she turns the pages: it starts with a couple of old, faded Polaroids of us as teenagers. Then there's a shot or two of places we'd go, which she's taken recently. It flows in chronological order of our life together: the trips to Europe, South America, India and all throughout the States.

Then she flips over a page; a photo of us in our apartment in Chicago appears.

I gulp, thinking of what happened in that apartment, and look up to Isobel, who is not perturbed at all. The picture to the right of this one is from the beach house in San Diego, the day before she fell. We're standing on the back porch, a deep orange sunset in the background, Isobel's stomach bulging with our baby girl.

She's included everything she could in this.

Everything.

On the last page there's one photograph, one I've never seen before.

It's North Pond: me in the chair, Isobel crouching beside me.

Everything about us.

What did she feel when she put this together?

"You put a lot into this," I say.

Isobel's countenance is pleasant and peaceful. "It's all part of your life, even the bad stuff. You used to try to forget everything, Cody, but you've learned that you can't. It's all part of the journey, and who you've become."

"That, I'm still figuring out."

Isobel laughs. "Aren't we always?"

She taps the camera. "Maybe it's time you used this thing."

"Maybe if you tried to turn it on, you'd see the battery is flat."

Her hand rests on my left. "You used it?"

"I did."

"You have no idea how great that is to hear."

"I'm glad. Thank you, Isobel."

"It's your birthday, you deserve presents."

"Not just for them … I went to see Janine and Larry."

"Oh …"

"Thank you for keeping in touch with them."

"You saw Larry?"

"He was who I took the photos with."

"It's hard, isn't it?" Her hand finds its way onto mine again. "I've tried, Cody. I've found him different homes, paid for his accommodation, but he never stays there – he just leaves to sit on the street. I still take him food most days after work." She pauses. "I'm sorry I've never told you. You made me promise, but I couldn't leave them. They've suffered too."

"I know." I drop my eyes to my lap, where crumbs have gathered around my crotch. "You don't have to apologize; I do."

"Maybe we both do."

I turn my hand so it is holding hers. "Maybe neither of us do anymore. Maybe we just have to try to be all that we can be."

"That's exactly what I'm trying to do, Cody."

"So am I."

Her thumb massages my palm. "It makes me happy to hear that."

I grip as much as I can. "It makes me happy that you're here."

"We're getting so serious." Isobel holds up the brown paper bag and slides out a bottle of Johnny Red. "Let's have a drink. Got your favorite."

"That's a great idea." I drive back toward the party with Isobel by my side.

"I'd love to see those photos you took some time, too." She fills the glasses. "Curious to see if you've still got it."

"You know I do." The bourbon warms my throat. "Like riding a bike."

The party, funnily enough, actually resembles something like a party as the night progresses.

A nursing home full of people over sixty, celebrating the thirty-third birthday of the youngest resident, who's a quadriplegic, where by nine o'clock at night everybody has disregarded the possible bowel consequences of consuming large amounts of alcohol.

Yep. Everyone is drunk – even Joe and Caren are tipsy.

Yep. I'm drunk, too – and so is Isobel.

Just when I thought the dancefloor was never going to start … I thought after last time, that ludicrous incident where I three-sixtied my way onto *Dancing With The Stars*, that it could never happen again … I'm cutting the rug with the oldies like there's no tomorrow (which there sort of isn't). My joystick has never had a workout like this: back, back and forth, rotate side to side, and spin. I'm killing it – a better dancer in the chair than I ever was on two legs.

Life's a rollercoaster. Enjoy the ride or … feel like vomiting.

Shit. I'm really drunk.

Take a breather. Gasp between laughs.

Isobel wipes sweat off her brow. "I didn't realize you could dance …"

"Moonwalking's never been so easy."

I'm seventeen again. Should wait longer between drinks. Should … don't.

It's just going down so well. Johnny Red just flows like a waterfall.

Isobel puts down my cup.

We're back on the dancefloor.

We're dancing …

God, she looks good. It's a decade ago on a dancefloor. In Berlin.

At Berghain. Drunk, and high among the clouds. The lights flashing fluorescent beams of color like swords across our faces. She's so damn stunning. The molly had me too damn horny. But knowing it was her I was looking at … Knowing her was the biggest turn-on ever. Her dress was white and figure-hugging tight, and when the light found it, every shade of color in a sexy Skittles rainbow. That white dress could do anything. She could do anything; in it, getting out of it, being her.

Grinding. Pushing. Pulsing. Teasing and foreplay on that dancefloor. My hand up her leg until it found her bare pussy, already wet. Her eyes fucking mine.

And she said to me, "Let's go."

The lights aren't pulsing, the music's not blasting. No spray-on dress. I'm not grinding, or playing with her. We're a decade older.

But we're dancing again.

And I'm more enthralled with her than ever.

Isobel, in only a tank top and skinny jeans. Me, bourbon seeping from my pores.

She looks at me and says, "Let's go."

What's ten years between dances?

Isobel leads me from the party, everyone else too drunk to notice.

"Isobel …" We enter the hallway. "What …"

Her forefinger presses on my lips. She's in control. I love it.

We're in my room.

The room is a bad gif, going from right to left over again.

I'm floating and chuckling drunkenly, my weight being lifted.

Isobel is giggling, too, and trying to get me into the hoists.

Smack, the floor. Ouch. My face.

"Come on, Cody. Help me."

I laugh. "I can't; I'm too drunk."

I'm caught in a wave at the beach, my body rolling with the barrel in freefall.

Smack. I face plant on the bed. "Good one, Froot Loop."

Isobel rolls me over onto my back. The room is still looping, from left to right, left to right. Isobel is on top of me. Her legs are either side of my body. The only sensation I can feel apart from my burning eyes, cloudy mind and dry mouth is the tingling in my pants.

Isobel starts grinding on me.

Her hands clutch my shoulders, and she closes her eyes.

"Isobel …" it sounds as if someone else is saying it. "What are we doing?"

Her breaths are heavy. "Shut up, Cody." Her face squashes, her muscles tensing in every which way, as she moves up and down on my cock.

Those heavy breaths become punctuated by soft moans. Isobel drops on top of me, her hands wrap around my back, and she whispers in my ear, "Cody, I'm coming."

Then she lies down, resting her head on my chest.

There's a ringing in my ear. I can barely hear the music from out in the recreation room. "Isobel, what just happened?"

"You're a grown man, Cody, figure it out."

So I do. A weak left forearm, but it manages to make it to her. Rubbing her crotch on top of her jeans. She rolls under my hand, pushing it down harder.

A click, a zipper, unzipping. In the moonlight the shine off her panties. White lace. We're virgins again. Old, used-up virgins.

She rolls over and plants her lips on mine. It's like water to me, this kiss. Drunk, sloppy, but like water in a desert. Everything inside it makes me want to cry.

A dull sensation. My pants are off, too. Isobel's hand is wrapped around my dick. Stroking it up and down. She takes my left and guides it down her knickers. She's so smooth, and soft, wet and warm.

We speak through breaths.

Isobel straddles me.

There is nothing in my mind right now except the warmth I can feel as I enter her. The warmth inside me, my heart, where I feel her most.

She lies down and moves back and forth, pressing her pubic bone into me. Then she sits up, and takes off her tank top, and unclips her bra.

At thirty-two, her breasts look better than ever. Her fingers wrap around my wrist, she moves my hand up and onto her breast. I fondle it softly, rub her nipple – I remember. She likes that a lot. Circles and circles. Pinch just a little.

There's liquor on my tongue, a mix of mine and hers. Our saliva rolling around, together.

This is the second time I've lost my virginity.

"Cody," she moans, "I'm going to come again."

She contracts around me, and I feel myself throb back against her. Everything is blurry for a moment. It's been years since I had an orgasm outside of my sleep.

This exhilaration, this relief, is unparalleled.

Isobel collapses onto the bed next to me. We lie for a time. Breathing, fogged by the moonlight. Quiet rumbles from the party come through under the door. The room is spinning a little. My mind's so still, though.

Isobel rolls over, her head on my chest. "It's been so long since I've felt lust like that."

"But … what about Jake?"

"He's not you, Cody."

"What are you saying, Isobel?"

"It was insane what you tried to do … trying to kill him … but in my fucked-up mind, it was kind of romantic. It showed me how badly you want to be with me. Plus, it was kind of, sexy, too." In the shine of her eyes I can see how drunk and honest she is. "Maybe we can love more than one person … But I think there's only ever one person we'll love like they're the only person in the world."

"I want to be with you, Isobel. More than anything. And as much as I regret what I tried to do because it put me in here away from you, I'd try again in a heartbeat. I would kill for you. To be us again. Just you and me. Together."

Saliva clacks in her mouth. "What do you think we're doing?"

The smell of bourbon. Her lips on mine. A slow, passionate kiss. Leave me here, forever, I wish.

She leans her head back down on my chest. Her fingernails run over my skin. I see it, but my mind is strong enough right now that I will my nerves to feel it.

My memory makes it real.

This moment makes it real.

No longer do I lie somewhere far away from her.

I lie with her.

Chapter 40

(NOW)

There's a fist punching the inside of my left temple, I've got cottonmouth, and my stomach is a tumble dryer. Yet, I'm warm, happy.

I'm hungover and I'm grateful. There truly is a first for everything.

Outside on the sidewalk, a brown paper bag is dancing along the concrete. I wonder where the night time has gone that was punctuated by the bottle it held. Where that bottle is, where the time has gone? Who drank it away?

Does the sunshine feel as promising on their cheek as it does on mine?

The whisper of warmth on my skin.

"Oh my god." Isobel returns from the bathroom and slumps down on the chair across the table from me. "I haven't been this hungover ever."

She buries her head into her arms, which are folded on the table top.

"You were quite drunk last night."

"So were you." Her voice is muffled.

A waitress comes to take our order.

"Coffee, please," Isobel says, sitting up. "Strong and black. No food."

"I'll have a lemon and sugar crepe, thanks. Strong coffee, too."

The waitress nods and takes our menus, returning moments later with the coffee.

Isobel sluggishly moves her chair around to the side of the table and takes my coffee cup. "Shit, we need a straw, don't we?"

"Nah. Gave them up a while ago."

"Well look at you." Joy covers her face. Her makeup is clumped, her eyeliner tar on a summer's day, her hair messed, but she looks so damn beautiful.

I take a sip of the coffee as she brings it to my mouth. "Look at you … You look terrible."

Isobel smirks. "You're one to talk. You could put groceries in the bags under your eyes."

"Coffee will fix that."

I sip at it for a bit. It's terrible, but still, it's coffee.

After a while Isobel puts down the cup and takes a long, desperate gulp of hers. "What a night …"

The words dangle out in the air for a time. Just off her tongue, waiting for me to finish the thought.

"Did you mean what you said?"

She takes another gulp of her coffee. "I was drunk, Cody … But, yeah, I meant it."

"So what happens now?"

My crepe arrives as Isobel looks onto the table, as if the words are scrawled onto the woodgrain.

Her hand rests on mine. "Remember years ago, when we were sitting near the Holika bonfire? Remember what I asked you?"

"Where do you see yourself in five years?"

"Remember how you answered?"

"Yeah. And I remember how you argued."

"Well … maybe now I think that you were right. Maybe we have no idea about the future, and maybe it doesn't matter."

I get through half of my crepe before I'm full. We pay and leave.

Outside, the late fall day is fresh but clear. Between gusts of cool breeze, sunshine touches my cheek.

On the way back to the home, Isobel picks at flowers. My wheels roll through puddles as I try to hit them with a burst of speed to splash Isobel, just so maybe she'll have to come inside and dry off. The chair doesn't quite have the power.

"So what are we going to do now?" I ask, hopefully, as we arrive at the front gates. "Maybe we should take a trip somewhere?"

"Croatian Islands?" she replies.

"Northern lights?" I say.

"Even just Myrtle Beach – we never got there."

I laugh. "That ever-elusive Florida coast."

"Lots of places to go."

There's a crazy impetuousness running through me. I'm serious. "So, why don't we just go? Like old times."

Isobel tosses petals to the ground one by one. "One day, babe."

"Well, what do you want to do?"

Isobel looks at her phone. "I've gotta head home. I'll see you soon."

The disappointment of a goodbye is usurped by the feeling of her hands on my cheeks, the sensation of her lips on mine.

She offers me one more smile and then goes over to her car and gets in.

From over the steering wheel she waves at me.

The car disappears down the road.

I look around, to the gravel driveway, the lush green grass, the trees clinging to their last leaves. I breathe in fresh air. Everything is quiet, still, out here by myself.

My mind is blank.

Unsure, unknowing.

Then I push my joystick and drive toward the front door.

Joe comes out and opens the door for me.

Time passes by the window – long, long minutes that become hours, my mind still unsure of what thoughts it should think.

White light of late afternoon in the sky outside, sunlight from behind clouds, infinite blankness.

Blankness, not nothing, but rather opportunity for anything.

Here I am, in love with the woman I've always loved. More awake to our love than ever. She told me, she showed me, that she still feels for me, too. That our passion was and always will be stronger than any other. That he's not me. Yet, I'm here, alone, and she's with him.

"I'm calling in that favor you owe me." I park in front of Joe, who's playing chess with Fay Washington.

He moves his pawn and takes her knight. "Really? Now? I'm in the middle of a game."

"Really. It's important."

"It's six o'clock." He points up to the wall clock. "Time for day trips has finished."

I ram the table, which shocks Fay. "That's why it's a favor not just part of your job."

Joe resets the fallen chess pieces, and then holds Fay's hands. "I've gotta head off for a bit, Fay. We'll finish our game later."

She nods, and then resumes playing by herself.

Joe opens the front door. "Has anyone told you how much of a jerk you've become?"

"Yeah, I've been told," I reply, and drive to the van. "Now hurry up. I need to go home."

⁂

Why is my chair so damn slow?!

It whirs up the front path, and then the ramp.

There's no plan for this. I just need to be there, with her, and I need to know if she wants to be with me, too.

Joe whips his keys out of his pocket, and finds the front door key. He holds it up. "Good luck, mate." He unlocks the door.

I drive in …

My finger drops from the joystick and I halt to a stop.

Jake and Isobel stop, too, frozen in poses.

Jake is down on his knee, holding her hand. A ring waiting to be put on her finger.

"Isobel, don't." I drive toward where they stand flabbergasted. "You can't."

Jake stands and towers over me. "She can."

"We're still married, idiot, and she still loves me. And I love her."

"She doesn't love you, she's in love with me. We're here, we're in love. You're gone. What are you forgetting, Cody, seriously?!"

He turns to her. "Isobel, I want this. I want to spend my life with you. I know we'll have to wait until you get a divorce …"

"Divorce?!" I cry. "Who in the hell said anything about a divorce?"

"You'll have to," Jake says. "So we can get married. Look, Cody, you need to accept this. Isobel has made her choice and she chose me. You have to move on."

"If she chose you, then why has she been sneaking out at night to see me?"

He turns to her, anxiously. "Is that true?"

Isobel stares him straight in the eyes. "It is."

Jake pauses for a second, and then shakes himself off. "I don't care… that doesn't matter now. Maybe you missed him … maybe it was hard without someone you've known for so long around. But I care about the future, and I care about a future with you."

"She said she still loves me."

My words hit him like a punch in the guts.

His lip trembles. "Isobel, Bel?"

"And we kissed," I intervene before she can answer. "We made love. In a way that you'll never make love."

"Shut up." Jake grits his teeth, becoming overwrought. "That's not true. What we have is amazing."

"It's nothing compared to what Isobel and I have."

In a chair, half his height, I feel dominant.

"We're going to be engaged, and we'll be planning a wedding …"

"Over my dead body!"

"And one day, we'll have a family …"

"You two need to shut up and stop fighting," Isobel says sternly.

"Isobel." Jake reaches for her hand. "Please …"

She pulls back. "Stop."

"Isobel," I say, steering toward her. "You need to tell him, you need to …"

"Shut up! Both of you, for goodness sake. Just shut up and stop telling me what I need to do, or what I want."

Jake and I freeze, like stunned mullets.

Isobel sits on the couch, her hands pinned between her thighs.

I turn in front of her.

Jake sits beside her on the couch. "You need to make a decision, Isobel, please."

"What did I just say?" She glowers at him. "I don't want you telling me what I need to do."

"This isn't fair." He sulks, meager and childish. "I've put so much into this … my heart, every bit of love and energy I had."

"And you still weren't enough," I say.

He glares at me. "Oh shut the fuck up, Cody."

"Isobel …" I drive a little bit closer, but she raises her hand.

Jake smirks at me.

"Cody's right, Jake," she says.

His smirk turns to dismay.

"I still have feelings for him."

Now I smirk.

"But, it's not that simple, Cody."

My smirk vanishes.

"You pushed me away, and so I went and found someone I connected with. How am I meant to just drop it because it's convenient for you now to love me?"

"It's not convenient," I choke the words out, "it's how I feel."

Isobel sits quietly, thinking for a long while. Jake and I wait in silence. He looks as nervous as I feel.

Taking a deep breath, Isobel stands. "You want me to make a decision, I get that … This whole thing has gotten out of control. Maybe I shouldn't have done to you both what I've done, but maybe I just did what I felt – I couldn't decide between you." She stops and shakes her head. "I've spent so long thinking about other people. Who's right for me? What can I do for them? How can we be happy? I've never stopped to think about myself, and what I can do for myself, how I can be the happiest I can. It's become a strain, and neither of you deserves to be left in limbo. In a perfect world, based on how I feel, maybe I'd choose both of you.

"This isn't a perfect world, though, and I can't do that."

She stares at Jake, and then at me.

"I can't choose either of you. I have to choose myself."

Chapter 41

(NOW)

Stones crunch under my tire.

"You look fresh," I say, stopping in front of Isobel.

She's leaning on her car, parked in the lot of the home.

"Thanks for not ignoring me." She scuffs her feet. "I know this might be hard."

"I ignored you for too long, Isobel. It's a mistake I'll never make again."

"I'm checking into a facility upstate. They have a place for me."

"I'm happy for you." Although they're true, it's difficult to say those words without adding how much I feel I need her right now. What else do I have if she's gone?

"I'll have no access to the outside for a while. I won't be using my phone, email or social media. I need a complete break to get myself sorted and start fresh."

"Have you said goodbye to Jake?"

She nods.

"How did he take it?"

"It upset him."

"He's a big boy, he'll get over it."

I don't believe it myself. If he feels half of what I feel for her, he won't. Isobel made me believe that someone could be my soulmate. I've never once believed in having a plural of that. There's no getting over your soulmate.

She takes my phone from the tray. "I'm putting in a post office box that you can send things to if you need to reach me."

The fear I'm feeling inside must be seeping from my eyes, because Isobel reaches forward and tries to catch it for me. "This isn't a forever thing, Cody."

What she doesn't realize is that it might be a forever thing. I'm a grenade with a faulty pin.

There's no way I can tell her now. I love her too much to ever hold her back again.

"I know," I say, white lies flowing from my mouth as tears begin to form in my eyes. "Just didn't see it coming."

A year ago, I wouldn't have thought I could ever cry in front of Isobel, again. Yet here I am, trying to contain my tears. I'm happy for it.

A cold gust of wind whistles through the lot. "There's still so much for you in this world, Cody. You've gotta understand that."

My tears subside.

The clouds part momentarily, early winter sun glazing my forehead. "I know. You helped me remember that."

Remembering her, and letting go of the guilt, pain and regret was the hardest thing I've ever had to do. And now I need to let go of her.

"There's a big wide world out there." Isobel gazes around the grounds of the home, stopping at the trees, her eyes off somewhere between their vacant branches.

"We got through a lot of it," I say. "But not all of it."

Isobel smiles pleasantly. "Still haven't gotten to Myrtle Beach."

"Maybe you can after you check out."

"You never know, hey."

"That's the future, isn't it?"

Isobel laughs. "It certainly is."

All that life to be lived, it's somewhere in front of her eyes. Out in the sky, where somewhere in the world the sun is shining.

She might go there – she could go anywhere … Anywhere, except back here. I know Isobel, and this isn't just a temporary thing. This is a fresh start.

For me, it's a watershed moment.

Letting go is such a hard thing.

But now, gazing upon my beautiful wife, a woman who once had wings that could fly so high, who's had to keep them clipped for so long, I see a woman who's got the courage to find a way to fix those wings. She wants to fly again, and I want that for her.

I want the best for her. For her to feel happy … to feel at peace for once in her life.

I need to let her go.

"I imagine so many great things yet to come," I say, though I'm clueless as to whether they'll come.

A squawk comes from the distance. A flock of ducks crosses the sky. They're leaving. Flying south for the winter. To a place where the sun is shining.

Isobel kneels in front of me. "You don't have to imagine." She leans in and takes my head in her hands, and kisses my forehead. "You just need to live."

She stands, and then walks to her car.

The clouds close in and light snowflakes begin to fall. The footage of Isobel walking away plays over in my mind.

"Goodbye Cody," she says, standing with one leg in the car.

"Goodbye, Isobel," I reply.

We share a look for a moment longer – reflective smiles.

And then then she gets in and closes the door.

The engine starts. For a second I think I see her eyes in the rear-view mirror, our eyes meeting again, saying the words that didn't get said.

"I love you, Isobel," I say aloud, and with every bit of feeling in my heart, which I hope manifests in my eyes.

I hope she can feel it, even if she deserves more.

The car turns, and her eyes and the mirror disappear.

I'm stuck there in that vision. In her rear-view mirror.

But who knows what the future holds, right? It's always been said that a leopard can't change its spots. But we're human, and we're infinitely complex, and in all our stupidity and genius, maybe some of us can change.

I've changed more times than I count.

I'll never walk again, but deep down inside me I want to believe that I can find the wings to fly free. Fly by myself. And with her.

Maybe there's more for me, still.

Maybe I can change again.

A hand plants on my shoulder.

"There's someone here to see you, mate."

Joe leaves and a chair slides up beside me.

"You're the last person I expected to see," I say to Jake, who's assumed my pose of staring blankly out the window.

"Yeah, this is the last place I thought I'd be today. I was packing up my stuff from the house and I noticed this photograph." He places the photo on my tray table. The one that's been stuck there near the refrigerator for years. Isobel and me at North Pond, and a bump we called Holi. The shot taken on self-timer. My favorite photograph.

"Thank you … I didn't expect this."

"Figured you'd want it. Looks special. You and Isobel when she was pregnant. Must have been an exciting time for you two."

"It was." My eyes drift back out to the trees. "She'll be well upstate by now. Far away from here. Far away from us."

"Did she come and see you before she left?"

"She did. How was it for you?"

"Was hard," he replies dolefully.

My jaw firms, thinking about the possibility of a future without Isobel. Then it releases, picturing her becoming all she can be. "She was just too good for us, wasn't she?"

Jake laughs. "She was. It was so stupid thinking we could win her from one another."

"I don't think a woman can be won. You have to earn the opportunity to have her in your life."

"She wasn't just any woman, though."

I shake my head. "Not by a long shot."

"Hey." He turns to me. "I'm sorry for getting you put here. It was all my idea. I pressured Isobel."

Though the clouds are heavy, thick, seemingly impenetrable, they part again for just a moment, flashing a patch of clear blue. "It's fine. I'm sorry for trying to kill you."

We both chuckle.

"You're not such a bad guy, Cody."

"Neither are you, Jake. I hated you for it, but I understand all too well why you fell in love with Isobel."

"Yeah, and I get why you never stopped trying." He sighs. "You haven't heard from her, have you?"

"No. And I don't think I will."

"I thought as much."

He slaps his hands on his knees, and then stands. "Well, I best be off."

"Hey, Jake. Thanks for bringing the photo."

He nods. "All the best, Cody."

With his hands stuffed in his pockets and head low, he walks away, out the front door, and he's gone.

He'll be gone from the house soon. I'll never go back there, nor will Isobel.

It's so quiet here.

There's nothing to do.

Just sit, and stare out the window.

"What's life, Codes?" Joe plonks in the chair beside me.

We pass some time, lost together outside the window.

"Viktor's settled down," he says. "New meds seem to be working."

"That's good to hear."

"Yeah, makes it pretty boring around here, though."

Another flock of ducks crosses the white of the clouds.

They're all heading south, to the warmth.

Ducks, the stupid animals that are full of hope. Just chasing the sunshine. Flying free, and chasing the sun.

"What the hell are we doing here?" I watch the last of them disappear out of sight. "We're not living."

"We're not," Joe agrees.

"So, what the hell is keeping us here?"

He takes a moment to think. "Nothing."

"It's ridiculous. Sitting around here, dying. Thinking about what we've lost. What is there for us to gain?"

Joe looks around the room. "Nothing in here."

"So why don't we go?"

Our eyes meet, the reality of this watershed moment burgeoning.

He stands. "Let's do it. Right now. No packing. Just go."

With Joe walking by my side, I drive from the window, toward the door.

Philomena comes from her office. "Are you two off for the afternoon?"

Joe chuckles. "Yeah, and for the rest of our lives."

He opens the door and I drive out into the front courtyard. Viktor is sitting by himself, rolling the stem of a flower through his fingers.

"Vik," I say as we near him. "We're leaving. You want to come?"

He glances up at me.

"This is your chance to leave," I continue, "be free like you've wanted for so long."

He stands. It's his time, too.

From the side of the building, Sophie appears with a basket full of flowers. "I found some more," she calls. "See, there are still plenty of flowers around."

Viktor turns his head to her, and then back to us. "I am already free."

He walks away, and as he meets Sophie she drops the basket, and he takes her in his arms. She reaches up and brings his head down. Their lips connect. They hold each other close, beaming peacefully. It's the most beautiful display of affection I've ever seen.

Joe slaps his hand on my shoulder. "It's never too late, hey mate."

I find myself smiling uncontrollably, so much so that my cheeks begin to hurt. "It's not."

Joe unlocks the van and I drive toward it.

Instead of stopping at the back, ready to be raised into it like a horse in a float, I go to the passenger side. "It's about time I rode up front."

Joe unbuckles me and lifts me into the seat.

He loads my chair into the back and then climbs into the driver's seat.

"We're really doing this, aren't we?" he asks, grinning with contained excitement.

"We're living," I reply.

The van starts up, stones crunch and we drive out of the parking lot of the home.

I watch it retreat in the side mirror. The gardens, the drapes, the rooms inside. My room. All the things that went on there. In the front garden, two white-haired lovers, rediscovering something they might have given up hope of ever finding again.

We drive along the motorway, out of the city and suburbs.

Into the dusk and the fading sunlight.

Chasing the sunshine.

Somewhere in the world, Isobel is breathing. She is living. I hope she is happy, feeling the sunshine wherever she is. Wherever she goes … she will always be right here inside my heart.

The window is down, a cool breeze blowing through my hair.

I glance beside me to the small, hobbit-like Australian man. Joe. The man who gave me so much advice when I wouldn't hear it, who lived and learned with me, who came to know me and help me rediscover who I was. I see his triumphs, his wisdom, his heartache, his pain, and his new beginnings. Most of all, though, I see my friend. The best friend I've ever had.

I'd never have known him if I'd never fallen from that roof.

"What's life?" he asked.

Stars shine lightly in the clear country sky.

At thirty-three, barely able to move from the neck down, barely able to physically feel, with so many memories behind me – of happiness, sadness, connection and loneliness – I'm here, with rekindled hope.

The stars shine brightly all around. A whole world, a universe of possibilities lie in front of me.

Tomorrow, I'm excited for it.

Today, I'm alive.

Life, it's a funny thing.

This Picture of Us

Joe parks the van. "So this is the spot?"

"It's even better," I wheeze. "It's better … when you get out there."

My breathing has shallowed since we left Florida four days ago.

The feeling of water in my chest is rising progressively.

It's happening.

Six months of adventure and freedom, chasing the sunshine throughout America and Mexico.

Six months and now it's here …

Every day, almost every moment, I've thought about Isobel. I've wondered how the adventure might have been with her there as well. I've wondered how she is doing, what she is doing, and what she is thinking.

Some weeks ago, I sat on the sand of Myrtle Beach, bathed by Florida sun. This was one place Isobel always wanted to come, and one we never got to. There with sand in between my toes, which I could see and remember enough to almost feel, I felt her there with me. As the water ebbed and flowed into the shore, I dictated to Joe a short letter, some sentiments full of hope. He sent it and I've wondered for the journey since whether she's received it, and whether she'll come.

I can only find out now.

I can only hope.

Clinging to whatever time there is left.

I'm out of the seat, and in my chair. Joe does the buckles up. "I really think I should take you to the hospital, mate …"

I cough. "What'll they do?"

"Just … make it easier."

"I don't want easy … I want it my way."

Solemnly, he nods. He knows this is how it must be. There's not another place to go. Not another sky to find. No more sun to chase.

No more ducks to see.

We start toward the archway of trees, my wheels crunching on leaves and breaking twigs.

Through the trees, we emerge into the field. The morning sun is a spark through the fresh, cool breeze. The grass floor looks softer than plush carpet. It opens as I steer through it, approaching the oak tree.

I park in the shade, beside a large root that sticks up like a wave suspended in motion. The same root I used to sit back against. Joe places my bag down beside the tree, unbuckles my seatbelt and lifts me from the chair, squatting to put me down between the root and the tree trunk.

He kneels in front of me. "Comfy?"

I nod.

"I'm going to stay until she gets here." He places my cell phone on my leg, under my left hand. "I'll be at the van if you need anything."

Now I shake my head. "Go, please. I want you to."

"Mate … what if she doesn't come?"

"She will."

"But," he grabs hold of my left hand, "I don't want you to be alone."

"I won't be." I grip his hand as best I can. "I'll never be alone again." Joe gives a sad smile. "My camera … can I have it, too?"

He removes the tray from the chair and sets it up on my lap. "This'll be better."

"What's …" I gasp in air, momentarily blocked. "What's next for you?"

There's a look of quiet contentment in his eyes as he looks around the field. "There's a big wide world out there, mate. Lots I never got to do with Rebecca."

Smiling, I'm reminded of my travels. "I know the feeling."

"There's a big old island home that I haven't seen in far too long. Dirt that hasn't touched my feet in too long. A sun like fire in the sky that my skin is yearning for. Animals I haven't seen … people, too."

He takes out the tiny urn of Rebecca's ashes from his pocket, and a picture of him and her at North Pond. "Think it's about time you saw where I came from, love." He looks at me, grinning. "I'm still a weirdo who talks to his dead wife."

"And ... I'm still a cripple who ... who thinks he can ..."

"A cripple who's shown me that he still can," Joe says before I can finish.

He leans in and takes my hand in his, shaking it. "Good luck, my friend."

"You too, mate."

This makes him laugh. "Never get sick of hearing a yank trying to say mate."

"Hey Joe ..." Goodbyes never get easier. This one's the hardest yet. "Thanks for everything ... for helping me live again."

"No, thank *you*, mate." Joe smiles peacefully. "You might not have realized it, but you helped me live again, too."

The only sound is that of air, the breeze through the field, through the branches and leaves.

And my breathing.

I lose myself in the tranquility of the field.

Shallower still. Water gathering like a plugged sink with a dripping tap.

Life, that funny thing. Without all the pain and loss, without the heartache, I'd have never had this friend.

Wishes, they can always exist. I've always missed what I could have had. But now ... what overwhelms me is gratitude.

Had, don't have – they don't matter.

Have is all that matters.

And Joe is a friend I have. My best friend.

Our eyes connect. There's excitement and anticipation in his deep brown buttons. I hope he can see the gleam in mine, too. We share this moment, an exchange between our hearts and minds. An understanding that only true friends can have.

His leather skin is wizened, but not yet too much for a little more sun to hit it. I can imagine the land he's soon to see again. The open expanses, the blue mountains. Sunrises that tell of a burning day ahead. The freshness of the air. The sound of birds, laughing and singing. Pastel dawns. Clear night skies, full of stars. The feeling of freedom.

I can feel it, too.

Joe leans in and hugs me. I bury my head into his shoulder and we stay like this for a precious moment that will never be long enough.

He stands, surveys the field for a moment and then looks down at me with a wry smile. "Ducks are just stupid, ya know."

And with that, he nods his head, tipping an invisible hat, and walks away.

Through the field.

At the archway, he stops and looks back to me once more.

He waves.

I lift my left hand and wave back.

Then he turns and goes through the archway.

Goodbye, my friend.

Just me now. Me and the wind blowing gently through the field.

Me, here with a lifetime of moments with people I love behind me. With hope that there are more in front of me.

Memories flick through my mind, a photo album of my life.

A young child, sitting in a police station, wondering why Mommy and Daddy haven't come to pick him up. Feeling so alone.

That little boy who found moments of warmth in an orphanage. Where I picked tomatoes, and found the instrument that I grew to love, that inspired my life and my yearning to create. Where I first caught a glimpse of the girl who would consume my life.

Those years that came in between. Waking up to sunrises upon concrete, or squeezing the cushiness out of cardboard. Where my photographs kept me fed and hopeful, and bought me a ticket to a better life.

That better life, where I finally found a real home. A new family, who showed that family is those people we connect with most, the people who hold the piece of the puzzle that we are missing, the piece that we need to be whole.

Then a runway, and how one fortuitous afternoon turned into a fate-like meeting.

Finding Isobel, the girl who'd become a woman, who I needed to know again.

How I learned with her what it is to have a soulmate.

And how life took a turn. The dashed hope. The broken dreams and connection that was beaten into indifference …

I think of it all, right up until this point. And I sit here with a longing, and a hope that there is more of our story to come.

Here, with a creeping sense of doubt.

She's not coming, is she?

I cough.

There's a gurgle inside my lungs.

I cough again.

No, she's not coming. Dreams are dreams because they are not real.

My eyes close for a moment.

Relax, breathe slowly.

Let it pass. Stay.

The sun is dulling to a light yellow. Clouds drift across the blue.

Was the letter enough? Should I have done more?

A small flock of birds launches into the sky from the archway of trees.

My body jolts.

Shallow breaths.

I blink my eyes, my heart thudding like a sledgehammer in my chest.

I blink again.

It's an illusion – it must be. My heart wanting so much it deceives my eyes.

Shallow breaths. Gasping.

Isobel is walking toward me as if this moment is a decade before. Through the grass, her hips swaying, her hair blowing across her face.

My finger shakes.

I press the capture button. The click goes off and I continue to snap her.

She looks so young and uninhibited, free, in her light, torn 501s and a white tank top. The necklace with the heart locket she used to wear is now around her neck again, hanging perfectly between the top of her breasts.

I wonder what pictures are inside it now …

More photos – I can't take enough.

She dips her head and looks back up at me, the corner of her soft pink lips curling upward. Her fingers twirl a lock of hair as she nears me, almost seductively.

I'm engrossed in the most minute of details: the tiny creases on the outside of her eyes, the way the afternoon light strikes her hazel eyes differently with each step she takes, showing shimmers of green, flickers of blue.

The photos flow as she gets nearer.

The most beautiful photo shoot we've ever done.

I'm snickering with uninhibited joy … between every breath …

Shallowing.

She pauses and poses for me. I snap her with her lips pouted, her hands gripping her waist.

I break out into laughter. I can't contain my exultation; how truly happy this moment feels.

"I like that you took photos of me," she says, as if we are kids again.

"I like taking photos of nice things," I reply.

Isobel sits beside me and wraps her arm around me, bringing my head into her shoulder. She leans hers on mine, and runs her fingers through my hair.

"I'm glad you wrote me," she says.

I cough and splutter, wheezing again. "I'm glad I did too."

"Are you okay?"

"I'm fine." I splutter again. "I'm great."

She sits up and holds my hand in hers. "Cody … what's going on?"

"Nothing …" I'm gasping. "Please just stay with me."

A layer of glass forms over her eyes. Her hand runs over my cheek, and she holds mine to hers, tears rolling over my skin.

I can feel her. I can feel myself. Everything we had together. Everything we have right now.

"The necklace … looks beautiful." Her hand is close enough to touch. "Look … look inside my pocket."

She rests my hand on my leg and then takes out the photo of us at North Pond. Cathartic laughter jumps from her mouth.

"Remember when this used to sit inside your necklace?"

Isobel runs the silver heart through her fingers. She unclips the locket. Inside is a photo of us at my last birthday, in the home, when we drunkenly opened up. The other half is empty.

"I thought that it was time to update it. I left one side for a memory that is still to come."

She's holding back tears.

"We're going to see some …" My body jolts. "There are so many things we're still going to do, babe. So many travels. So many memories."

Now her tears come. "I know, hon."

"I … It might have taken me a while to wake up … But I'm more awake than ever. I still love you, Isobel … More than ever."

"Cody …" She wraps her hands around my left. "I never stopped."

"I'm just sorry … that I didn't realize this sooner."

"I'm sorry I wasn't here …"

"You never have anything to be sorry for. You gave me the greatest times of my life, the love we had. I'm so thankful I got to love you, Isobel, so thankful we got our life together."

She brings my hand back up to her cheek. "So am I, Cody. There's no more to be sorry for."

Her skin is so soft, like silk beneath my fingertips.

Our lips come together, melting into one another. Every single second of pain, apathy and heartbreak feels absolved with this kiss.

"Hold me," I say. Her cheek on mine, the touch of her skin relieving. "And let me hold you."

Isobel buries her head into my shoulder, and I lean mine on hers. She wraps my arm around her body. It's heavy, but my heart feels so light it could fly.

The afternoon light is fading.

My breaths. Fading.

My love, growing stronger.

Everything, fading, and growing.

"Never forget the passion, Cody."

"Never." My whisper floats on the breeze.

We're given one opportunity to take hold of life and do everything that makes us happy. To immerse ourselves in the wonders of the world and the beauty of the people we find ourselves endeared to. We capture moments and memories in photographs and in our minds, feelings in our hearts. Every moment is unique, though, and infinitely uncaptured – we can never have them again, not more than that picture, that memory. We need to continue to make more of those moments as we live each day. Treasure the people we love.

The prime of our lives is always the moment we are in.

Maybe I left it late to remember this. Maybe I almost missed out on the opportunity to recapture life.

But right now, I can feel Isobel.

Not just her skin, her body, her hair, her lips on mine, her hand in mine, the sweat between our bodies. More than that, I feel our hearts, our minds, connected eternally.

I feel everything.

Right now, I'm here. I'm in love. I'm capturing all that I can.

With Isobel in my arms, I close my eyes, more alive than ever.

Thank you for reading *These Pictures of Us.*

It was a fun and interesting journey writing this novel. I often put myself through different situations to feel what my characters were feeling. I must thank the countless cafes and bars in Melbourne who put up with me occupying a seat for hours on end, and anyone who had to put up with my fluctuating moods as I immersed myself in the novel and the ups-and-downs it takes.

I hope you enjoyed the story. Don't hesitate to drop me a line.

Thanks again

Tommy